PENGUIN MODERN CLAS

The Man in the High C

PHILIP K. DICK was born in Chicago in 1928, but lived most of his life in California, briefly attending the University of California at Berkeley in 1947. Among the most prolific and eccentric of science fiction writers, his works blend philosophical speculation with elements of the surreal, and typically feature androids, drugs and hallucinations.

By the time of his death in 1982, he had written over thirty science-fiction novels and 112 short stories, many of which have been adapted for film or television. His most famous books include *Do Androids Dream of Electric Sheep?* (1968, later the inspiration for the film *Blade Runner*), *Ubik* (1969) and *A Scanner Darkly* (1977). *The Man in the High Castle* (1962), perhaps his most painstakingly constructed and chilling novel, won a Hugo Award in 1963.

PHILIP K. DICK

The Man in the High Castle

PENGUIN BOOKS

PENGUIN CLASSICS

UK | USA | Canada | Ireland | Australia
India | New Zealand | South Africa

Penguin Books is part of the Penguin Random House group of companies
whose addresses can be found at global.penguinrandomhouse.com.

First published in the United States of America 1962
Published in Penguin Books 1965
This edition published in Penguin Classics 2015

019

Copyright © Philip K. Dick, 1962

Printed and bound in Great Britain by Clays Ltd, Elcograf S.p.A.

A CIP catalogue record for this book is available from the British Library

ISBN: 978-0-241-24610-8

*To my wife Anne, without whose silence
this book would never have been written*

Acknowledgements

The version of the *I Ching* or *Book of Changes* used and quoted in this novel is the Richard Wilhelm translation rendered into English by Cary F. Baynes, published by Pantheon Books, Bollingen Series XIX, 1950, by the Bollingen Foundation Inc., New York.

The *haiku* on page 48 is by Yosa Buson, translated by Harold G. Henderson, from the *Anthology of Japanese Literature*, Volume One, compiled and edited by Donald Keene, Grove Press, 1955, New York.

The *waka* on page 135 is by Chiyo, translated by Daisetz T. Suzuki, from *Zen and Japanese Culture*, by Daisetz T. Suzuki, published by Pantheon Books, Bollingen Series LXIV, 1959, by the Bollingen Foundation Inc., New York.

I have made much use of *The Rise and Fall of the Third Reich, A History of Nazi Germany*, by William L. Shirer, Secker & Warburg, 1960; *Hitler, a Study in Tyranny*, by Alan Bullock, Odhams, 1952 (Pelican Books, 1962); *The Goebbels Diaries, 1942–1943*, edited and translated by Louis P. Lochner, Doubleday & Co. Inc., 1948; *The Tibetan Book of the Dead*, compiled and edited by W. Y. Evans-Wentz, Oxford University Press, 1960; *The Foxes of the Desert*, by Paul Carell, Macdonald, 1960. And I owe personal thanks to the eminent Western writer Will Cook for his help with material dealing with historic artifacts and the U.S. Frontier Period.

I

For a week Mr R. Childan had been anxiously watching the mail. But the valuable shipment from the Rocky Mountain States had not arrived. As he opened up his store on Friday morning and saw only letters on the floor by the mail slot he thought, I'm going to have an angry customer.

Pouring himself a cup of instant tea from the five-cent wall dispenser he got a broom and began to sweep; soon he had the front of American Artistic Handcrafts Inc. ready for the day, all spick and span with the cash register full of change, a fresh vase of marigolds, and the radio playing background music. Outdoors along the sidewalk businessmen hurried towards their offices along Montgomery Street. Far off, a cable car passed; Childan halted to watch it with pleasure. Women in their long colourful silk dresses . . . he watched them, too. Then the phone rang. He turned to answer it.

'Yes,' a familiar voice said to his answer. Childan's heart sank. 'This is Mr Tagomi. Did my Civil War recruiting poster arrive yet, sir? Please recall; you promised it sometime last week.' The fussy, brisk voice, barely polite, barely keeping the code. 'Did I not give you a deposit, sir, Mr Childan, with that stipulation? This is to be a gift, you see. I explained that. A client.'

'Extensive inquiries,' Childan began, 'which I've had made at my own expense, Mr Tagomi, sir, regarding the promised parcel, which you realize originates outside of this region and is therefore –'

But Tagomi broke in. 'Then it has not arrived.'

'No, Mr Tagomi, sir.'

An icy pause.

'I can wait no furthermore,' Tagomi said.

'No sir.' Childan gazed morosely through the store window at the warm bright day and the San Francisco office buildings.

'A substitute, then. Your recommendation, Mr Chil*dan*?' Tagomi deliberately mispronounced the name; insult within the code that made Childan's ears burn. Place pulled, the dreadful mortification of their situation. Robert Childan's aspirations and fears and torments rose up and exposed themselves, swamped him, stopping his tongue. He stammered, his hand sticky on the phone. The air of his store smelled of the marigolds; the music played on, but he felt as if he were falling into some distant sea.

'Well . . .' he managed to mutter. 'Butter churn. Ice-cream maker circa 1900.' His mind refused to think. Just when you forget about it; just when you fool yourself. He was thirty-eight years old, and he could remember the pre-war days, the other times. Franklin D. Roosevelt and the World's Fair; the former better world. 'Could I bring various desirable items out to your business location?' he mumbled.

An appointment was made for two o'clock. Have to shut store, he knew as he hung up the phone. No choice. Have to keep goodwill of such customers; business depends on them.

Standing shakily, he became aware that someone — a couple — had entered the store. Young man and girl, both handsome, well-dressed. Ideal. He calmed himself and moved professionally, easily, in their direction, smiling. They were bending to scrutinize a counter display, had picked up a lovely ashtray. Married, he guessed. Live out in City of the Winding Mists, the new exclusive apartments on Skyline overlooking Belmont.

'Hello,' he said, and felt better. They smiled at him without any superiority, only kindness. His displays — which really were the best of their kind on the Coast — had awed them a little; he saw that and was grateful. They understood.

'Really excellent pieces, sir,' the young man said.

Childan bowed spontaneously.

Their eyes, warm not only with human bond but with the shared enjoyment of the art objects he sold, their mutual tastes and satisfactions, remained fixed on him; they were thanking him for having things like these for them to see, pick up and examine, handle perhaps without even buying. Yes, he thought, they know what sort of store they are in; this is not tourist trash, not redwood plaques reading MUIR WOODS, MARIN COUNTY, P.S.A., or funny signs or girly rings or postcards of views of the Bridge. The girl's eyes especially, large, dark. How easily, Childan thought, I could fall in love with a girl like this. How tragic my life, then; as if it weren't bad enough already. The stylish black hair, lacquered nails, pierced ears for the long dangling brass handmade ear-rings.

'Your ear-rings,' he murmured. 'Purchased here, perhaps?'

'No,' she said. 'At home.'

Childan nodded. No contemporary American art; only the past could be represented here, in a store such as his. 'You are here for long?' he asked. 'To our San Francisco?'

'I'm stationed here indefinitely,' the man said. 'With Standard of Living for Unfortunate Areas Planning Commission of Inquiry.' Pride showed on his face. Not the military. Not one of the gum-chewing boorish draftees with their greedy peasant faces, wandering up Market Street, gaping at the bawdy shows, the sex movies, the shooting galleries, the cheap nightclubs with photos of middle-aged blondes holding their nipples between their wrinkled fingers and leering . . . the honky-tonk jazz slums that made up most of the flat part of San Francisco, rickety tin and board shacks that had sprung up from the ruins even before the last bomb fell. No – this man was of the elite. Cultured, educated, even more so than Mr Tagomi, who was after all a high official with the ranking Trade Mission on the Pacific Coast. Tagomi was an old man. His attitudes had formed in the War Cabinet days.

'Had you wished American traditional ethnic art objects

as a gift?' Childan asked. 'Or to decorate perhaps a new apartment for your stay here?' If the latter . . ᵥ his heart picked up.

'An accurate guess,' the girl said. We are starting to decorate. A bit undecided. Do you think you could inform us?'

'I could arrange to arrive at your apartment, yes,' Childan said. 'Bringing several hand cases, I can suggest in context, at your leisure. This, of course, is our speciality.' He dropped his eyes so as to conceal his hope. There might be thousands of dollars involved. 'I am getting in a New England table, maple, all wood-pegged, no nails. Immense beauty and worth. And a mirror from the time of the 1812 War. And also the aboriginal art : a group of vegetable-dyed goat-hair rugs.'

'I myself,' the man said, 'prefer the art of the cities.'

'Yes,' Childan said eagerly. 'Listen, sir. I have a mural from W.P.A. post-office period, original, done on board, four sections, depicting Horace Greeley. Priceless collector's item.'

'Ah,' the man said, his dark eyes flashing.

'And a Victrola cabinet of 1920 made into a liquor cabinet.'

'Ah.'

'And, sir, listen : *framed signed picture of Jean Harlow.*' The man goggled at him.

'Shall we make arrangements?' Childan said, seizing this correct psychological instant. From his inner coat pocket he brought his pen, notebook. 'I shall take your name and address, sir and lady.'

Afterwards, as the couple strolled from his store, Childan stood, hands behind his back, watching the street. Joy. If all business days were like this . . . but it was more than business, the success of his store. It was a chance to meet a young Japanese couple socially, on a basis of acceptance of him as a man rather than him as a *yank* or, at best, a tradesman who sold art objects. Yes, these new young people, of the rising generation, who did not remember the days before the war or even the war itself – they were the hope of the world, Place difference did not have the significance for them.

It will end, Childan thought. Someday. The very idea of place. Not governed and governing, but people.

And yet he trembled with fear, imagining himself knocking at their door. He examined his notes. The Kasouras. Being admitted, no doubt offered tea. Would he do the right thing? Know the proper act and utterance at each moment? Or would he disgrace himself, like an animal, by some dismal faux pas?

The girl's name was Betty. Such understanding in her face, he thought. The gentle, sympathetic eyes. Surely, even in the short time in the store, she had glimpsed his hopes and defeats.

His hopes – he felt suddenly dizzy. What aspirations bordering on the insane if not the suicidal did he have? But it was known, relations between Japanese and *yanks,* although generally it was between a Japanese man and a *yank* woman. This . . . he quailed at the idea. And she was married. He whipped his mind away from the pageant of his involuntary thoughts and began busily opening the morning's mail.

His hands, he discovered, were still shaking. And then he recalled his two o'clock appointment with Mr Tagomi; at that, his hands ceased shaking and his nervousness became determination. I've got to come up with something acceptable, he said to himself. Where? How? What? A phone call. Sources. Business ability. Scrape up a fully restored 1929 Ford including fabric top (black). Grand slam to keep patronage forever. Crated original mint trimotor airmail plane discovered in barn in Alabama, etc. Produce mummified head of Mr B. Bill, including flowing white hair; sensational American artifact. Make my reputation in top connoisseur circles throughout Pacific, not excluding Home Islands.

To inspire himself, he lit up a marijuana cigarette, excellent Land-O-Smiles brand.

*

In his room on Hayes Street, Frank Frink lay in bed wondering how to get up. Sun glared past the blind onto the heap of clothes that had fallen to the floor. His glasses, too. Would he step on them? Try to get to bathroom by other route, he thought. Crawl or roll. His head ached but he did not feel sad. Never look back, he decided. Time? The clock on the dresser. Eleven-thirty! Good grief. But still he lay.

I'm fired, he thought.

Yesterday he had done wrong at the factory. Spouted the wrong kind of talk to Mr Wyndam-Matson, who had a dished-in face with Socrates-type nose, diamond ring, gold fly zipper. In other words, a power. A throne. Frink's thoughts wandered groggily.

Yes, he thought, and now they'll blacklist me; my skill is no use – I have no trade. Fifteen years' experience. Gone.

And now he would have to appear at the Labourers' Justification Commission for a revision of his work category. Since he had never been able to make out Wyndam-Matson's relationship to the *pinocs* – the puppet white government at Sacramento – he could not fathom his ex-employer's power to sway the real authorities, the Japanese. The L.J.C. was *pinoc* run. He would be facing four or five middle-aged plump white faces, on the order of Wyndam-Matson's. If he failed to get justification there, he would make his way to one of the Import-Export Trade Missions which operated out of Tokyo, and which had offices throughout California, Oregon, Washington, and the parts of Nevada included in the Pacific States of America. But if he failed successfully to plead there . . .

Plans roamed his mind as he lay in bed gazing up at the ancient light fixture in the ceiling. He could for instance slip across into the Rocky Mountain States. But it was loosely banded to the P.S.A., and might extradite him. What about the South? His body recoiled. Ugh. Not that. As a white man he would have plenty of place, in fact more than he had here in the P.S.A. But . . , he did not want that kind of place.

And, worse, the South had a cat's cradle of ties, economic, ideological, and god knew what, with the Reich. And Frank Frink was a Jew.

His original name was Frank Fink. He had been born on the East Coast, in New York, and in 1941 he had been drafted into the Army of the United States of America, right after the collapse of Russia. After the Japs had taken Hawaii he had been sent to the West Coast. When the war ended, there he was, on the Japanese side of the settlement line. And here he was today, fifteen years later.

In 1947, on Capitulation Day, he had more or less gone berserk. Hating the Japs as he did, he had vowed revenge; he had buried his Service weapons ten feet underground, in a basement, well-wrapped and oiled, for the day he and his buddies arose. However, time was a great healer, a fact he had not taken into account. When he thought of the idea now, the great blood bath, the purging of the *pinocs* and their masters, he felt as if he were reviewing one of those stained yearbooks from his high school days, coming upon an account of his boyhood aspirations. Frank 'Goldfish' Frink is going to be a palaeontologist and vows to marry Norma Prout. Norma Prout was the class *schönes Mädchen*, and he really had vowed to marry her. That was all so goddam long ago, like listening to Fred Allen or seeing a W. C. Fields movie. Since 1947 he had probably seen or talked to six hundred thousand Japanese, and the desire to do violence to any or all of them had simply never materialized, after the first few months. It was just not relevant any more.

But wait. There was one, a Mr Omuro, who had bought control of a great area of rental property in downtown San Francisco, and who for a time had been Frank's landlord. There was a bad apple, he thought. A shark who had never made repairs, had partitioned rooms smaller and smaller, raised rents . . . Omuro had gouged the poor, especially the nearly destitute jobless ex-servicemen during the depression years of the early 'fifties. However, it had been one of the Japanese trade missions which had cut off Omuro's head for his profiteering; And nowadays such a violation of the harsh, rigid, but just Japanese civil law was unheard of. It was a credit to the incorruptibility of the Jap occupation officials, especially those who had come in after the War Cabinet had fallen.

Recalling the rugged, stoic honesty of the Trade Missions, Frink felt reassured. Even Wyndam-Matson would be waved off like a noisy fly. W.-M. Corporation owner or not. At least, so he hoped. I guess I really have faith in this Co-Prosperity Pacific Alliance stuff, he said to himself. Strange. Looking back to the early days . . . it had seemed such an obvious fake, then. Empty propaganda. But now . . .

He rose from the bed and unsteadily made his way to the bathroom. While he washed and shaved, he listened to the mid-day news on the radio.

'Let us not deride this effort,' the radio was saying as he momentarily shut off the hot water.

No, we won't, Frink thought bitterly. He knew which particular effort the radio had in mind. Yet, there was after all something humorous about it, the picture of stolid, grumpy Germans walking around on Mars, on the red sand where no humans had ever stepped before. Lathering his jowls, Frink began a chanting satire to himself. *Gott, Herr Kreisleiter. Ist dies vielleicht der Ort wo man das Konzentrationslager bilden kann? Das Wetter ist so schön. Heiss, aber doch schön* . . .

The radio said : 'Co-Prosperity Civilization must pause and consider whether in our quest to provide a balanced equity of mutual duties and responsibilities coupled with remunerations . . .' Typical jargon from the ruling hierarchy, Frink noted. '. . . we have not failed to perceive the future arena in which the affairs of man will be acted out, be they Nordic, Japanese, Negroid . . .' On and on it went.

As he dressed, he mulled with pleasure his satire. *The weather is schön, so schön. But there is nothing to breathe* . . .

However, it was a fact; the Pacific had done nothing towards colonization of the planets. It was involved – bogged down, rather – in South America. While the Germans were busy bustling enormous robot construction systems across space, the Japs were still burning off the jungles in the interior of Brazil, erecting eight-floor clay apartment houses for ex-headhunters. By the time the Japs got their first space-ship off the ground the Germans would have the entire solar system sewed up tight. Back in the quaint old history-book days, the Germans had missed out while the rest of Europe put the final touches on their colonial empires. However, Frink reflected, they were not going to be last this time; they had learned.

And then he thought about Africa, and the Nazi experiment there. And his blood stopped in his veins, hesitated, at last went on.

That huge empty ruin.

The radio said : '... we must consider with pride however our emphasis on the fundamental physical needs of peoples of all place, their subspiritual aspirations which must be ...'

Frink shut the radio off. Then, calmer, he turned it back on.

Christ on the crapper, he thought. Africa. For the ghosts of dead tribes. Wiped out to make a land of – what? Who knew? Maybe even the master architects in Berlin did not know. Bunch of automatons, building and toiling away. Building? Grinding down. Ogres out of a palaeontology exhibit, at their task of making a cup from an enemy's skull, the whole family industriously scooping out the contents – the raw brains – first, to eat. Then useful utensils of men's leg bones. Thrifty, to think not only of eating the people you did not like, but eating them out of their own skull. The first technicians! Prehistoric man in a sterile white lab coat in some Berlin university lab, experimenting with uses to which other people's skull, skin, ears, fat could be put. Ja, Herr Doktor. A new use for the big toe; see, one can adapt the joint for a quick-acting cigarette lighter mechanism. Now, if only Herr Krupp can produce it in quantity ...

It horrified him, this thought : the ancient gigantic cannibal near-man flourishing now, ruling the world once more. We spent a million years escaping him, Frink thought, and now he's back. And not merely as the adversary . . . but as the master.

'. . . we can deplore,' the radio, the voice of the little yellow-bellies from Tokyo was saying. God, Frink thought; and we called them monkeys, these civilized bandy-legged shrimps who would no more set up gas ovens than they would melt their wives into sealing wax. '. . . and we have deplored often in the past the dreadful waste of humans in this fanatical striving which sets the broader mass of men wholly outside the legal community.' They, the Japs, were so strong on law. '. . , To quote a Western saint familiar to all : "What profit it a man if he gain the whole world but in this enter-prise lose his soul?"' The radio paused, Frink, tying his tie, also paused. It was the morning ablution.

I have to make my pact with them here, he realized. Black-listed or not, it'd be death for me if I left Japanese-controlled land and showed up in the South or in Europe – anywhere in the Reich.

I'll have to come to terms with old Wyndam-Matson.

Seated on his bed, a cup of lukewarm tea beside him, Frink got down his copy of the *I Ching*. From their leather tube he took the forty-nine yarrow stalks. He considered, until he had his thoughts properly controlled and his ques-tions worked out.

Aloud he said, 'How should I approach Wyndam-Matson in order to come to decent terms with him?' He wrote the question down on the tablet, then began whipping the yarrow stalks from hand to hand until he had the first line, the beginning. An eight. Half the sixty-four hexagrams eliminated already. He divided the stalks and obtained the second line. Soon, being so expert, he had all six lines; the hexagram lay before him, and he did not need to identify it by the chart. He could recognize it as Hexagram Fifteen. Ch'ien. Modesty. Ah. The low will be raised up, the high brought down, powerful families humbled; he did not have to refer to the text – he knew it by heart. A good omen. The oracle was giving him favourable counsel.

And yet he was a bit disappointed. There was something fatuous about Hexagram Fifteen. Too goody-goody. *Naturally* he should be modest. Perhaps there was an idea in it, however. After all, he had no power over old W.-M. He could not compel him to take him back. All he could do was adopt the point of view of Hexagram Fifteen; this was that sort of moment, when one had to petition, to hope, to await with faith. Heaven in its time would raise him up to his old job or perhaps even to something better.

He had no lines to read, no nines or sixes; it was static. So he was through. It did not move into a second hexagram.

A new question, then. Setting himself, he said aloud, 'Will I ever see Juliana again?'

That was his wife. Or rather his ex-wife. Juliana had divorced him a year ago, and he had not seen her in months; in fact he did not even know where she lived. Evidently she had left San Francisco. Perhaps even the P.S.A. Either their mutual friends had not heard from her or they were not telling him.

Busily he manoeuvred the yarrow stalks, his eyes fixed on the tallies. How many times he had asked about Juliana, one question or another? Here came the hexagram, brought forth by the passive chance workings of the vegetable stalks. Random, and yet rooted in the moment in which he lived, in which his life was bound up with all other lives and particles in the universe. The necessary hexagram picturing in its pattern of broken and unbroken lines the *situation*. He, Juliana, the factory on Gough Street, the Trade Missions that ruled, the exploration of the planets, the billion chemical heaps in Africa that were now not even corpses, the aspirations of the thousands around him in the shanty warrens of San Francisco, the mad creatures in Berlin with their calm faces and manic plans – all connected in this moment of casting the yarrow stalks to select the exact wisdom appropriate in a book begun in the thirtieth century B.C. A book created by the sages of China over a period of five thousand years, winnowed, perfected, that superb cosmology – and science – codified before Europe had even learned to do long division.

The hexagram. His heart dropped. Forty-four. Kou. Coming to Meet. Its sobering judgement. *The maiden is powerful. One should not marry such a maiden.* Again he had gotten it in connection with Juliana.

Oy vey, he thought, settling back. So she was wrong for me; I know that. I didn't ask that. Why does the oracle have to remind me? A bad fate for me, to have met her and been in love – be in love – with her.

Juliana – the best-looking woman he had ever married. Soot-black eyebrows and hair : trace amounts of Spanish blood distributed as pure colour, even to her lips. Her rubbery, soundless walk; she had worn saddle shoes left over from high school. In fact all her clothes had a dilapidated quality and the definite suggestion of being old and often washed. He and she had been so broke so long that despite her looks she had had to wear a cotton sweater, cloth zippered jacket, brown tweed skirt, and bobby socks, and she hated him and it because it made her look, she had said, like a woman who played tennis or (even worse) collected mushrooms in the woods.

But above and beyond everything else, he had originally been drawn by her screwball expression; for no reason, Juliana greeted strangers with a portentous, nudnik, Mona Lisa smile that hung them up between responses, whether to say hello or not. And she was so attractive that more often than not they did say hello, whereupon Juliana glided by. At first he had thought it was just plain bad eyesight, but finally he had decided that it revealed a deep-dyed otherwise concealed stupidity at her core. And so finally her borderline flicker of greeting to strangers had annoyed him, as had her plantlike, silent, I'm-on-a-mysterious-errand way of coming and going. But even then, towards the end, when they had been fighting so much, he still never saw her as anything but a direct, literal invention of God's, dropped into his life for reasons he would never know. And on that account – a sort of religious intuition or faith about her – he could not get over having lost her.

She seemed so close right now . . . as if he still had her. That spirit, still busy in his life, padding through his room in search of – whatever it was Juliana sought. And in his mind whenever he took up the volumes of the oracle.

Seated on his bed, surrounded by lonely disorder, preparing to go out and begin his day, Frank Frink wondered who else in the vast complicated city of San Francisco was at this same moment consulting the oracle. And were they all getting as gloomy advice as he? Was the tenor of the Moment as adverse for them as it was for him?

2

Mr Nobusuke Tagomi sat consulting the divine Fifth Book of Confucian wisdom, the Taoist oracle called for centuries the *I Ching* or *Book of Changes*. At noon that day, he had begun to become apprehensive about his appointment with Mr Childan, which would occur in two more hours.

His suite of offices on the twentieth floor of the Nippon Times Building on Taylor Street overlooked the Bay. Through the glass wall he could watch ships entering, passing beneath the Golden Gate Bridge. At this moment a freighter could be seen beyond Alcatraz, but Mr Tagomi did not care. Going to the wall he unfastened the cord and lowered the bamboo blinds over the view. The large central office became darker; he did not have to squint against the glare. Now he could think more clearly.

It was not within his power, he decided, to please his client. No matter what Mr Childan came up with : the client would not be impressed. Let us face that, he had said to himself. But we can keep him from becoming displeased, at least.

We can refrain from insulting him by a mouldy gift.

The client would soon reach San Francisco airport by avenue of the high-place new German rocket, the Messerschmitt 9-E. Mr Tagomi had never ridden on such a ship; when he met Mr Baynes he would have to take care to appear blasé, no matter how large the rocket turned out to be. Now to practice. He stood in front of the mirror on the office wall, creating a face of composure, mildly bored, inspecting his own cold features for any give-away. Yes, they are very noisy, Mr Baynes, sir. One cannot read. But then the flight from Stockholm to San Francisco is only forty-five minutes. Perhaps then a word about German mechanical failures? I suppose you heard the radio. That crash over Madagascar. I must say, there is something to be said for the old piston planes.

Essential to avoid politics. For he did not know Mr Baynes's views on leading issues of the day. Yet they might arise. Mr Baynes, being Swedish, would be a neutral. Yet he had chosen Lufthansa rather than S.A.S. A cautious ploy ... Mr Baynes, sir, they say Herr Bormann is quite ill. That a new Reichs Chancellor will be chosen by the Partei this autumn. Rumour only? So much secrecy, alas, between Pacific and Reich.

In the folder on his desk, clipping from *New York Times* of a recent speech by Mr Baynes. Mr Tagomi now studied it critically, bending due to slight failure of correction by his contact lenses. The speech had to do with need of exploring once more – ninety-eighth time? – for sources of water on the moon. 'We may still solve this heartbreaking dilemma,' Mr Baynes was quoted. 'Our nearest neighbour, and so far the most unrewarding except for military purposes.' *Sic!* Mr Tagomi thought, using high-place Latin word. Clue to Mr Baynes. Looks askance at merely military. Mr Tagomi made a mental note.

Touching the intercom button Mr Tagomi said, 'Miss Ephreikian, I would like you to bring in your tape recorder, please.'

The outer office door slid to one side and Miss Ephreikian,

today pleasantly adorned with blue flowers in her hair, appeared.

'Bit of lilac,' Mr Tagomi observed. Once, he had professionally flower-raised back home on Hokkaido.

Miss Ephreikian, a tall, brown-haired Armenian girl, bowed.

'Ready with Zip-Track Speed Master?' Mr Tagomi asked.

'Yes, Mr Tagomi.' Miss Ephreikian seated herself, the portable battery-operated tape recorder ready.

Mr Tagomi began. 'I inquired of the oracle, "Will the meeting between myself and Mr Childan be profitable?" and obtained to my dismay the ominous hexagram The Preponderance of the Great. The ridgepole is sagging. Too much weight in the middle; all unbalanced. Clearly away from the Tao.' The tape recorder whirred.

Pausing, Mr Tagomi reflected.

Miss Ephreikian watched him expectantly. The whirring ceased.

'Have Mr Ramsey come in for a moment, please,' Mr Tagomi said.

'Yes, Mr Tagomi.' Rising, she put down the tape recorder; her heels tapped as she departed from the office.

With a large folder of bills-of-lading under his arm, Mr Ramsey appeared. Young, smiling, he advanced, wearing the natty U.S. Midwest Plains string tie, checkered shirt and tight beltless blue jeans considered so high-place among the style-conscious of the day. 'Howdy, Mr Tagomi,' he said. 'Right nice day, sir.'

Mr Tagomi bowed.

At that, Mr Ramsey stiffened abruptly and also bowed.

'I've been consulting the oracle,' Mr Tagomi said, as Miss Ephreikian reseated herself with her tape recorder. 'You understand that Mr Baynes, who as you know is arriving shortly in person, holds to the Nordic ideology regarding so-called Oriental culture. I could make the effort to dazzle him into a better comprehension with authentic works of

Chinese scroll art or ceramics of our Tokugawa Period . . . but it is not our job to convert.'

'I see,' Mr Ramsey said; his Caucasian face twisted with painful concentration.

'Therefore we will cater to his prejudice and graft a priceless American artifact to him instead.'

'Yes.'

'You, sir, are of American ancestry. Although you have gone to the trouble of darkening your skin colour.' He scrutinized Mr Ramsey.

'A tan achieved by a sun lamp,' Mr Ramsey murmured. 'For merely acquiring vitamin D.' But his expression of humiliation gave him away. 'I assure you that I retain authentic roots with –' Mr Ramsey stumbled over the words. 'I have not cut off all ties with – native ethnic patterns.'

Mr Tagomi said to Miss Ephreikian. 'Resume, please.' Once more the tape recorder whirred. 'In consulting the oracle and obtaining Hexagram Ta Kuo, Twenty-eight, I further received the unfavourable line Nine in the fifth place. It reads :

> A withered poplar puts forth flowers.
> An older woman takes a husband.
> No blame. No praise.

'This clearly indicates that Mr Childan will have nothing of worth to offer us at two.' Mr Tagomi paused. 'Let us be candid. I cannot rely on my own judgement regarding American art objects. That is why a –' He lingered over his choice of terms. 'Why you, Mr Ramsey, who are shall I say *native born*, are required. Obviously we must do the best we can.'

Mr Ramsey had no answer. But, despite his efforts to conceal, his features showed hurt, anger, a frustrated and mute reaction.

'Now,' Mr Tagomi said. 'I have further consulted the oracle. For purposes of policy, I cannot divulge to you, Mr Ramsey, the question.' In other words, his tone meant, you and your *pinoc* kind are not entitled to share the important matters which we deal in. 'It is sufficient to say, however, that I received a most provocative response. It has caused me to ponder at length.'

Both Mr Ramsey and Miss Ephreikian watched him intently.

'It deals with Mr Baynes,' Mr Tagomi said.

They nodded.

'My question regarding Mr Baynes produced through the occult workings of the Tao the Hexagram Sheng, Forty-six. A good judgement. And lines Six at the beginning and Nine in the second place.' His question had been, Will I be able to deal with Mr Baynes successfully? And the Nine in the second place had assured him that he would. It read :

> If one is sincere,
> It furthers one to bring even a small offering.
> No blame.

Obviously Mr Baynes would be satisfied by whatever gift the ranking Trade Mission grafted to him through the good offices of Mr Tagomi. But Mr Tagomi, in asking the question, had had a deeper query in the back of his mind, one of which he was barely conscious. As so often, the oracle had perceived that more fundamental query and, while answering the other, had taken it upon itself to answer the subliminal one, too.

'As we know,' Mr Tagomi said, 'Mr Baynes is bringing us detailed account of new injection moulds developed in Sweden. Were we successfully to sign agreement with his firm, we could no doubt replace many present metals, quite scarce, with plastics.'

For years, the Pacific had been trying to get basic assistance in the synthetics field from the Reich. However, the big German chemical cartels, I.G. Farben in particular, had harboured their patents; had, in fact, created a world monopoly in plastics, especially in the development of the polyesters. By this means, Reich trade had kept an edge over Pacific trade, and in technology the Reich was at least ten years ahead. The interplanetary rockets leaving Festung

Europa consisted mainly of heat-resistant plastics, very light in weight, so hard that they survived even major meteor impact. The Pacific had nothing of this sort; natural fibres such as wood were still used, and of course the ubiquitous pot metals. Mr Tagomi cringed as he thought about it; he had seen at trade fairs some of the advanced German work, including an all-synthetics automobile, the D.S.S. – Der Schnelle Spuk – which sold, in P.S.A. currency, for about six hundred dollars.

But his underlying question, one which he could never reveal to the *pinocs* flitting about Trade Mission offices, had to do with an aspect of Mr Baynes suggested by the original coded cable from Tokyo. First of all, coded material was infrequent, and dealt usually with matters of security, not with trade deals. And the cipher was the metaphor type, utilizing poetic allusion, which had been adopted to baffle the Reich monitors – who could crack any literal code, no matter how elaborate. So clearly it was the Reich whom the Tokyo authorities had in mind, not quasi-disloyal cliques in the Home Islands. The key phrase, 'Skim milk is his diet', referred to *Pinafore*, to the eerie song that expounded the doctrine, '. . . Things are seldom what they seem/Skim milk masquerades as cream.' And the *I Ching*, when Mr Tagomi had consulted it, had fortified his insight. Its commentary :

Here a strong man is presupposed. It is true he does not fit in with his environment, inasmuch as he is too brusque and pays too little attention to form. But as he is upright in character, he meets with response . . .

The insight was, simply, that Mr Baynes was not what he seemed; that his actual purpose in coming to San Francisco was not to sign a deal for injection moulds. That, in fact, Mr Baynes was a spy.

But for the life of him, Mr Tagomi could not figure out what sort of spy, for whom or for what.

At one-forty that afternoon, Robert Childan with enormous reluctance locked the front door of American Artistic Handcrafts Inc. He lugged his heavy cases to the kerb, hailed a pedecab, and told the *chink* to take him to the Nippon Times Building.

The *chink*, gaunt-faced, hunched over and perspiring, gasped a place-conscious acknowledgement and began loading Mr Childan's bags aboard. Then, having assisted Mr Childan himself into the carpet-lined seat, the *chink* clicked on the meter, mounted his own seat and pedalled off along Montgomery Street, among the cars and buses.

The entire day had been spent finding the item for Mr Tagomi, and Childan's bitterness and anxiety almost overwhelmed him as he watched the buildings pass. And yet – triumph. The separate skill, apart from the rest of him : he had found the right thing, and Mr Tagomi would be mollified and his client, whoever he was, would be overjoyed. I always give satisfaction, Childan thought. To my customers.

He had been able to procure, miraculously, an almost mint copy of Volume One, Number One of *Tip Top Comics.* Dating from the 'thirties, it was a choice piece of Americana ; one of the first funny books, a prize collectors searched for constantly. Of course, he had other items with him, to show first. He would lead up gradually to the funny book, which lay well-protected in a leather case packed in tissue paper at the centre of the largest bag.

The radio of the pedecab blared out popular tunes, competing with the radios of other cabs, cars, and buses. Childan did not hear; he was used to it. Nor did he take notice of the enormous neon signs with their permanent ads obliterating the front of virtually every large building. After all, he had his own sign; at night it blazed on and off in company with all the others of the city. What other way did one advertise? One had to be realistic.

In fact, the uproar of radios, traffic noises, the signs, and people lulled him. They blotted out his inner worries. And it was pleasurable to be pedalled along by another human being, to feel the straining muscles of the *chink* transmitted

27

in the form of regular vibrations; a sort of relaxing machine, Childan reflected. To be pulled instead of having to pull. And – to have, if even for a moment, higher place.

Guiltily, he woke himself. Too much to plan; no time for a midday doze. Was he absolutely properly dressed to enter the Nippon Times Building? Possibly he would faint in the high-speed elevator. But he had motion-illness tablets with him, a German compound. The various modes of address . . . he knew them. Whom to treat politely, whom rudely. Be brusque with the doorman, elavator operator, reception-ist, guide, any janitorial person. Bow to any Japanese, of course, even if it obliged him to bow hundreds of times. But the *pinocs*. Nebulous area. Bow, but look straight through them as if they did not exist. Did that cover every situation, then? What about a visiting foreigner? Germans often could be seen at the Trade Missions, as well as neutrals.

And then, too, he might see a slave.

German or South ships docked at the port of San Fran-cisco all the time, and blacks occasionally were allowed off for short intervals. Always in groups of fewer than three. And they could not be out after nightfall; even under Pacific law, they had to obey the curfew. But also slaves unloaded at the docks, and these lived perpetually ashore, in shacks under the wharves, above the waterline. None would be in the Trade Mission offices, but if any unloading were taking place – for instance, should he carry his own bags to Mr Tagomi's office? Surely not. A slave would have to be found, even if he had to stand waiting an hour. Even if he missed his appointment. It was out of the question to let a slave see him carrying something; he had to be quite careful of that. A mistake of that kind would cost him dearly; he would never have place of any sort again, among those who saw.

In a way, Childan thought, I would almost enjoy carrying my own bags into the Nippon Times Building in broad daylight. What a grand gesture. It is not actually illegal; I would not go to jail. And I would show my real feelings, the side of a man which never comes out in public life. But . . .

I could do it, he thought, if there weren't those damn black slaves lurking around; I could endure those above me seeing it, their scorn – after all, they scorn me and humiliate me every day. But to have those beneath see me, to feel their contempt. Like this *chink* pedalling away ahead of me. If I hadn't taken a pedecab, if he had seen me trying to *walk* to a business appointment ...

One had to blame the Germans for the situation. Tendency to bite off more than they could chew. After all, they had barely managed to win the war, and at once they had gone off to conquer the solar system, while at home they had passed edicts which . . . well, at least the idea was good. And after all, they had been successful with the Jews and Gypsies and Bible Students. And the Slavs had been rolled back two thousand years' worth, to their heartland in Asia. Out of Europe entirely, to everyone's relief. Back to riding yaks and hunting with bow and arrow. And those great glossy magazines printed in Munich and circulated around to all the libraries and news-stands . . . one could see the full-page colour pictures for oneself : the blue-eyed, blond-haired Aryan settlers who now industriously tilled, culled, ploughed, and so forth in the vast grain bowl of the world, the Ukraine. Those fellows certainly looked happy. And their farms and cottages were clean. You didn't see pictures of drunken dull-witted Poles any more, slouched on sagging porches or hawking a few sickly turnips at the village market. All a thing of the past, like rutted dirt roads that once turned to slop in the rainy season, bogging down the carts.

But Africa. They had simply let their enthusiasm get the better of them there, and you had to admire that, although more thoughtful advice would have cautioned them to perhaps let it wait a bit until, for instance, Project Farmland had been completed. Now *there* the Nazis had shown genius; the artist in them had truly emerged. The Mediterranean Sea bottled up, drained, made into tillable farmland, through the use of atomic power – what daring! How the sniggerers had been set back on their heels, for instance certain scoffing merchants along Montgomery Street. And as a matter of fact, Africa had almost been successful . . . but in a project of that sort, *almost* was an ominous word to begin to hear. Rosenberg's well-known powerful pamphlet issued in 1958; the word had first shown up, then. *As to the Final Solution of the African Problem, we have almost achieved our objectives. Unfortunately, however –*

Still, it had taken two hundred years to dispose of the American aborigines, and Germany had almost done it in Africa in fifteen years. So no criticism was legitimately in order. Childan had, in fact, argued it out recently while having lunch with certain of those other merchants. They expected miracles, evidently, as if the Nazis could remould the world by magic. No, it was science and technology and that fabulous talent for hard work; the Germans never stopped applying themselves. And when they did a task, they did it *right*.

And anyhow, the flights to Mars had distracted world attention from the difficulty in Africa. So it all came back to what he had told his fellow store owners; what the Nazis have which we lack is – nobility. Admire them for their love of work or their efficiency . . . but it's the dream that stirs one. Space flights first to the moon, then to Mars; if that isn't the oldest yearning of mankind, our finest hope for glory. Now, the Japanese on the other hand. I know them pretty well; I do business with them, after all, day in and day out. They are – let's face it – Orientals. Yellow people. We whites have to bow to them because they hold the power. But we watch Germany; we see what can be done where whites have conquered, and it's quite different.

'We approach the Nippon Times Building, sir,' the *chink* said, his chest heaving from the exertion of the hill climbing. He slowed, now.

To himself, Childan tried to picture Mr Tagomi's client. Clearly the man was unusually important; Mr Tagomi's tone on the telephone, his immense agitation, had communicated the fact. Image of one of Childan's own very important clients or rather, customers, swam up into his mind, a man who had done a good deal to create for Childan a reputation among the high-placed personages residing in the Bay Area.

Four years ago, Childan had not been the dealer in the rare and desirable which he was now; he had operated a small rather dimly lighted secondhand bookshop on Geary. His neighbouring stores sold used furniture, or hardware, or did laundry. It was not a nice neighbourhood. At night strong-arm robberies and sometimes rape took place on the sidewalk, despite the efforts of the San Francisco Police Department and even the Kempeitai, the Japanese higher-ups. All store windows had iron gratings fitted over them once the business day had ended, this to prevent forcible entry. Yet, into this district of the city had come an elderly Japanese ex-Army man, a Major Ito Humo. Tall, slender, white-haired, walking and standing stiffly, Major Humo had given Childan his first inkling of what might be done with his line of merchandise.

'I am a collector,' Major Humo had explained. He had spent an entire afternoon searching among the heaps of old magazines in the store. In his mild voice he had explained something which Childan could not quite grasp at the time : to many wealthy, cultured Japanese, the historic objects of American popular civilization were of equal interest along-side the more formal antiques. *Why* this was so, the major himself did not know; he was particularly addicted to the collecting of old magazines dealing with U.S. brass buttons, as well as the buttons themselves. It was of the order of coin or stamp collecting; no rational explanation could ever be given. And high prices were being paid by wealthy collectors.

'I will give you an example,' the major had said. 'Do you know what is meant by "Horrors of War" cards?' He had eyed Childan with avidity.

Searching his memory, Childan had at last recalled. The cards had been dispensed, during his childhood, with bubble gum. A cent apiece. There had been a series of them, each card depicting a different horror.

'A dear friend of mine,' the major had gone on, 'collects

"Horrors of War". He lacks but one, now. The *Sinking of the Panay*. He has offered a substantial sum of money for that particular card.'

'Flip cards,' Childan had said suddenly.

'Sir?'

'We flipped them. There was a head and a tail side on each card.' He had been about eight years old. 'Each of us had a pack of flip cards. We stood, two of us, facing each other. Each of us dropped a card so that it flipped in the air. The boy whose card landed with the head side up, the side with the picture, won both cards.' How enjoyable to recall those good days, those early happy days of his childhood.

Considering, Major Humo had said, 'I have heard my friend discuss his "Horrors of War" cards, and he has never mentioned this. *It is my opinion that he does not know how these cards actually were put to use.*'

Eventually, the major's friend had shown up at the store to hear Childan's historically firsthand account. That man, also a retired officer of the Imperial Army, had been fascinated.

'Bottle caps!' Childan had exclaimed without warning.

The Japanese had blinked uncomprehendingly.

'We used to collect the tops from milk bottles. As kids. The round tops that gave the name of the dairy. There must have been thousands of dairies in the United States. Each one printed a special top.'

The officer's eyes had glinted with the instinct. 'Do you possess any of your sometime collection, sir?'

Naturally, Childan did not. But ₁ . ₂ probably it was still possible to obtain the ancient, long-forgotten tops from the days before the war when milk had come in glass bottles rather than throwaway pasteboard cartons.

And so, by stages, he had gotten into the business. Others had opened similar places, taking advantage of the ever-growing Japanese craze for Americana . . . but Childan had always kept his edge.

'Your fare,' the *chink* was saying, bringing him out of his meditation, 'is a dollar, sir.' He had unloaded the bags and was waiting.

Absentmindedly, Childan paid him. Yes, it was quite likely that the client of Mr Tagomi resembled Major Humo; at least, Childan thought tartly, from my point of view. He had dealt with so many Japanese . . . but he still had difficulty telling them apart. There were the short squat ones, built like wrestlers. Then the druggistlike ones. The tree-shrub-flower-gardener ones . . . he had his categories. And the young ones, who were to him not like Japanese at all. Mr Tagomi's client would probably be portly, a business-man, smoking a Philippine cigar.

And then, standing before the Nippon Times Building, with his bags on the sidewalk beside him, Childan suddenly thought with a chill: Suppose his client isn't Japanese! Everything in the bags had been selected with them in mind, their tastes –

But the man had to be Japanese. A Civil War recruiting poster had been Mr Tagomi's original order; surely only a Japanese would care about such débris. Typical of their mania for the trivial, their legalistic fascination with docu-ments, proclamations, ads. He remembered one who had devoted his leisure time to collecting newspaper ads of American patent medicines of the 1900s.

There were other problems to face. Immediate problems. Through the high doors of the Nippon Times Building men and women hurried, all of them well dressed; their voices reached Childan's ears, and he started into motion. A glance upwards at the towering edifice, the highest building in San Francisco. Wall of offices, windows, the fabulous design of the Japanese architects – and the surrounding garden of dwarf evergreens, rocks, the karesansui landscape, sand imi-tating a dried-up stream winding past roots, among simple, irregular flat stones . . .

He saw a black who had carried baggage, now free. At once Childan called, 'Porter!'

The black trotted towards him, smiling.

'To the twentieth floor,' Childan said in his harshest

voice. 'Suite B. At once.' He indicated the bags and then strode on towards the doors of the building. Naturally he did not look back.

A moment later he found himself being crowded into one of the express elevators; mostly Japanese around him, their clean faces shining slightly in the brilliant light of the elevator. Then the nauseating upwards thrust of the elevator, the rapid click of doors passing; he shut his eyes, planted his feet firmly, prayed for the flight to end. The black, of course, had taken the bags up on a service elevator. It would not have been within the realm of reason to permit him here. In fact – Childan opened his eyes and looked momentarily – he was one of the few whites in the elevator.

When the elevator let him off on the twentieth floor, Childan was already bowing mentally, preparing himself for the encounter in Mr Tagomi's offices.

3

At sunset, glancing up, Juliana Frink saw the dot of light in the sky shoot in an arc, disappear to the west. One of those Nazi rocket ships, she said to herself. Flying to the Coast. Full of big shots. And here I am down below. She waved, although the rocket ship of course had already gone.

Shadows advancing from the Rockies. Blue peaks turning to night. A flock of slow birds, migratory, made their way parallel with the mountains. Here and there a car turned its headlights on; she saw the twin dots along the highway. Lights, too, of a gas station. Houses.

For months now she had been living here in Canon City, Colorado. She was a judo instructor.

Her workday had ended and she was preparing to take a shower. She felt tired. All the showers were in use, by customers of Ray's Gym, so she had been standing, waiting outdoors in the coolness, enjoying the smell of mountain air, the quiet. All she heard now was the faint murmur from the hamburger stand down the road by the highway's edge. Two huge diesel trucks had parked, and the drivers, in the gloom, could be seen moving about, putting on their leather jackets before entering the hamburger stand.

She thought: Didn't Diesel throw himself out the window of his stateroom? Commit suicide by drowning himself on an ocean voyage? Maybe I ought to do that. But here there was no ocean. But there is always a way. Like in Shakespeare. A pin stuck through one's shirt front, and good-bye Frink. The girl who need not fear marauding homeless from the desert. Walks upright in consciousness of many pinched-nerve possibilities in grizzled salivating adversary. Death instead by, say, sniffing car exhaust in highway town, perhaps through long hollow straw.

Learned that, she thought, from Japanese. Imbibed placid attitude towards mortality, along with money-making judo. How to kill, how to die. Yang and yin. But that's behind, now; this is Protestant land.

It was a good thing to see the Nazi rockets go by overhead and not stop, not take any interest of any sort in Canon City, Colorado. Nor in Utah or Wyoming or the eastern part of Nevada, none of the open empty desert states or pasture states. We have no value, she said to herself. We can live out our tiny lives. If we want to. If it matters to us.

From one of the showers, the noise of a door unlocking. A shape, large Miss Davis, finished with her shower, dressed, purse under her arm. 'Oh, were you waiting, Mrs Frink? I'm sorry.'

'It's all right,' Juliana said.

'You know, Mrs Frink, I've gotten so much out of judo. Even more than out of Zen. I wanted to tell you.'

'Slim your hips the Zen way,' Juliana said. 'Lose pounds through painless satori. I'm sorry, Miss Davis. I'm woolgathering.'

Miss Davis said, 'Did they hurt you much?'

'Who?'

'The Japs. Before you learned to defend yourself.'

'It was dreadful,' Juliana said. 'You've never been out there, on the Coast. Where they are.'

'I've never been outside of Colorado,' Miss Davis said, her voice fluttering timidly.

'It could happen here,' Juliana said. 'They might decide to occupy this region, too.'

'Not this late!'

'You never know what they're going to do,' Juliana said. 'They hide their real thoughts.'

'What – did they make you do?' Miss Davis, hugging her purse against her body with both arms, moved closer, in the evening darkness, to hear.

'Everything,' Juliana said.

'Oh God. I'd fight,' Miss Davis said.

Juliana excused herself and walked to the vacant shower; someone else was approaching it with a towel over her arm.

Later, she sat in a booth at Tasty Charley's Broiled Hamburgers, listlessly reading the menu. The jukebox played some hillbilly tune; steel guitar and emotion-choked moaning . . . the air was heavy with grease smoke. And yet, the place was warm and bright, and it cheered her, The presence of the truck drivers at the counters, the waitress, the big Irish fry cook in his white jacket at the register making change.

Seeing her, Charley approached to wait on her himself. Grinning, he drawled, 'Missy want tea now?'

'Coffee,' Juliana said, enduring the fry cook's relentless humour.

'Ah so,' Charley said, nodding.

'And the hot steak sandwich with gravy.'

'Not have bowl rat's-nest soup? Or maybe goat brains fried in olive oil?' A couple of the truck drivers, turning on their stools, grinned along with the gag, too. And in addition they took pleasure in noticing how attractive she was. Even lacking the fry cook's kidding, she would have found the truck drivers scrutinizing her. The months of active judo had given her unusual muscle tone; she knew how well she held herself and what it did for her figure.

It all has to do with the shoulder muscles, she thought as she met their gaze. Dancers do it, too. It has nothing to do with size. Send your wives around to the gym and we'll teach them. And you'll be so much more content in life.

'Stay away from her,' the fry cook warned the truck drivers with a wink. 'She'll throw you on your can.'

She said to the younger of the truck drivers, 'Where are you in from?'

'Missouri,' both men said.

'Are you from the United States?' she asked.

'I am,' the older man said, 'Philadelphia. Got three kids there. The oldest is eleven.'

'Listen,' Juliana said. 'Is it – easy to get a good job back there?'

The younger truck driver said, 'Sure. If you have the right colour skin.' He himself had a dark brooding face with curly black hair. His expression had become set and bitter.

'He's a wop,' the older man said.

'Well,' Juliana said, 'didn't Italy win the war?' She smiled at the young truck driver but he did not smile back. Instead, his sombre eyes glowed even more intensely, and suddenly he turned away.

I'm sorry, she thought. But she said nothing. I can't save you or anybody else from being dark. She thought of Frank. I wonder if he's dead yet. Said the wrong thing; spoke out of line. No, she thought. Somehow he likes Japs. Maybe he identifies with them because they're ugly. She had always told Frank that he was ugly. Large pores. Big nose. Her own skin was finely knit, unusually so. Did he fall dead without me? A fink is a finch, a form of bird. And they say birds die.

'Are you going back on the road tonight?' she asked the young Italian truck driver.

'Tomorrow.'

'If you're not happy in the U.S. why don't you cross over permanently?' she said. 'I've been living in the Rockies for a long time and it isn't so bad. I lived on the Coast, in San Francisco. They have the skin thing there, too.'

Glancing briefly at her as he sat hunched at the counter, the young Italian said, 'Lady, it's bad enough to have to spend one day or one night in a town like this. Live here? Christ – if I could get any other kind of job, and not have to be on the road eating my meals in places like this –' Noticing that the fry cook was red, he ceased speaking and began to drink his coffee.

The older truck driver said to him, 'Joe, you're a snob.'

'You could live in Denver,' Juliana said. 'It's nicer up there.' I know you East Americans, she thought. You like the big time. Dreaming your big schemes. This is just the sticks to you, the Rockies. Nothing has happened here since before the war. Retired old people, farmers, the stupid, slow, poor . . . and all the smart boys have flocked east to New York, crossed the border legally or illegally. Because, she thought, that's where the money is, the big industrial money. The expansion. German investment has done a lot . . . it didn't take long for them to build the U.S. back up.

The fry cook said in a hoarse angry voice, 'Buddy, I'm not a Jew-lover, but I seen some of those Jew refugees fleeing your U.S. in '49, and you can have your U.S. If there's a lot of building back there and a lot of loose easy money it's because they stole it from those Jews when they kicked them out of New York, that goddam Nazi Nuremberg Law. I lived in Boston when I was a kid, and I got no special use for Jews, but I never thought I'd see that Nazi racial law get passed in the U.S., even if we did lose the war. I'm surprised you aren't in the U.S. Armed Forces, getting ready to invade some little South American republic as a front for the Germans, so they can push the Japanese back a little bit more –'

Both truck drivers were on their feet, their faces stark. The older man picked up a ketchup bottle from the counter and held it upright by the neck. The fry cook without turning his back to the two men reached behind him until his fingers touched one of his meat forks. He brought the fork out and held it.

Juliana said, 'Denver is getting one of those heat-resistant runways so that Lufthansa rockets can land there.'

None of the three men moved or spoke. The other customers sat silently.

Finally, the fry cook said, 'One flew over around sundown.'

'It wasn't going to Denver,' Juliana said. 'It was going west, to the Coast.'

By degrees, the two truck drivers reseated themselves. The older man mumbled, 'I always forget; they're a little yellow out here.'

The fry cook said, 'No Japs killed Jews, in the war or after. No Japs built ovens.'

'Too bad they didn't,' the older truck driver said. But, picking up his coffee cup, he resumed eating.

Yellow, Juliana thought. Yes, I suppose it's true. We love the Japs out here.

'Where are you staying?' she asked, speaking to the young truck driver, Joe. 'Overnight.'

'I don't know,' he answered. 'I just got out of the truck to come in here. I don't like this whole state. Maybe I'll sleep in the truck.'

'The Honey Bee Motel isn't too bad,' the fry cook said.

'Okay,' the young truck driver said. 'Maybe I'll stay there. If they don't mind me being Italian.' He had a definite accent, although he tried to hide it.

Watching him, Juliana thought, It's idealism that makes him that bitter. Asking too much out of life. Always moving on, restless and griped. I'm the same way; I couldn't stay on the West Coast and eventually I won't be able to stand it here. Weren't the old-timers like that? But, she thought, now the frontier isn't here; it's the other planets.

She thought: He and I could sign up for one of those colonizing rocket ships. But the Germans would disbar him because of his skin and me because of my dark hair. Those pale skinny Nordic S.S. fairies in those training castles in Bavaria. This guy – Joe whatever – hasn't even got the right expression on his face; he should have that cold but somehow enthusiastic look, as if he believed in nothing and yet somehow had absolute faith. Yes, that's how they are. They're not idealists like Joe and me; they're cynics with utter faith. It's a sort of brain defect, like a lobotomy – that maiming those German psychiatrists do as a poor substitute for psychotherapy.

Their trouble, she decided, is with sex; they did something foul with it back in the 'thirties, and it has gotten worse. Hitler started it with his – what was she? His sister? Aunt? Niece? And his family was inbred already; his mother and father were cousins. They're all committing incest, going back to the original sin of lusting for their own mothers. That's why they, those elite S.S. fairies, have that angelic simper, that blond babylike innocence; they're saving themselves for Mama. Or for each other.

And who is Mama for them? she wondered. The leader, Herr Bormann, who is supposed to be dying? Or – the Sick One.

Old Adolf, supposed to be in a sanatorium somewhere, living out his life of senile paresis. Syphilis of the brain, dating back to his poor days as a bum in Vienna . . . long black coat, dirty underwear, flophouses.

Obviously, it was God's sardonic vengeance, right out of some silent movie. That awful man struck down by an internal filth, the historic plague for man's wickedness.

And the horrible part was that the present-day German Empire was a product of that brain. First a political party, then a nation, then half the world. And the Nazis themselves had diagnosed it, identified it; that quack herbal medicine man who had treated Hitler, that Dr Morell who had dosed Hitler with a patent medicine called Dr Koester's Antigas Pills – he had originally been a specialist in venereal disease. The entire world knew it, and yet the Leader's gabble was still sacred, still Holy Writ. The views had infected a civilization by now, and, like evil spores, the blind blond Nazi queens were swishing out from Earth to the other planets, spreading the contamination.

What you get for incest : madness, blindness, death.

Brrr. She shook herself.

'Charley,' she called to the fry cook. 'You about ready with my order?' She felt absolutely alone; getting to her feet she walked to the counter and seated herself by the register.

No one noticed her except the young Italian truck driver; his dark eyes were fixed on her. Joe, his name was. Joe what? she wondered.

Closer to him, now, she saw that he was not as young as she had thought. Hard to tell; the intensity all around him disturbed her judgement. Continually he drew his hand through his hair, combing it back with crooked, rigid fingers. There's something special about this man, she thought. He breathes – death. It upset her, and yet attracted her. Now the older truck driver inclined his head and whispered to him. Then they both scrutinized her, this time with a look that was not the ordinary male interest.

'Miss,' the older one said. Both men were quite tense, now. 'Do you know what this is?' He held up a flat white box, not too large.

'Yes,' Juliana said. 'Nylon stockings. Synthetic fibre made only by the great cartel in New York, I.G. Farben. Very rare and expensive.'

'You got to hand it to the Germans; monopoly's not a bad idea.' The older truck driver passed the box to his companion, who pushed it with his elbow along the counter towards her.

'You have a car?' the young Italian asked her, sipping his coffee.

From the kitchen, Charley appeared; he had her plate.

'You could drive me to this place.' The wild, strong eyes still studied her, and she became increasingly nervous, and yet increasingly transfixed. 'This motel, or wherever I'm supposed to stay tonight. Isn't that so?'

'Yes,' she said. ' I have a car. An old Studebaker.'

The fry cook glanced from her to the young truck driver, and then set her plate before her at the counter.

The loudspeaker at the end of the aisle said, 'Achtung, meine Damen und Herren.' In his seat, Mr Baynes started, opened his eyes. Through the window to his right he could see, far below, the brown and green of land, and then blue. The Pacific. The rocket, he realized, had begun its long slow descent.

In German first, then Japanese, and at last English, the loudspeaker explained that no one was to smoke or to untie himself from his padded seat. The descent, it explained, would take eight minutes.

The retro-jets started then, so suddenly and loudly, shaking the ship so violently, that a number of passengers gasped. Mr Baynes smiled, and in the aisle seat across from him, another passenger, a younger man with close-cropped blond hair, also smiled.

'Sie fürchten dasz –' the young man began, but Mr Baynes said at once, in English :

'I'm sorry; I don't speak German.' The young German gazed at him questioningly, and so he said the same thing in German.

'No German?' the young German said, amazed, in accented English.

'I am Swedish,' Baynes said.

'You embarked at Tempelhof.'

'Yes, I was in Germany on business. My business carries me to a number of countries.'

Clearly, the young German could not believe that anyone in the modern world, anyone who had international business dealings and rode – could afford to ride – on the latest Lufthansa rocket, could or would not speak German. To Baynes he said, 'What line are you in, mein Herr?'

'Plastics. Polyesters. Resins. Ersatz – industrial uses. Do you see? No consumers' commodities.'

'Sweden has a *plastics* industry?' Disbelief.

'Yes, a very good one. If you will give me your name I

will have a firm brochure mailed to you.' Mr Baynes brought out his pen and pad.

'Never mind. It would be wasted on me. I am an artist, not a commercial man. No offence. Possibly you have seen my work while on the Continent, Alex Lotze.' He waited.

'Afraid I do not care for modern art,' Mr Baynes said. 'I like the old prewar cubists and abstractionists. I like a picture to mean something, not merely to represent the ideal.' He turned away.

'But that's the task of art,' Lotze said. 'To advance the spirituality of man, over the sensual. Your abstract art represented a period of spiritual decadence, of spiritual chaos, due to the disintegration of society, the old plutocracy. The Jewish and capitalist millionaires, the international set that supported the decadent art. Those times are over; art has to go on – it can't stay still.'

Baynes nodded, gazing out the window.

'Have you been to the Pacific before?' Lotze asked.

'Several times.'

'Not I. There is an exhibition in San Francisco of my work, arranged by Dr Goebbels' office, with the Japanese authorities. A cultural exchange to promote understanding and goodwill. We must ease tensions between the East and West, don't you think? We must have more communication, and art can do that.'

Baynes nodded. Below, beyond the ring of fire from the rocket, the city of San Francisco and the Bay could now be seen.

'Where does one eat in San Francisco?' Lotze was saying. 'I have reservations at the Palace Hotel, but my understanding is that one can find good food in the international section, such as the Chinatown.'

'True,' Baynes said.

'Are prices high in San Francisco? I am out of pocket for this trip. The Ministry is very frugal.' Lotze laughed.

'Depends on the exchange rate you can manage. I presume you're carrying Reichsbank drafts. I suggest you go to the Bank of Tokyo on Samson Street and exchange there.'

'Danke sehr,' Lotze said. 'I would have done it at the hotel.'

The rocket had almost reached the ground. Now Baynes could see the airfield itself, hangars, parking lots, the autobahn from the city, the houses . . . very lovely view, he thought. Mountains and water, and a few bits of fog drifting in at the Golden Gate.

'What is that enormous structure below?' Lotze asked. 'It is half-finished, open at one side. A spaceport? The Nipponese have no spacecraft, I thought.'

With a smile, Baynes said, 'That's Golden Poppy Stadium. The baseball park.'

Lotze laughed. 'Yes, they love baseball. Incredible. They have begun work on that great structure for a pastime, an idle time-wasting sport –'

Interrupting, Baynes said, 'It is finished. That's its permanent shape. Open on one side. A new architectural design. They are very proud of it.'

'It looks,' Lotze said, gazing down, 'as if it was designed by a Jew.'

Baynes regarded the man for a time. He felt, strongly for a moment, the unbalanced quality, the psychotic streak, in the German mind. Did Lotze actually mean what he said? Was it a truly spontaneous remark?

'I hope we will see one another later on in San Francisco,' Lotze said as the rocket touched the ground. 'I will be at loose ends without a countryman to talk to.'

'I'm not a countryman of yours,' Baynes said.

'Oh, yes; that's so. But racially, you're quite close. For all intents and purposes the same.' Lotze began to stir around in his seat, getting ready to unfasten the elaborate belts.

Am I racially kin to this man? Baynes wondered. So closely so that for all intents and purposes it is the same? Then it is in me, too, the psychotic streak. A psychotic world we live in. The madmen are in power. How long have we known this? Faced this? And – how many of us do know it? Not Lotze. Perhaps if you know you are insane then you are not insane. Or you are becoming sane, finally. Waking up. I suppose only a few are aware of all this. Isolated persons here and there. But the broad masses . . . what do they think? All these hundreds of thousands in this city, here. Do they imagine that they live in a sane world? Or do they guess, glimpse, the truth . . .?

But, he thought, what does it mean, *insane*? A legal definition. What do I mean? I feel it, see it, but what is it?

He thought, It is something they do, something they are. It is their unconsciousness. Their lack of knowledge about others. Their not being aware of what they do to others, the destruction they have caused and are causing. No, he thought. That isn't it. I don't know; I sense it, intuit it. But – they are purposelessly cruel . . . is that it? No, God, he thought. I can't find it, make it clear. Do they ignore parts of reality? Yes. But it is more. It is their plans. Yes, their plans. The conquering of the planets. Something frenzied and demented, as was their conquering of Africa, and before that, Europe and Asia.

Their view; it is cosmic. Not a man here, a child there, but an abstraction : race, land. *Volk. Land. Blut. Ehre.* Not of honourable men but of *Ehre* itself, honour; the abstract is real, the actual is invisible to them. *Die Güte*, but not good men, this good man. It is their sense of space and time. They see through the here, the now, into the vast black deep beyond, the unchanging. And that is fatal to life. Because eventually there will be no life; there was once only the dust particles in space, the hot hydrogen gases, nothing more, and it will come again. This is an interval, *ein Augenblick*. The cosmic process is hurrying on, crushing life back into the granite and methane; the wheel turns for all life. It is all temporary. And these – these madmen – respond to the granite, the dust, the longing of the inanimate; they want to aid *Natur*.

And, he thought, I know why. They want to be the agents, not the victims, of history. They identify with God's power and believe they are godlike. That is their basic madness. They are overcome by some archetype; their egos have expanded psychotically so that they cannot tell where they begin and the godhead leaves off. It is not hubris, not pride; it is inflation of the ego to its ultimate – confusion between him who worships and that which is worshipped. Man has not eaten God; God has eaten man.

What they do not comprehend is man's *helplessness.* I am weak, small, of no consequence to the universe. It does not notice me; I live on unseen. But why is that bad? Isn't it better that way? Whom the gods notice they destroy. Be small . . . and you will escape the jealousy of the great.

As he unfastened his own belt, Baynes said, 'Mr Lotze, I have never told anyone this. I am a Jew. Do you understand?'

Lotze stared at him piteously.

'You would not have known,' Baynes said, 'because I do not in any physical way appear Jewish; I have had my nose altered, my large greasy pores made smaller, my skin chemically lightened, the shape of my skull changed. In short, physically I cannot be detected. I can and have often walked in the highest circles of Nazi society. No one will ever discover me. And –' He paused, standing close, very close to Lotze and speaking in a low voice which only Lotze could hear. 'And there are others of us. Do you hear? We did not die. We still exist. We live on unseen.'

After a moment Lotze stuttered, 'The Security Police –'

'The S.D. can go over my record,' Baynes said. 'You can report me. But I have very high connections. Some of them are Aryan, some are other Jews in top positions in Berlin. Your report will be discounted, and then, presently, I will report you. And through these same connections, you will find yourself in Protective Custody.' He smiled, nodded and walked up the aisle of the ship, away from Lotze, to join the other passengers.

Everyone descended the ramp, onto the cold, windy field. At the bottom, Baynes found himself once more momentarily near Lotze.

'In fact,' Baynes said, walking beside Lotze, 'I do not

like your looks, Mr Lotze, so I think I will report you any-how.' He strode on, then, leaving Lotze behind.

At the far end of the field, at the concourse entrance, a large number of people were waiting. Relatives, friends of passengers, some of them waving, peering, smiling, looking anxious, scanning faces. A heavy-set middle-aged Japanese man, well dressed in a British overcoat, pointed Oxfords, bowler, stood a little ahead of the others, with a younger Japanese beside him. On his coat lapel he wore the badge of the ranking Pacific Trade Mission of the Imperial Government. There he is, Baynes realized. Mr N. Tagomi, come personally to meet me.

Starting forward, the Japanese called, 'Herr Baynes – good evening.' His head tilted hesitantly.

'Good evening, Mr Tagomi,' Baynes said, holding out his hand. They shook, then bowed. The younger Japanese also bowed, beaming.

'Bit cold, sir, on this exposed field,' Mr Tagomi said. 'We shall begin return trip to downtown city by Mission helicopter. Is that so? Or do you need to use the facilities, and so forth?' He scrutinized Mr Baynes's face anxiously.

'We can start right now,' Baynes said. 'I want to check in at my hotel. My baggage, however –'

'Mr Kotomichi will attend to that,' Mr Tagomi said. 'He will follow. You see, sir, at this terminal it takes almost an hour waiting in line to claim baggage. Longer than your trip.'

Mr Kotomichi smiled agreeably.

'All right,' Baynes said.

Mr Tagomi said, 'Sir, I have a gift to graft.'

'I beg your pardon?' Baynes said.

'To invite your favourable attitude.' Mr Tagomi reached into his overcoat pocket and brought out a small box. 'Selected from among the finest *objets d'art* of America available.' He held out the box.

'Well,' Baynes said. 'Thanks.' He accepted the box.

'All afternoon assorted officials examined the alternatives,' Mr Tagomi said. 'This is most authentic of dying old U.S.

47

culture, a rare retained artifact carrying flavour of bygone halcyon day.'

Mr Baynes opened the box. In it lay a Mickey Mouse wristwatch on a pad of black velvet.

Was Mr Tagomi playing a joke on him? He raised his eyes, saw Mr Tagomi's tense, concerned face. No, it was not a joke. 'Thank you very much,' Baynes said. 'This is indeed incredible.'

'Only few, perhaps ten, authentic 1938 Mickey Mouse watches in all world today,' Mr Tagomi said, studying him, drinking in his reaction, his appreciation. 'No collector known to me has one, sir.'

They entered the air terminal and together ascended the ramp.

Behind them Mr Kotomichi said, '*Harusame ni nuretsutsu yane no temari kana ...*'

'What is that?' Mr Baynes said to Mr Tagomi.

'Old poem,' Mr Tagomi said. 'Middle Tokugawa Period.'

Mr Kotomichi said, '*As the spring rains fall, soaking in them, on the roof, is a child's rag ball.*'

4

As Frank Frink watched his ex-employer waddle down the corridor and into the main work area of W.-M. Corporation he thought to himself, The strange thing about Wyndam-Matson is that he does not look like a man who owns a factory. He looks like a Tenderloin bum, a wino, who has been given a bath, new clothes, a shave, haircut, shot of vitamins, and sent out into the world with five dollars to find a new life. The old man had a weak, shifty, nervous, even ingratiating manner, as if he regarded everyone as a potential enemy stronger than he, whom he had to fawn on and pacify. 'They're going to get me,' his manner seemed to say.

And yet old W.-M. was really very powerful. He owned

controlling interests in a variety of enterprises, speculations, real estate. As well as the W.-M. Corporation factory.

Following after the old man, Frink pushed open the big metal door to the main work area. The rumble of machinery, which he had heard around him every day for so long – sight of men at the machines, air filled with flash of light, waste dust, movement. There went the old man. Frink increased his pace.

'Hey, Mr W.-M.!' he called.

The old man had stopped by the hairy-armed shop foreman, Ed McCarthy. Both of them glanced up as Frink came towards them.

Moistening his lips nervously, Wyndam-Matson said, 'I'm sorry, Frank; I can't do anything about taking you back. I've already gone ahead and hired someone to take your place, thinking you weren't coming back. After what you said.' His small round eyes flickered with what Frink knew to be an almost hereditary evasiveness. It was in the old man's blood.

Frink said, 'I came for my tools. Nothing else.' His own voice, he was glad to hear, was firm, even harsh.

'Well, let's see,' W.-M. mumbled, obviously hazy in his own mind as to the status of Frink's tools. To Ed McCarthy he said, 'I think that would be in your department, Ed. Maybe you can fix Frank here up. I have other business.' He glanced at his pocket watch. 'Listen, Ed. I'll discuss that invoice later; I have to run along.' He patted Ed McCarthy on the arm and then trotted off, not looking back.

Ed McCarthy and Frink stood together.

'You came to get your job back,' McCarthy said after a time.

'Yes,' Frink said.

'I was proud of what you said yesterday.'

'So was I,' Frink said. 'But – Christ, I can't work it out anywhere else.' He felt defeated and hopeless. 'You know that.' The two of them had, in the past, often talked over their problems.

McCarthy said, ' I don't know that. You're as good with that flex-cable machine as anybody on the Coast. I've seen you whip out a piece in five minutes, including the rouge polishing. All the way from the rough Cratex. And except for the welding –'

'I never said I could weld,' Frink said.

'Did you ever think of going into business on your own?'

Frink, taken by surprise, stammered, 'What doing?'

'Jewellery.'

'Aw, for Christ's sake!'

'Custom, original pieces, not commercial.' McCarthy beckoned him over to a corner of the shop, away from the noise. 'For about two thousand bucks you could set up a little basement or garage shop. One time I drew up designs for women's ear-rings and pendants. You remember – real modern contemporary.' Taking scratch paper, he began to draw, slowly, grimly.

Peering over his shoulder, Frink saw a bracelet design, an abstract with flowing lines. 'Is there a market?' All he had ever seen were the traditional – even antique – objects from the past. 'Nobody wants contemporary American; there isn't any such thing, not since the war.'

'Create a market,' McCarthy said, with an angry grimace.

'You mean sell it myself?'

'Take it into retail shops. Like that – what's it called? On Montgomery Street, that big ritzy art object place.'

'American Artistic Handcrafts,' Frink said. He never went into fashionable, expensive stores such as that. Few Americans did; it was the Japanese who had the money to buy from such places.

'You know what retailers like that are selling?' McCarthy said. 'And getting a fortune for? Those goddam silver belt buckles from New Mexico that the Indians make. Those goddam tourist trash pieces, all alike. Supposedly native art.'

For a long time Frink regarded McCarthy. 'I know what else they sell,' he said finally. 'And so do you.'

'Yes,' McCarthy said.

They both knew – because they had both been directly involved, and for a long time.

W.-M. Corporation's stated legal business consisted in turning out wrought-iron staircases, railings, fireplaces, and ornaments for new apartment buildings, all on a mass basis, from standard designs. For a new forty-unit building the same piece would be executed forty times in a row. Ostensibly, W.-M. Corporation was an iron foundry. But in addition, it maintained another business from which its real profits were derived.

Using an elaborate variety of tools, materials, and machines, W.-M. Corporation turned out a constant flow of forgeries of pre-war American artifacts. These forgeries were cautiously but expertly fed into the wholesale art object market, to join the genuine objects collected throughout the continent. As in the stamp and coin business, no one could possibly estimate the percentage of forgeries in circulation. And no one – especially the dealers and the collectors themselves – wanted to.

When Frink had quit, there lay half-finished on his bench a Colt revolver of the Frontier period; he had made the moulds himself, done the casting, and had been busy hand-smoothing the pieces. There was an unlimited market for small arms of the American Civil War and Frontier period; W.-M. Corporation could sell all that Frink could turn out. It was his speciality.

Walking slowly over to his bench, Frink picked up the still-rough and burred ramrod of the revolver. Another three days and the gun would be finished. Yes, he thought, it was good work. An expert could have told the difference . . . but the Japanese collectors weren't authorities in the proper sense, had no standards or tests by which to judge.

In fact, as far as he knew, it had never occurred to them to ask themselves if the so-called historic art objects for sale in West Coast shops were genuine. Perhaps some day they would . . . and then the bubble would burst, the market would collapse even for the authentic pieces. A Gresham's Law : the fakes would undermine the value of the real. And that no doubt was the motive for the failure to investigate; after all, everyone was happy. The factories, here and there in the various cities, which turned out the pieces, they made their profits. The wholesalers passed them on, and the dealers displayed and advertised them. The collectors shelled out their money and carried their purchases happily home, to impress their associates, friends, and mistresses.

Like postwar boodle paper money, it was fine until questioned. Nobody was hurt – until the day of reckoning. And then everyone, equally, would be ruined. But meanwhile, nobody talked about it, even the men who earned their living turning out the forgeries; they shut their own minds to *what* they made, kept their attention on the mere technical problems,

'How long since you tried to do original designing?' McCarthy asked.

Frink shrugged, 'Years. I can copy accurately as hell. But –'

'You know what I think? I think you've picked up the Nazi idea that Jews can't create. That they can only imitate and sell. Middlemen.' He fixed his merciless scrutiny on Frink.

'Maybe so,' Frink said.

'Try it. Do some original designs. Or work directly on the metal. Play around. Like a kid plays.'

'No,' Frink said.

'You have no faith,' McCarthy said. 'You've completely lost faith in yourself – right? Too bad. Because I know you could do it.' He walked away from the workbench,

It is too bad, Frink thought. But nevertheless it's the truth. It's a fact. I can't get faith or enthusiasm by willing it. Deciding to.

That McCarthy, he thought, is a damn good shop foreman. He has the knack of needling a man, getting him to put out his best efforts, to do his utmost in spite of himself. He's a natural leader; he almost inspired me, for a moment, there. But – McCarthy had gone off, now; the effort had failed.

Too bad I don't have my copy of the oracle here, Frink thought. I could consult it on this; take the isssue to it for its five thousand years of wisdom. And then he recalled that there was a copy of the *I Ching* in the lounge of the business office of W.-M. Corporation. So he made his way from the work area, along the corridor, hurriedly through the business office to the lounge.

Seated in one of the chrome and plastic lounge chairs, he wrote his question out on the back of an envelope : 'Should I attempt to go into the creative private business outlined to me just now?' And then he began throwing the coins.

The bottom line was a seven, and so was the second and then the third. The bottom trigram is Ch'ien, he realized. That sounded good; Ch'ien was the creative. Then line Four, an eight. Yin. And line Five, also eight, a yin line. Good lord, he thought excitedly; one more yin line and I've got Hexagram Eleven, T'ai, Peace. Very favourable judgement. Or – his hands trembled as he rattled the coins. A yang line and hence Hexagram Twenty-six, Ta Ch'u, the Taming Power of the Great. Both have favourable judgements, and it has to be one or the other. He threw the three coins.

Yin. A six. It was Peace.

Opening the book, he read the judgement.

> PEACE. The small departs,
> The great approaches.
> Good fortune. Success.

So I ought to do as Ed McCarthy says. Open my little business. Now the six at the top, my one moving line. He turned the page. What was the text? He could not recall; probably favourable because the hexagram itself was so favourable. Union of heaven and earth – but the first and last lines were outside the hexagram always, so possibly the six at the top . . .

His eyes picked out the line, read it in a flash.

> The wall falls back into the moat.
> Use no army now.
> Make your commands known within your own town.
> Perseverance brings humiliation.

My busted back! he exclaimed, horrified. And the commentary.

The change alluded to in the middle of the hexagram has begun to take place. The wall of the town sinks back into the moat from which it was dug. The hour of doom is at hand ...

It was, beyond doubt, one of the most dismal lines in the entire book, of more than three thousand lines. And yet the judgement of the hexagram was good.

Which was he supposed to follow?

And how could they be so different? It had never happened to him before, good fortune and doom mixed together in the oracle's prophecy; what a weird fate, as if the oracle had scraped the bottom of the barrel, tossed up every sort of rag, bone, and turd of the dark, then reversed itself and poured in the light like a cook gone barmy. I must have pressed two buttons at once, he decided; jammed the works and got this *schlimazl's*-eye view of reality. Just for a second – fortunately. Didn't last.

Hell, he thought, it has to be one or the other; it can't be both. You can't have good fortune and doom simultaneously.

Or ... can you?

The jewellery business will bring good fortune; the judgement refers to that. But the line, the goddam line; it refers to something deeper, some future catastrophe probably not even connected with the jewellery business. Some evil fate that's in store for me *anyhow* ...

War! he thought. Third World War! All frigging two billion of us killed, our civilization wiped out. Hydrogen bombs falling like hail.

Oy gewalt! he thought. What's happening? Did I start it in motion? Or is someone else tinkering, someone I don't even know? Or – the whole lot of us. It's the fault of those physicists and that synchronicity theory, every particle being connected with every other; you can't fart without changing the balance in the universe. It makes living a funny joke with nobody around to laugh. I open a book and get a report on future events that even God would like to file and forget. And who am I? The wrong person; I can tell you that.

I should take my tools, get my motors from McCarthy, open my shop, start my piddling business, go on despite the horrible line. Be working, creating in my own way right up to the end, living as best I can, as actively as possible, until the wall falls back into the moat for all of us, all mankind. That's what the oracle is telling me. Fate will poleaxe us eventually anyhow, but I have my job in the meantime; I must use my mind, my hands.

The judgement was for me alone, for my work. But the line; it was for us all.

I'm too small, he thought. I can only read what's written, glance up and then lower my head and plod along where I left off as if I hadn't seen; the oracle doesn't expect me to start running up and down the streets, squalling and yammering for public attention.

Can *anyone* alter it? he wondered. All of us combined ... or one great figure ... or someone strategically placed, who happens to be in the right spot. Chance. Accident. And our lives, our world, hanging on it.

Closing the book, he left the lounge and walked back to the main work area. When he caught sight of McCarthy, he waved him over to one side where they could resume talk.

'The more I think about it,' Frink said, 'the more I like your idea.'

'Fine,' McCarthy said. 'Now listen. Here's what you do. You have to get money from Wyndam-Matson.' He winked, a slow, intense, frightened twitch of his eyelid. 'I figured out how. I'm going to quit and go in with you. My designs, see. What's wrong with that? I know they're good.'

'Sure,' Frink said, a little dazed.

'I'll see you after work tonight,' McCarthy said. 'At my

apartment. You come over around seven and have dinner with Jean and me – if you can stand the kids.'

'Okay,' Frink said.

McCarthy gave him a slap on the shoulder and went off.

I've gone a long way, Frink said to himself. In the last ten minutes. But he did not feel apprehensive; he felt, now, excitement.

It sure happened fast, he thought as he walked over to his bench and began collecting his tools. I guess that's how those kinds of things happen. Opportunity, when it comes –

All my life I've waited for this. When the oracle says 'something must be achieved' – it means this. The time is truly great. What is the time, now? What is this moment? Six at the top in Hexagram Eleven changes everything to Twenty-six, Taming Power of the Great. Yin becomes yang; the line moves and a new Moment appears. And I was so off stride I didn't even notice!

I'll bet that's why I got that terrible line; that's the only way Hexagram Eleven can change to Hexagram Twenty-six, by that moving six at the top. So I shouldn't get my ass in such an uproar.

But, despite his excitement and optimism, he could not get the line completely out of his mind.

However, he thought ironically, I'm making a damn good try; by seven tonight maybe I'll have managed to forget it like it never happened.

He thought, I sure hope so. Because this get-together with Ed is big. He's got some surefire idea; I can tell. And I don't intend to find myself left out.

Right now I'm nothing, but if I can swing this, then maybe I can get Juliana back. I know what she wants – she deserves to be married to a man who matters, an important person in the community, not some *meshuggener*. Men used to be men, in the old days; before the war for instance. But all that's gone now.

No wonder she roams around from place to place, from man to man, seeking. And not even knowing what it is herself, what her biology needs. But I know, and through this

big-time action with McCarthy – whatever it is – I'm going
to achieve it for her.

At lunchtime, Robert Childan closed up American Artistic Handcrafts Inc. Usually he crossed the street and ate at
the coffee shop. In any case he stayed away no more than
half an hour, and today he was gone only twenty minutes.
Memory of his ordeal with Mr Tagomi and the staff of the
Trade Mission still kept his stomach upset.

As he returned to his store he said to himself, Perhaps new
policy of not making calls. Do all business within store.

Two hours showing. Much too long. Almost four hours in
all; too late to reopen store. An entire afternoon to sell one
item, one Mickey Mouse watch; expensive treasure, but –
He unlocked the store door, propped it open, went to hang
up his coat in the rear.

When he re-emerged he found that he had a customer.
A white man. Well, he thought. Surprise.

'Good day, sir,' Childan said, bowing slightly. Probably
a *pinoc*. Slender, rather dark man. Well dressed, fashionable.
But not at ease. Slight shine of perspiration.

'Good day,' the man murmured, moving around the store
to inspect the displays. Then, all at once, he approached
the counter. He reached into his coat, produced a small
shiny leather cardcase, set down a multicoloured, elaborately
printed card.

On the card, the Imperial emblem. And military insignia.
The Navy. Admiral Harusha. Robert Childan examined it,
impressed.

'The admiral's ship,' the customer explained, 'lies in San
Francisco Bay at this moment. The carrier *Syokaku*.'

'Ah,' Childan said.

'Admiral Harusha has never before visited the West
Coast,' the customer explained. 'He has many wishes while
here, one of which is to pay personal visit to your famous
store. All the time in the Home Islands he has heard of
American Artistic Handcrafts Inc.'

Childan bowed with delight.

'However,' the man continued, 'due to pressure of appointments, the admiral cannot pay personal visit to your esteemed store. But he has sent me; I am his gentleman.'

'The admiral is a collector?' Childan said, his mind working at top speed.

'He is a lover of the arts. He is a connoisseur. But not a collector. What he desires is for gift purposes; to wit : he wishes to present each officer of his ship a valuable historic artifact, a side arm of the epic American Civil War.' The man paused. 'There are twelve officers in all.'

To himself, Childan thought, Twelve Civil War side arms. Cost to buyer : almost ten thousand dollars. He trembled.

'As is well known,' the man continued, 'your shop sells such priceless antique artifacts from the pages of American history. Alas, all too rapidly vanishing into limbo of time.'

Taking enormous care in his words – he could not afford to lose this, to make one single slip – Childan said, 'Yes, it is true. Of all the stores in P.S.A., I possess finest stock imaginable of Civil War weapons. I will be happy to serve Admiral Harusha. Shall I gather superb collection of such and bring aboard the *Syokaku*? This afternoon, possibly?'

The man said, 'No. I shall inspect them here.'

Twelve. Childan computed. He did not possess twelve – in fact, he had only three. But he could acquire twelve, if luck were with him, through various channels within the week. Air express from the East, for instance. And local wholesale contacts.

'You, sir,' Childan said, 'are knowledgeable in such weapons?'

'Tolerably,' the man said. 'I have a small collection of hand weapons, including tiny secret pistol made to look like domino. Circa 1840.'

'Exquisite item,' Childan said, as he went to the locked safe to get several guns for Admiral Harusha's gentleman's inspection.

When he returned, he found the man writing out a bank cheque. The man paused and said, 'The admiral desires to pay in advance. A deposit of fifteen thousand P.S.A. dollars.'

The room swam before Childan's eyes. But he managed to keep his voice level; he even made himself sound a trifle bored. 'If you wish. It is not necessary; a mere formality of business.' Laying down a leather and felt box he said, 'Here is exceptional Colt ·44 of 1860.' He opened the box. 'Black powder and ball. This issued to U.S. Army. Boys in blue carried these into for instance Second Bull Run.'

For a considerable time the man examined the Colt ·44. Then, lifting his eyes, he said calmly, 'Sir, this is an imitation.'

'Eh?' Childan said, not comprehending.

'This piece is no older than six months. Sir, your offering is a fake. I am cast into gloom. But see. The wood here. Artificially aged by an acid chemical. What a shame.' He laid the gun down.

Childan picked the gun up and stood holding it between his hands. He could think of nothing to say. Turning the gun over and over, he at last said, 'It can't be.'

'An imitation of the authentic historic gun. Nothing more. I am afraid, sir, you have been deceived. Perhaps by some unscrupulous churl. You must report this to the San Francisco police.' The man bowed. 'It grieves me. You may have other imitations, too, in your shop. It is possible, sir, that you, the owner, dealer in such items, *cannot distinguish the forgeries from the real?*'

There was silence.

Reaching down, the man picked up the half-completed cheque which he had been making out. He returned it to his pocket, put his pen away, and bowed. 'It is a shame, sir, but I clearly cannot, alas, conduct my business with American Artistic Handcrafts Inc. after all. Admiral Harusha will be disappointed. Nevertheless, you can see my position.'

Childan stared down at the gun.

'Good day, sir,' the man said. 'Please accept my humbly meant advice; hire some expert to scrutinize your acquisitions. Your reputation . . . I am sure you understand.'

Childan mumbled, 'Sir, if you could please –'

'Be tranquil, sir. I will not mention this to anyone. I – shall tell the admiral that unfortunately your shop was closed today. After all –' The man paused at the doorway. 'We are both, after all, white men.' Bowing once more, he departed.

Alone, Childan stood holding the gun.

It can't be, he thought.

But it must be. Good God in heaven. I am ruined. I have lost a fifteen-thousand-dollar sale. And my reputation, if this gets out. If that man, Admiral Harusha's gentleman, is not discreet.

I will kill myself, he decided. I have lost place. I cannot go on; that is a fact.

On the other hand, perhaps that man erred.

Perhaps he lied.

He was sent by United States Historic Objects to destroy me. Or by West Coast Art Exclusives.

Anyhow, one of my competitors.

The gun is no doubt genuine.

How can I find out? Childan racked his brains. Ah. I will have the gun analysed at the University of California Penology Department. I know someone there, or at least I once did. This matter came up before once. Alleged non-authenticity of ancient breechloader.

In haste, he telephoned one of the city's bonded messenger and delivery services, told them to send a man over at once. Then he wrapped the gun and wrote out a note to the University lab, telling them to make professional estimate of the gun's age at once and inform him by phone. The delivery man arrived; Childan gave him the note and parcel, the address, and told him to go by helicopter. The man departed, and Childan began pacing about his store, waiting ... waiting.

At three o'clock the University called.

'Mr Childan,' the voice said, 'you wanted this weapon tested for authenticity, this 1860 Army Model Colt ·44.' A pause, while Childan gripped the phone with apprehension. 'Here's the lab report. It's a reproduction cast from plastic moulds except for the walnut. Serial numbers all wrong. The frame not casehardened by the cyanide process. Both brown and blue surfaces achieved by a modern quick-acting technique, the whole gun artificially aged, given a treatment to make it appear old and worn.'

Childan said thickly, 'The man who brought it to me for appraisal –'

'Tell him he's been taken,' the University technician said. 'And very taken. It's a good job. Done by a real pro. See, the authentic gun was given its – you know the blue-metal parts? Those were put in a box of leather strips, sealed, with cyanide gas, and heated. Too cumbersome, nowadays. But this was done in a fairly well-equipped shop. We detected particles of several polishing and finishing compounds, some quite unusual. Now we can't prove this, but we know there's a regular industry turning out these fakes. There must be. We've seen so many.'

'No,' Childan said. 'That is only a rumour. I can state that to you as absolute fact, sir.' His voice rose and broke screechingly. 'And I am in a position to know. Why do you think I sent it to you? I could perceive its fakery, being qualified by years of training. Such as this is a rarity, an oddity. Actually a joke. A prank.' He broke off, panting. 'Thank you for confirming my own observations. You will bill me. Thank you.' He rang off at once.

Then, without pausing, he got out his records. He began tracing the gun. How had it come to him? *From whom?*

It had come, he discovered, from one of the largest wholesale suppliers in San Francisco. Ray Calvin Associates, on Van Ness. At once he phoned them.

'Let me talk to Mr Calvin,' he said. His voice had now become a trifle steadier.

Presently a gruff voice, very busy. 'Yes.'

'This is Bob Childan. At A.A.H. Inc. On Montgomery. Ray, I have a matter of delicacy. I wish to see you, private conference, some time today in your office or et cetera. Believe me, sir. You had better heed my request.' Now, he discovered, he was bellowing into the phone.

'Okay,' Ray Calvin said.

'Tell no one. This is absolutely confidential.'

'Four o'clock?'

'Four it is,' Childan said. 'At your office. Good day.' He slammed the receiver down so furiously that the entire phone fell from the counter to the floor; kneeling, he gathered it up and replaced it in its spot.

There was half an hour ahead before he should start; he had all that time to pace, helpless, waiting. What to do? An idea. He phoned the San Francisco office of the Tokyo *Herald*, on Market Street.

'Sirs,' he said, 'please tell me if the carrier *Syokaku* is in the harbour, and if so, how long. I would appreciate this information from your estimable newspaper.'

An agonizing wait. Then the girl was back.

'According to our reference room, sir,' she said in a giggling voice, 'the carrier *Syokaku* is at the bottom of the Philippine Sea. It was sunk by an American submarine in 1945. Any more questions we can help you with, sir?' Obviously they, at the newspaper office, appreciated the wild-goose variety of prank that had been played on him.

He hung up. No carrier *Syokaku* for seventeen years. Probably no Admiral Harusha. The man had been an impostor. And yet –

The man had been right. The Colt ·44 was a fake.

It did not make sense.

Perhaps the man was a speculator; he had been trying to corner the market in Civil War period side arms. An expert. And he had recognized the fake. He was the professional of professionals.

It would take a professional to know. Someone in the business. Not a mere collector.

Childan felt a tiny measure of relief. Then few others would detect. Perhaps no one else. Secret safe.

Let matter drop?

He considered. No. Must investigate. First of all, get back investment; get reimbursement from Ray Calvin. And –

must have all other artifacts in stock examined by University lab.

But – suppose many of them are non-authentic?

Difficult matter.

Only way is this, he decided. He felt grim, even desperate. Go to Ray Calvin. Confront him. Insist that he pursue matter back to source. Maybe he is innocent, too. Maybe not. In any case, tell him *no more fakes or I will not buy through him ever again.*

He will have to absorb the loss, Childan decided. Not I. If he will not, then I will approach other retail dealers, tell them; ruin his reputation. Why should I be ruined alone? Pass it on to those responsible, hand hot potato back along line.

But it must be done with utmost secrecy. Keep matter strictly between ourselves.

5

The telephone call from Ray Calvin puzzled Wyndam-Matson. He could not make sense out of it, partly because of Calvin's rapid manner of speech and partly because at the moment the call came – eleven-thirty in the evening – Wyndam-Matson was entertaining a lady visitor in his apartment at the Muromachi Hotel.

Calvin said, 'Look here, my friend, we're sending back that whole last shipment from you people. And I'd send back stuff before that, but we've paid for everything except the last shipment. Your billing date May eighteenth.'

Naturally, Wyndam-Matson wanted to know why.

'They're lousy fakes,' Calvin said.

'But you knew that.' He was dumbfounded. 'I mean, Ray, you've always been aware of the situation.' He glanced around; the girl was off somewhere, probably in the powder room.

Calvin said, 'I knew they were fakes. I'm not talking about that. I'm talking about the lousy part. Look, I'm really not concerned whether some gun you send us *really* was used in the Civil War or not; all I care about is that it's a satisfactory Colt ·44, item whatever-it-is in your catalogue. It has to meet standards. Look, do you know who Robert Childan is?'

'Yes.' He had a vague memory, although at the moment he could not quite pin the name down. Somebody important.

'He was in here today. To my office. I'm calling from my office, not home; we're still going over it. Anyhow, he came in and rattled off some long account. He was mad as hell. Really agitated. Well, evidently some big customer of his, some Jap admiral, came in or had his man come in. Childan talked about a twenty-thousand-dollar order, but that's probably an exaggeration. Anyhow, what did happen – I have no cause to doubt this part – is that the Japanese came in, wanted to buy, took one look at one of those Colt ·44 items you people turn out, saw it to be a fake, put his money back in his pants pocket, and left. Now. What do you say?'

There was nothing that Wyndam-Matson could think of to say. But he thought to himself instantly. It's Frink and McCarthy. They said they'd do something, and this is it. But – he could not figure out what they had done; he could not make sense out of Calvin's account.

A kind of superstitious fright filled him. Those two – how could they doctor an item made last February? He had presumed they would go to the police or the newspapers, or even the *pinoc* government at Sac, and of course he had all those taken care of. Eerie. He did not know what to tell Calvin; he mumbled on for what seemed an endless time and at last managed to wind up the conversation and get off the phone.

When he hung up he realized, with a start, that Rita had come out of the bedroom and had listened to the whole conversation; she had been pacing irritably back and forth, wearing only a black silk slip, her blonde hair falling loosely over her bare, slighly freckled shoulders.

'Tell the police,' she said.

Well, he thought, it probably would be cheaper to offer them two thousand or so. They'd accept it; that was probably all they wanted. Little fellows like that thought small; to them it would seem like a lot. They'd put it in their new business, lose it, be broke again inside a month.

'No,' he said.

'Why not? Blackmail's a crime.'

It was hard to explain to her. He was accustomed to paying people; it was part of the overhead, like the utilities. If the sum was small enough ₁ . . but she did have a point. He mulled it over.

I'll give them two thousand, but I'll also get in touch with that guy at the Civic Centre I know, that police inspector. I'll have them look into both Frink and McCarthy and see if there's anything of use. So if they come back and try again – I'll be able to handle them.

For instance, he thought, somebody told me Frink's a kike₁ Changed his nose and name. All I have to do is notify the German consul here. Routine business. He'll request the Jap authorities for extradition. They'll gas the bugger soon as they get him across the Demarcation Line. I think they've got one of those camps in New York, he thought. Those oven camps.

'I'm surprised,' the girl said, 'that anyone could blackmail a man of your stature.' She eyed him.

'Well, I'll tell you,' he said. 'This whole damn historicity business is nonsense. Those Japs are bats. I'll prove it.' Getting up, he hurried into his study, returned at once with two cigarette lighters which he set down on the coffee table₁ 'Look at these. Look the same, don't they? Well, listen. One has historicity in it.' He grinned at her. 'Pick them up. Go ahead₁ One's worth, oh, maybe forty or fifty thousand dollars on the collectors' market.'

The girl gingerly picked up the two lighters and examined them.

'Don't you feel it?' he kidded her. 'The historicity?'

She said, 'what is "historicity"?'

'When a thing has history in it. Listen. One of those two Zippo lighters was in Franklin D. Roosevelt's pocket when he was assassinated. And one wasn't. One has historicity, a hell of a lot of it. As much as any object ever had. And one has nothing. Can you feel it?' He nudged her. 'You can't. You can't tell which is which. There's no "mystical plasmic presence", no "aura" around it.'

'Gee,' the girl said, awed. 'Is that really true? That he had one of those on him that day?'

'Sure. And I know which it is. You see my point. It's all a big racket; they're playing it on themselves. I mean, a gun goes through a famous battle, like the Meuse-Argonne, and it's the same as if it hadn't, *unless you know.* It's in here.' He tapped his head. 'In the mind, not the gun. I used to be a collector. In fact, that's how I got into this business. I collected stamps. Early British colonies.'

The girl now stood at the window, her arms folded, gazing out at the lights of downtown San Francisco. 'My mother and dad used to say we wouldn't have lost the war if he had lived,' she said.

'Okay,' Wyndam-Matson went on. 'Now suppose say last year the Canadian Government or somebody, anybody, finds the plates from which some old stamp was printed. And the ink. And a supply of –'

'I don't believe either of those two lighters belonged to Franklin Roosevelt,' the girl said.

Wyndam-Matson giggled. 'That's my point! I'd have to prove it to you with some sort of document. A paper of authenticity. And so it's all a fake, a mass delusion. The paper proves its worth, not the object itself!'

'Show me the paper.'

'Sure.' Hopping up, he made his way back into the study. From the wall he took the Smithsonian Institution's framed certificate; the paper and the lighter had cost him a fortune, but they were worth it – because they enabled him to prove that he was right, that the word 'fake' meant nothing really, since the word 'authentic' meant nothing really.

'A Colt ·44 is a Colt ·44,' he called to the girl as he hurried back into the living room. 'It has to do with bore and design, not when it was made. It has to do with –'

She held out her hand. He gave her the document.

'So it is genuine,' she said finally.

'Yes. This one.' He picked up the lighter with the long scratch across its side.

'I think I'd like to go now,' the girl said. 'I'll see you again some other evening.' She set down the document and lighter and moved towards the bedroom, where her clothes were.

'Why?' he shouted in agitation, following after her. 'You know it's perfectly safe; my wife won't be back for weeks – I explained the whole situation to you. A detached retina.'

'It's not that.'

'What, then?'

Rita said, 'Please call a pedecab for me. While I dress.'

'I'll drive you home,' he said grumpily.

She dressed, and then, while he got her coat from the closet, she wandered silently about the apartment. She seemed pensive, withdrawn, even a little depressed. The past makes people sad, he realized. Damn it; why did I have to bring it up? But hell, she's so young – I thought she'd hardly know the name.

At the bookcase she knelt. 'Did you read this?' she asked, taking a book out.

Nearsightedly he peered. Lurid cover. Novel. 'No,' he said. 'My wife got that. She reads a lot.'

'You should read it.'

Still feeling disappointed, he grabbed the book, glanced at it. *The Grasshopper Lies Heavy*. 'Isn't this one of those banned-in-Boston books?' he said.

'Banned through the United States. And in Europe, of course.' She had gone to the hall door and stood there now, waiting.

'I've heard of this Hawthorne Abendsen.' But actually he had not. All he could recall about the book was – what? That it was very popular right now. Another fad. Another mass craze. He bent down and stuck it back in the shelf. 'I don't have time to read popular fiction. I'm too busy with work.' Secretaries, he thought acidly, read that junk, at home in bed at night. It stimulates them. Instead of the real thing. Which they're afraid of. But of course really crave.

'One of those love stories,' he said as he sullenly opened the hall door.

'No,' she said. 'A story about war.' As they walked down the hall to the elevator she said, 'He says the same thing. As my mother and dad.'

'Who? That Abbotson?'

'That's his theory. If Joe Zangara had missed him, he would have pulled America out of the Depression and armed it so that –' She broke off. They had arrived at the elevator, and other people were waiting.

Later, as they drove through the nocturnal traffic in Wyndam-Matson's Mercedes-Benz, she resumed.

'Abendsen's theory is that Roosevelt would have been a terribly strong President. As strong as Lincoln. He showed it in the year he was President, all those measures he introduced. The book is fiction. I mean, it's in novel form. Roosevelt isn't assasssinated in Miami; he goes on and is re-elected in 1936, so he's President until 1940, until during the war. Don't you see? He's still President when Germany attacks England and France and Poland. And he sees all that. He makes America strong. Garner was a really awful President. A lot of what happened was his fault. And then in 1940, instead of Bricker, a Democrat would have been elected –'

'According to this Abelson,' Wyndam-Matson broke in. He glanced at the girl beside him. God, they read a book, he thought, and they spout on forever.

'His theory is that instead of an Isolationist like Bricker, in 1940 after Roosevelt, Rexford Tugwell would have been President.' Her smooth face, reflecting the traffic lights, glowed with animation; her eyes had become large and she gestured as she talked. 'And he would have been very active in continuing the Roosevelt anti-Nazi policies. So Germany would have been afraid to come to Japan's help in 1941. They would not have honoured their treaty. Do you see?'

Turning towards him on the seat, grabbing his shoulder with intensity, she said, 'And so Germany and Japan would have lost the war !'

He laughed.

Staring at him, seeking something in his face – he could not tell what, and anyhow he had to watch the other cars – she said, 'It's not funny. It really would have been like that, The U.S. would have been able to lick the Japanese . And –'

'How?' he broke in.

'He has it all laid out.' For a moment she was silent. 'It's in fiction form,' she said. 'Naturally, it's got a lot of fictional parts; I mean, it's got to be entertaining or people wouldn't read it. It has a human-interest theme; there's these two young people, the boy is in the American Army. The girl – well, anyhow, President Tugwell is really smart. He understands what the Japs are going to do.' Anxiously, she said, 'It's all right to talk about this; the Japs have let it be circulated in the Pacific. I read that a lot of them are reading it. It's popular in the Home Islands. It's stirred up a lot of talk.'

Wyndam-Matson said, 'Listen. What does he say about Pearl Harbor?'

'President Tugwell is so smart that he has all the ships out to sea. So the U.S. fleet isn't destroyed.'

'I see.'

'So, there really isn't any Pearl Harbor. They attack, but all they get is some little boats.'

'It's called "The Grasshopper something?" '

'*The Grasshopper Lies Heavy*. That's a quote from the Bible.'

'And Japan is defeated because there's no Pearl Harbor. Listen. Japan would have won anyhow. Even if there had been no Pearl Harbor.'

'The U.S. fleet – in this book – keeps them from taking the Philippines and Australia.'

'They would have taken them anyhow; their fleet was superior. I know the Japanese fairly well, and it was their destiny to assume dominance in the Pacific. The U.S. was on the decline ever since World War One. Every country on the Allied side was ruined in that war, morally and spiritually.'

With stubbornness, the girl said, 'And if the Germans hadn't taken Malta, Churchill would have stayed in power and guided England to victory.'

'How? Where?'

'In North Africa – Churchill would have defeated Rommel finally.'

Wyndam-Matson guffawed.

'And once the British had defeated Rommel, they could move their whole army back and up through Turkey to join remnants of Russian armies and make a stand – in the book, they halt the Germans' eastward advance into Russia at some town on the Volga. We never heard of this town, but it really exists because I looked it up in the atlas.'

'What's it called?'

'Stalingrad. And the British turn the tide of the war, there. So, in the book, Rommel never would have linked up with those German armies that came down from Russia, von Paulus', armies; remember? And the Germans never would have been able to go on into the Middle East and get the needed oil, or on into India like they did and link up with the Japanese. And –'

'No strategy on earth could have defeated Erwin Rommel,' Wyndam-Matson said. 'And no events like this guy dreamed up, this town in Russia very heroically called "Stalingrad", no holding action could have done any more than delay the outcome; it couldn't have changed it. Listen. *I met Rommel.* In New York, when I was there on business, in 1948.' Actually, he had only seen the Military Governor of the U.S.A. at a reception in the White House, and at a distance. 'What a man. What dignity and bearing. So I know what I'm talking about,' he wound up.

'It was a dreadful thing,' Rita said, 'when General Rommel was relieved of his post and that awful Lammers was appointed in his place. That's when that murdering and those concentration camps really began.'

'They existed when Rommel was Military Governor.'

'But –' She gestured. 'It wasn't official. Maybe those S.S. hoodlums did those acts then . . . but he wasn't like the rest of them; he was more like those old Prussians. He was harsh –'

'I'll tell you who really did a good job in the U.S.A.,' Wyndam-Matson said, 'who you can look to for the economic revival. Albert Speer. Not Rommel and not the Organization Todt. Speer was the best appointment the Partei made in North America; he got all those businesses and corporations and factories – everything! – going again, and on an efficient basis. I wish we had that out here – as it is, we've got five outfits competing in each field, and at terrific waste. There's nothing more foolish than economic competition.'

Rita said, 'I couldn't live in those work camps, those dorms they have back East. A girl friend of mine; she lived there. They censored her mail – she couldn't tell me about it until she moved back out here again. They had to get up at six-thirty in the morning to *band* music.'

'You'd get used to it. You'd have clean quarters, adequate food, recreation, medical care provided. What do you want? Egg in your beer?'

Through the cool night fog of San Francisco, his big German-made car moved quietly.

On the floor Mr Tagomi sat, his legs folded beneath him. He held a handleless cup of oolong tea, into which he blew now and then as he smiled up at Mr Baynes.

'You have a lovely place here,' Baynes said presently. 'There is a peacefulness here on the Pacific Coast. It is completely different from – back there.' He did not specify.

'"God speaks to man in the sign of the Arousing,"' Mr Tagomi murmured.

'Pardon?'

'The oracle. I'm sorry. Fleece-seeking cortical response.'

Woolgathering, Baynes thought. That's the idiom he means. To himself he smiled.

'We are absurd,' Mr Tagomi said, 'because we live by a five-thousand-year-old book. We ask it questions as if it were alive. It *is* alive. As is the Christian Bible; many books are actually alive. Not in metaphoric fashion. Spirit animates it. Do you see?' He inspected Mr Baynes's face for his reaction.

Carefully phrasing his words, Baynes said, 'I – just don't know enough about religion. It's out of my field. I prefer to stick to subjects I have some competence in.' As a matter of fact, he was not certain what Mr Tagomi was talking about. I must be tired, Mr Baynes thought. There has been, since I got here this evening, a sort of . . . gnomish quality about everything. A smaller-than-life quality, with a dash of the droll. What is this five-thousand-year-old book? The Mickey Mouse watch, Mr Tagomi himself, the fragile cup in Mr Tagomi's hand . . . and, on the wall facing Mr Baynes, an enormous buffalo head, ugly and menacing.

'What is that head?' he asked suddenly.

'That,' Mr Tagomi said, 'is nothing less than the creature which sustained the aboriginal in bygone days.'

'I see.'

'Shall I demonstrate art of buffalo slaying?' Mr Tagomi put his cup down on the table and rose to his feet. Here in his own home in the evening he wore a silk robe, slippers, and white cravat. 'Here am I aboard iron horse.' He squatted in the air. 'Across lap, trusty Winchester rifle 1866 issue from my collection.' He glanced inquiringly at Mr Baynes. 'You are travel-stained, sir.'

'Afraid so,' Baynes said. It is all a little overwhelming for me. A lot of business worries . . .' And other worries, he thought. His head ached. He wondered if the fine I.G. Farben analgesics were available here on the Pacific Coast; he had become accustomed to them for his sinus headaches.

'We must all have faith in something,' Mr Tagomi said. 'We cannot know the answers. We cannot see ahead, on our own.'

Mr Baynes nodded.

'My wife may have something for your head,' Mr Tagomi

said, seeing him remove his glasses and rub his forehead. 'Eye muscles causing pain. Pardon me.' Bowing, he left the room.

What I need is sleep, Baynes thought. A night's rest. Or is it that I'm not facing the situation? Shrinking, because it is hard.

When Mr Tagomi returned – carrying a glass of water and some sort of pill – Mr Baynes said, 'I really am going to have to say good night and get to my hotel room. But I want to find out something first. We can discuss it further tomorrow, if that's convenient with you. Have you been told about a third party who is to join us in our discussions?'

Mr Tagomi's face registered surprise for an instant; then the surprise vanished and he assumed a careless expression. 'There was nothing said to that effect. However – it is interesting, of course.'

'From the Home Islands.'

'Ah,' Mr Tagomi said. And this time the surprise did not appear at all. It was totally controlled.

'An elderly retired businessman,' Mr Baynes said. 'Who is journeying by ship. He has been on his way for two weeks, now. He has a prejudice against air travel.'

'The quaint elderly,' Mr Tagomi said.

'His interests keep him informed as to the Home Islands markets. He will be able to give us information, and he was coming to San Francisco for a vacation in any case. It is not terribly important. But it will make our talks more accurate.'

'Yes,' Mr Tagomi said. 'He can correct errors regarding home market. I have been away two years.'

'Did you want to give me that pill?'

Starting, Mr Tagomi glanced down, saw that he still held the pill and water. 'Excuse me. This is powerful. Called zaracaine. Manufactured by drug firm in District of China.' As he held his palm out, he added, 'Non-habit-forming.'

'This old person,' Mr Baynes said as he prepared to take the pill, 'will probably contact your Trade Mission direct. I will write down his name so that your people will know not to turn him away. I have not met him, but I understand he's a little deaf and a little eccentric. We want to be sure he doesn't become – miffed.' Mr Tagomi seemed to understand. 'He loves rhododendrons. He'll be happy if you can provide someone to talk to him about them for half an hour or so, while we arrange our meeting. His name. I will write it down.'

Taking his pill, he got out his pen and wrote.

'Mr Shinjiro Yatabe,' Mr Tagomi read, accepting the slip of paper. He dutifully put it away in his pocketbook.

'One more point.

Mr Tagomi slowly picked at the rim of his cup, listening.

'A delicate trifle. The old gentleman – it is embarrassing. He is almost eighty. Some of his ventures, towards the end of his career, were not successful. Do you see?'

'He is not well-off any longer,' Mr Tagomi said. 'And perhaps he draws a pension.'

'That is it. And the pension is painfully small. He therefore augments it by means here and there.'

'A violation of some petty ordinance,' Mr Tagomi said. 'The Home Government and its bureaucratic officialdom. I grasp the situation. The old gentleman receives a stipend for his consultation with us, and he does not report it to his Pension Board. So we must not reveal his visit. They are only aware that he takes a vacation.'

'You are a sophisticate,' Mr Baynes said.

Mr Tagomi said, 'This situation has occurred before. We have not in our society solved the problem of the aged, more of which persons occur constantly as medical measures improve. China teaches us rightly to honour the old. However, the Germans cause our neglect to seem close to outright virtue. I understand they murder the old.'

'The Germans,' Baynes murmured, again rubbing his forehead. Had the pill had an effect? He felt a little drowsy.

'Being from Scandinavia, you no doubt have had much contact with the Festung Europa. For instance, you embarked at Tempelhof. Can one take an attitude like this? You are a neutral. Give me your opinion, if you will.'

'I don't understand what attitude you mean,' Mr Baynes said.

'Towards the old, the sick, the feeble, the insane, the useless in all variations. "Of what use is a newborn baby?" some Anglo-Saxon philosopher reputedly asked. I have committed that utterance to memory and contemplated it many times. Sir, there is no use. In general.'

Mr Baynes murmured some sound or other; he made it the noise of noncommittal politeness.

'Isn't it true,' Mr Tagomi said, 'that no man should be the instrument for another's needs?' He leaned forward urgently. 'Please give me your neutral Scandinavian opinion.'

'I don't know,' Mr Baynes said.

'During the war,' Mr Tagomi said, 'I held minor post in District of China. In Shanghai. There, at Hongkew, a settlement of Jews, interned by Imperial Government for duration. Kept alive by JOINT relief. The Nazi minister at Shanghai requested we massacre the Jews. I recall my superiors' answer. It was, "Such is not in accord with humanitarian considerations." They rejected the request as barbaric. It impressed me.'

'I see,' Mr Baynes murmured. Is he trying to draw me out? he asked himself. Now he felt alert. His wits seemed to come together.

'The Jews,' Mr Tagomi said, 'were described always by the Nazis as Asian and non-white. Sir, the implication was never lost on personages in Japan, even among the War Cabinet. I have not ever discussed this with Reich citizens whom I have encountered –'

Mr Baynes interrupted, 'Well, I'm not a German. So I can hardly speak for Germany.' Standing, he moved towards the door. 'I will resume the discussion with you tomorrow. Please excuse me. I cannot think.' But, as a matter of fact, his thoughts were now completely clear. I have to get out of here, he realized. This man is pushing me too far.

'Forgive stupidity of fanaticism,' Mr Tagomi said, at once moving to open the door. 'Philosophical involvement blinded me to authentic human fact. Here.' He called something in Japanese, and the front door opened. A young Japanese appeared, bowing slightly, glancing at Mr Baynes.

My driver, Mr Baynes thought.

Perhaps my quixotic remarks on the Lufthansa flight, he thought suddenly. To that – whatever his name was. Lotze. Got back to the Japanese here, somehow. Some connection.

I wish I hadn't said that to Lotze, he thought. I regret. But it's too late.

I am not the right person. Not at all. Not for this.

But then he thought, A Swede would say that to Lotze. It is all right. Nothing has gone wrong; I am being overly scrupulous. Carrying the habits of the previous situation into this. Actually I can do a great deal of open talking. *That* is the fact I have to adapt to.

And yet, his conditioning was absolutely against it. The blood in his veins. His bones, his organs, rebelled. Open your mouth, he said to himself. Something. Anything. An opinion. You must, if you are to succeed.

He said, 'Perhaps they are driven by some desperate subconscious archetype. In the Jungian sense.'

Mr Tagomi nodded. 'I have read Jung. I understand.'

They shook hands. 'I'll telephone you tomorrow morning,' Mr Baynes said. 'Good night, sir.' He bowed, and so did Mr Tagomi.

The young smiling Japanese, stepping forward, said something to Mr Baynes which he could not understand.

'Eh?' Baynes said, as he gathered up his overcoat and stepped out onto the porch.

Mr Tagomi said, 'He is addressing you in Swedish, sir. He has taken a course at Tokyo University on the Thirty Years' War, and is fascinated by your great hero, Gustavus Adolphus.' Mr Tagomi smiled sympathetically. 'However, it is plain that his attempts to master so alien a linguistic have been hopeless. No doubt he uses one of those phonograph record courses; he is a student, and such courses, being cheap, are quite popular with students.'

The young Japanese, obviously not understanding English, bowed and smiled.

'I see,' Baynes murmured, 'Well, I wish him luck.' I have my own linguistic problems, he thought. Evidently᠌

Good lord – the young Japanese student, while driving him to his hotel, would no doubt attempt to converse with him in Swedish the entire way. A language which Mr Baynes barely understood, and then only when it was spoken in the most formal and correct manner, certainly not when attempted by a young Japanese who tried to pick it up from a phonograph record course.

He'll never get through to me, Mr Baynes thought. And he'll keep trying, because this is his chance; probably he will never see a Swede again. Mr Baynes groaned inwardly. What an ordeal it was going to be, for both of them.

6

Early in the morning, enjoying the cool, bright sunlight, Mrs Juliana Frink did her grocery shopping. She strolled along the sidewalk, carrying the two brown paper bags, halting at each store to study the window displays. She took her time.

Wasn't there something she was supposed to pick up at the drugstore? She wandered in. Her shift at the judo parlour did not begin until noon; this was her free time, today. Seating herself on a stool at the counter she put down her shopping bags and began to go over the different magazines.

The new *Life*, she saw, had a big article called : TELEVISION IN EUROPE : GLIMPSE OF TOMORROW. Turning to it, interested, she saw a picture of a German family watching television in their living room. Already, the article said, there was four hours of image broadcast during the day from Berlin. Some day there would be television stations in all the major European cities. And, by 1970, one would be built in New York.

The article showed Reich electronic engineers at the New York site, helping the local personnel with their problems. It was easy to tell which were the Germans. They had that healthy, clean, energetic, assured look. The Americans, on the other hand – they just looked like people. They could have been anybody.

One of the German technicians could be seen pointing off somewhere, and the Americans were trying to make out what he was pointing at. I guess their eyesight is better than ours, she decided. Better diet over the last twenty years. As we've been told; they can see things no one else can. Vitamin A, perhaps?

I wonder what it's like to sit home in your living room and see the whole world on a little grey glass tube. If those Nazis can fly back and forth between here and Mars, why can't they get television going? I think I'd prefer that, to watch those comedy shows, actually see what Bob Hope and Durante look like, than to walk around on Mars.

Maybe that's it, she thought as she put the magazine back on the rack. The Nazis have no sense of humour, so why should they want television? Anyhow, they killed most of the really great comedians. Because most of them were Jewish. In fact, she realized, they killed off most of the entertainment field. I wonder how Hope gets away with what he says. Of course, he has to broadcast from Canada. And it's a little freer up there. But Hope really says things. Like that joke about Göring . . . the one where Göring buys Rome and had it shipped to his mountain retreat and then set up again. And revives Christianity so his pet lions will have something to –

'Did you want to buy that magazine, miss?' the little dried-up old man who ran the drugstore called, with suspicion.

Guiltily, she put down the *Reader's Digest* which she had begun to thumb through.

Again strolling along the sidewalk with her shopping bags, Juliana thought, Maybe Göring will be the new

Führer when that Bormann dies. He seems sort of different from the others. The only way that Bormann got it in the first place was to weasel in when Hitler was falling apart, and only those actually near Hitler realized how fast he was going. Old Göring was off in his mountain palace. Göring should have been Führer after Hitler, because it was his Luftwaffe that knocked out those English radar stations and then finished off the R.A.F. Hitler would have had them bomb London, like they did Rotterdam.

But probably Goebbels will get it, she decided. That was what everyone said. As long as that awful Heydrich doesn't. He'd kill us all. He's really bats.

The one I like, she thought, is that Baldur von Schirach. He's the only one who looks normal, anyhow. But he hasn't got a chance.

Turning, she ascended the steps to the front door of the old wooden building in which she lived.

When she unlocked the door of her apartment she saw Joe Cinnadella still lying where she had left him, in the centre of the bed, on his stomach, his arms dangling. He was still asleep.

No, she thought. He can't still be here; the truck's gone. Did he miss it? Obviously.

Going into the kitchen, she set her grocery bags on the table among the breakfast dishes.

But did he *intend* to miss it? she asked herself. That's what I wonder.

What a peculiar man . . . he had been so active with her, going on almost all night. And yet it had been as if he were not actually there, doing it but never being aware. Thoughts on something else, maybe.

From habit, she began putting food away in the old G.E. turret-top refrigerator. And then she began clearing the breakfast table.

Maybe he's done it so much, she decided. It's second nature; his body makes the motions, like mine now as I put these plates and silver in the sink. Could do it with three-fifths of his brain removed, like the leg of a frog in biology class.

'Hey,' she called. 'Wake up.'

In the bed, Joe stirred, snorted.

'Did you hear the Bob Hope show the other night?' she called. 'He told this really funny joke, the one where this German major is interviewing some Martians. The Martians can't provide racial documentation about their grandparents being Aryan, you know. So the German major reports back to Berlin that Mars is populated by Jews.' Coming into the living room where Joe lay in the bed, she said, 'And they're about one foot tall, and have two heads . . . you know how Bob Hope goes on.'

Joe had opened his eyes. He said nothing; he stared at her unwinkingly. His chin, black with stubble, his dark, ache-filled eyes . . . she also became quiet, then.

'What is it?' she said at last. 'Are you afraid?' No, she thought; that's Frank who's afraid. This is – I don't know what.

'The rig went on,' Joe said, sitting up.

'What are you going to do?' She seated herself on the edge of the bed, drying her arms and hands with the dish towel.

'I'll catch him on the return. He won't say anything to anybody; he knows I'd do the same for him.'

'You've done this before?' she asked.

Joe did not answer. You meant to miss it, Juliana said to herself. I can tell; all at once I know.

'Suppose he takes another route back?' she said.

'He always takes Fifty. Never Forty. He had an accident on Forty once; some horses got out in the road and he ploughed into them. In the Rockies.' Picking up his clothes from the chair he began to dress.

'How old are you, Joe?' she asked as he contemplated his naked body.

'Thirty-four.'

Then, she thought, you must have been in the war. She saw no obvious physical defects; he had, in fact, quite a good, lean body, with long legs. Joe, seeing her scrutiny, scowled and turned away, 'Can't I watch?' she asked, wondering why not. All night with him, and then this modesty. 'Are we bugs?' she said. 'We can't stand the sight of each other in the daylight – we have to squeeze into the walls?'

Grunting sourly, he started towards the bathroom in his underpants and socks, rubbing his chin.

This is my home, Juliana thought. I'm letting you stay here, and yet you won't allow me to look at you. Why do you want to stay, then? She followed after him, into the bathroom; he had begun running hot water in the bowl, to shave.

On his arm, she saw a tattoo, a blue letter C.

'What's that?' she asked. 'Your wife? Connie? Corinne?'

Joe, washing his face, said, 'Cairo.'

What an exotic name, she thought with envy. And then she felt herself flush. 'I'm really stupid,' she said. An Italian, thirty-four years old, from the Nazi part of the world . . . he had been in the war, all right. But on the Axis side. And he had fought at Cairo; the tattoo was their bond, the German and Italian veterans of that campaign – the defeat of the British and Australian army under General Gott at the hands of Rommel and his Afrika Korps.

She left the bathroom, returned to the living room and began making the bed; her hands flew.

In a neat stack on the chair lay Joe's possessions, clothes and small suitcase, personal articles. Among them she noticed a velvet-covered box, a little like a glasses' case; picking it up, she opened it and peeked inside.

You certainly did fight at Cairo, she thought as she gazed down at the Iron Cross Second Class with the word and the date – June 10, 1945 – engraved at its top. They didn't all get this; only the valiant ones. I wonder what you did . . . you were only seventeen years old, then.

Joe appeared at the door of the bathroom just as she lifted the medal from its velvet box; she became aware of him and jumped guiltily. But he did not seem angry.

'I was just looking at it,' Juliana said. 'I've never seen one before. Did Rommel pin it on you himself?'

'General Bayerlein gave them out. Rommel had already been transferred to England, to finish up there.' His voice was calm. But his hand once more had begun the monotonous pawing at his forehead, fingers digging into his scalp in that combing motion which seemed to be a chronic nervous tic.

'Would you tell me about it?' Juliana asked, as he returned to the bathroom and his shaving.

As he shaved and, after that, took a long hot shower, Joe Cinnadella told her a little; nothing like the sort of account she would have liked to hear. His two older brothers had served in the Ethiopian campaign, while he at thirteen had been in a Fascist youth organization in Milan, his home town. Later, his brothers had joined a crack artillery battery, that of Major Ricardo Pardi, and when World War Two began, Joe had been able to join them. They had fought under Graziani. Their equipment, especially their tanks, had been dreadful. The British had shot them down, even senior officers, like rabbits. Doors of the tanks had to be held shut with sandbags during battle, to keep them from flying open. Major Pardi, however, had reclaimed discarded artillery shells, polished and greased them, and fired them; his battery had halted General Wavell's great desperate tank advance in '43.

'Are your brothers still alive?' Juliana asked.

His brothers had been killed in '44, strangled with wire by British commandos, the Long Range Desert Group which had operated behind Axis lines and which had become especially fanatic during the last phases of the war when it was clear that the Allies could not win.

'How do you feel about the British now?' she asked haltingly.

Joe said, 'I'd like to see them do to England what they did in Africa.' His tone was flat.

'But it's been – eighteen years,' Juliana said. 'I know the British especially did terrible things. But –'

'They talk about the things the Nazis did to the Jews,' Joe said. 'The British have done worse. In the Battle of London.' He became silent. 'Those fire weapons, phosphorus and oil; I saw a few of the German troops, afterward. Boat after boat burned to a cinder. Those pipes under the water – turned the sea to fire. And on civilian populations, by those mass fire-bombing raids that Churchill thought were going to save the war at the last moment. Those terror attacks on Hamburg and Essen and –'

'Let's not talk about it,' Juliana said. In the kitchen, she started cooking bacon; she turned on the small white plastic Emerson radio which Frank had given her on her birthday. 'I'll fix you something to eat.' She dialled, trying to find some light, pleasant music.

'Look at this,' Joe said. In the living room, he sat on the bed, his small suitcase beside him; he had opened it and brought out a ragged, bent book which showed signs of much handling. He grinned at Juliana. 'Come here. You know what somebody says? This man –' He indicated the book. 'This is very funny. Sit down.' He took hold of her arm, drew her down beside him. 'I want to read to you. Suppose they had won. What would it be like? We don't have to worry; this man has done all the thinking for us.' Opening the book, Joe began turning pages slowly. 'The British Empire would control all Europe. All the Mediterranean. No Italy at all. No Germany, either. Bobbies and those funny little soldiers in tall fur hats, and the king as far as the Volga.'

In a low voice, Juliana said, 'Would that be so bad?'

'You read the book?'

'No,' she admitted, peering to see the cover. She had heard about it, though; a lot of people were reading it. 'But Frank and I – my former husband and I – often talked about how it would have been if the Allies had won the war.'

Joe did not seem to hear her; he was staring down at the copy of *The Grasshopper Lies Heavy*. 'And in this,' he went on, 'you know how it is that England wins? Beats the Axis?'

She shook her head, feeling the growing tension of the man beside her. His chin now had begun to quiver; he licked his lips again and again, dug at his scalp ɪ . . when he spoke his voice was hoarse.

'He has Italy betray the Axis,' said Joe.

'Oh,' she said.

'Italy goes over to the Allies. Joins the Anglo-Saxons and opens up what he calls the 'soft underbelly' of Europe. But that's natural for him to think that. We all know the cowardly Italian Army that ran every time they saw the British. Drinking vino. Happy-go-lucky, not made for fighting. This fellow –' Joe closed the book, turned it around to study the back cover. 'Abendsen. I don't blame him. He writes this fantasy, imagines how the world would be if the Axis had lost. How else could they lose except by Italy being a traitor?' His voice grated. 'The Duce – he was a clown; we all know that.'

'I have to turn the bacon.' She slid away from him and hurried back to the kitchen.

Following after her, still carrying the book, Joe went on, 'And the U.S. comes in. After it licks the Japs. And after the war, the U.S. and Britain divide the world. Exactly like Germany and Japan did in reality.'

Juliana said, 'Germany, Japan, and Italy.'

He stared at her.

'You left out Italy.' She faced him calmly. Did you forget, too? she said to herself. Like everybody else? The little empire in the Middle East . . . the musical-comedy New Rome.

Presently she served him a platter of bacon and eggs, toast and marmalade, coffee. He ate readily.

'What did they serve you in North Africa?' she asked as she, too, seated herself.

Joe said, 'Dead Donkey.'

'That's hideous.'

With a twisted grin, Joe said, 'Asino Morte. The bully beef cans had the initials A.M. stamped on them. The Germans called it Alter Mann. Old Man.' He resumed his rapid eating.

I would like to read this, Juliana thought as she reached to take the book from under Joe's arm. Will he be here that long? The book had grease on it; pages were torn. Finger marks all over it. Read by truck drivers on the long haul, she thought. In the one-arm beaneries late at night . . . I'll bet you're a slow reader, she thought. I'll bet you've been poring over this book for weeks, if not months.

Opening the book at random, she read :

. . . now in his old age he viewed tranquillity, domain such as the ancients would have coveted but not comprehended, ships from the Crimea to Madrid, and all the Empire, all with the same coin, speech, flag. The great old Union Jack dipping from sunrise to sunset: it had been fulfilled at last, that about the sun and the flag.

'The only book I carry around,' Juliana said, 'isn't actually a book; it's the oracle, the *I Ching* – Frank got me hooked on it and I use it all the time to decide. I never let it out of my sight. Ever.' She closed the copy of *The Grasshopper*. 'Want to see it? Want to use it?'

'No,' Joe said.

Resting her chin on her folded arms on the table surface and gazing at him sideways, she said, 'Have you moved in here permanently? And what are you up to?' Brooding over the insults, the slanders. You petrify me, she thought, with your hatred of life. But – you have something. You're like a little animal, not important but smart. Studying his limited, clever dark face she thought, How could I ever have imagined you as younger than me? But even that's true, your childishness; you are still the baby brother, worshipping your two older brothers and your Major Pardi and General Rommel, panting and sweating to break loose and get the Tommies. Did they actually garrotte your brothers with loops of wire? We heard that, the atrocity stories and photos released after the war . . . She shuddered. But the

British commandos were brought to trial and punished long ago.

The radio had ceased playing music; there seemed to be a news programme, racket of shortwave from Europe. The voice faded and became garbled. A long pause, nothing at all. Just silence. Then the Denver announcer, very clear, close by. She reached to turn the dial, but Joe stopped her hand.

'. . . news of Chancellor Bormann's death shocked a stunned Germany which had been assured as recently as yesterday . . .'

She and Joe jumped to their feet.

'. . . all Reich stations cancelled scheduled programmes and listeners heard the solemn strains of the chorus of the S.S. Division *Das Reich* raised in the anthem of the Partei, the *Horst Wessel Lied*. Later, in Dresden, where the acting Partei Secretary and chiefs of the Sicherheitsdienst, the national security police which replaced the Gestapo following . . .'

Joe turned the volume up.

'. . . reorganization of the government at the instigation of the late Reichsführer Himmler, Albert Speer and others, two weeks of official mourning were declared, and already many shops and businesses have closed, it was reported. As yet no word has come as to the expected convening of the Reichstag, the formal parliament of the Third Reich, whose approval is required . . .'

'It'll be Heydrich,' Joe said.

'I wish it would be that big blond fellow, that Schirach,' she said. 'Christ, so he finally died. Do you think Schirach has a chance?'

'No,' Joe said shortly.

'Maybe there'll be a civil war now,' she said. 'But those guys are so old now. Göring and Goebbels – all those old Party boys.'

The radio was saying, '. . . reached at his retreat in the alps near Brenner . . .'

Joe said, 'This'll be Fat Hermann.'

'. . . said merely that he was grief-stricken by the loss not only of a soldier and patriot and faithful Partei Leader, but also, as he has said many times over, of a personal friend, whom, one will recall, he backed in the interregnum dispute shortly after the war when it appeared for a time that elements hostile to Herr Bormann's ascension to supreme authority –'

Juliana shut the radio off.

'They're just babbling,' she said. 'Why do they use words like that? Those terrible murderers are talked about as if they were like the rest of us.'

'They are like us,' Joe said. He reseated himself and once more ate. 'There isn't anything they've done we wouldn't have done if we'd been in their places. They saved the world from Communism. We'd be living under Red rule now, if it wasn't for Germany. We'd be worse off.'

'You're just talking,' Juliana said. 'Like the radio. Babbling.'

'I been living under the Nazis,' Joe said. 'I know what it's like. Is that just talk, to live twelve, thirteen years – longer than that – almost fifteen years? I got a work card from O.T.; I worked for Organization Todt since 1947, in North Africa and the U.S.A. Listen –' He jabbed his finger at her. 'I got the Italian genius for earthworks; O.T. gave me a high rating. I wasn't shovelling asphalt and mixing concrete for the autobahns; I was helping design. Engineer. One day Doctor Todt came by and inspected what our work crew did. He said to me, "You got good hands." That's a big moment, Juliana. Dignity of labour; they're not talking only words. Before them, the Nazis, everyone looked down on manual jobs; myself, too. Aristocratic. The Labour Front put an end to that. I seen my own hands for the first time.' He spoke so swiftly that his accent began to take over; she had trouble understanding him. 'We all lived out there in the woods, in Upper State New York, like brothers. Sang songs. Marched to work. Spirit of the war, only rebuilding, not breaking down. Those were the best days of all, rebuilding after the war – fine, clean, long-lasting rows of public buildings block by block, whole new downtown, New York and Baltimore. Now of course that work's past. Big cartels like New Jersey Krupp und Sohnen running the show. But that's not Nazi; that's just old European powerful. Worse, you hear? Nazis like Rommel and Todt a million times better men than industrialists like Krupp and bankers, all those Prussians; ought to have been gassed. All those gentlemen in vests.'

But, Juliana thought, those gentlemen in vests are in for ever. And your idols, Rommel and Doctor Todt; they just came in after hostilities, to clear the rubble, build the autobahns, start industry humming. They even let the Jews live, lucky surprise – amnesty so the Jews could pitch in. Until '49, anyhow . . , and then good-bye Todt and Rommel, retired to graze.

Don't I know? Juliana thought. Didn't I hear all about it from Frank? You can't tell me anything about life under the Nazis; my husband was – is – a Jew. I know that Doctor Todt was the most modest, gentle man that ever lived; I know all he wanted to do was provide work – honest, reputable work – for the millions of bleak-eyed, despairing American men and women picking through the ruins after the war. I know he wanted to see medical plans and vacation resorts and adequate housing for everyone, regardless of race; he was a builder, not a thinker . . . and in most cases he managed to create what he had wanted – he actually got it. But . . .

A preoccupation, in the back of her mind, now rose decidedly. 'Joe. This *Grasshopper* book; isn't it banned in the East Coast?'

He nodded.

'How could you be reading it, then?' Something about it worried her. 'Don't they still shoot people for reading –'

'It depends on your social group. On the good old armband.'

That was so. Slavs, Poles, Puerto Ricans, were the most limited as to what they could read, do, listen to. The Anglo-Saxons had it much better; there was public education for their children, and they could go to libraries and museums and concerts. But even so . . . *The Grasshopper* was not merely classified; it was forbidden, and to everyone.

Joe said, 'I read it in the toilet. I hid it in a pillow. In fact, I read it *because* it was banned.'

'You're very brave,' she said.

Doubtfully he said, 'You mean that sarcastically?'

'No.'

He relaxed a little. 'It's easy for you people here; you live a safe, purposeless life, nothing to do, nothing to worry about. Out of the stream of events, left over from the past; right?' His eyes mocked her.

'You're killing yourself,' she said, 'with cynicism. Your idols got taken away from you one by one and now you have nothing to give your love to.' She held his fork toward him; he accepted it. Eat, she thought. Or give up even the biological processes.

As he ate, Joe nodded at the book and said, 'That Abendsen lives around here, according to the cover. In Cheyenne. Gets perspective on the world from such a safe spot, wouldn't you guess? Read what it says; read it aloud.'

Taking the book, she read the back part of the jacket. 'He's an ex-service man. He was in the U.S. Marine Corps in World War Two, wounded in England by a Nazi Tiger Tank. A sergeant. It says he's got practically a fortress that he writes in, guns all over the place.' Setting the book down, she said, 'And it doesn't say so here, but I heard someone say that he's almost a sort of paranoid; charged barbed wire around the place, and it's set in the mountains. Hard to get to.'

'Maybe he's right,' Joe said, 'to live like· that, after writing that book. The German bigwigs hit the roof when they read it.'

'He was living that way before; he wrote the book there. His place is called –' She glanced at the book jacket. 'The High Castle. That's his pet name for it.'

'Then they won't get him,' Joe said, chewing rapidly. 'He's on the lookout. Smart.'

She said, 'I believe he's got a lot of courage to write that book. If the Axis had lost the war, we'd be able to say and write anything we wanted, like we used to; we'd be one country and we'd have a fair legal system, the same one for all of us.'

To her surprise, he nodded reasonably to that.

'I don't understand you,' she said. 'What do you believe? What is it you want? You defend those monsters, those freaks who slaughtered the Jews, and then you –' Despairing, she caught hold of him by the ears; he blinked in surprise and pain as she rose to her feet, tugging him up with her.

They faced each other, wheezing, neither able to speak.

'Let me finish this meal you fixed for me,' Joe said at last.

'Won't you say? You won't tell me? You do know what it is, yourself; you understand and you just go on eating, pretending you don't have any idea what I mean.' She let go of his ears; they had been twisted until they were now bright red.

'Empty talk,' Joe said. 'It doesn't matter. Like the radio, what you said of it. You know the old brownshirt term for people who spin philosophy? *Eierkopf*. Egghead. Because the big double-domed empty heads break so easily . . . in the street brawls.'

'If you feel like that about me,' Juliana said, 'why don't you go on? What are you staying here for?'

His enigmatic grimace chilled her.

I wish I had never let him come with me, she thought. And now it's too late; I know I can't get rid of him – he's too strong.

Something terrible is happening, she thought. Coming out of him. And I seem to be helping it.

'What's the matter?' He reached out, chucked her beneath the chin, stroked her neck, put his fingers under her shirt and pressed her shoulders affectionately. 'A mood. Your problem – I'll analyse you free.'

'They'll call you a Jew analyst.' She smiled feebly. 'Do you want to wind up in an oven?'

'You're scared of men. Right?'

'I don't know.'

'It was possible to tell last night. Only because I –' He cut his sentence off. 'Because I took special care to notice your wants.'

'Because you've gone to bed with so many girls,' Juliana said, 'that's what you started to say.'

'But I know I'm right. Listen; I'll never hurt you, Juliana. On my mother's body – I give you my word. I'll be specially considerate, and if you want to make an issue out of my experience – I'll give you the advantage of that. You'll lose your jitters; I can relax you and improve you, in not very much time, either. You've just had bad luck.'

She nodded, cheered a bit. But she still felt cold and sad, and she still did not know quite why.

To begin his day, Mr Nobusuke Tagomi took a moment to be alone. He sat in his office in the Nippon Times Building and contemplated.

Already, before he had left his house to come to his office, he had received Ito's report on Mr Baynes. There was no doubt in the young student's mind; Mr Baynes was not a Swede. Mr Baynes was most certainly a German national.

But Ito's ability to handle Germanic languages had never impressed either the Trade Missions or the Tokkoka, the Japanese secret police. The fool possibly has sniffed out nothing to speak of, Mr Tagomi thought to himself. Maladroit enthusiasm, combined with romantic doctrines. Detect, always with suspicion.

Anyhow, the conference with Mr Baynes and the elderly individual from the Home Islands would begin soon, in due course, whatever national Mr Baynes was. And Mr Tagomi liked the man. That was, he decided, conceivably the basic talent of the man highly placed – such as himself. To know a good man when he met him. Intuition about people. Cut through all ceremony and outward form. Penetrate to the heart.

The heart, locked within two yin lines of black passion.

Strangled, sometimes, and yet, even then, the light of yang, the flicker at the centre. I like him, Mr Tagomi said to himself. German or Swede. I hope the zaracaine helped his headache. Must recall to inquire, first off the bat.

His desk intercom buzzed.

'No,' he said brusquely into it. 'No discussion. This is moment for Inner Truth. Introversion.'

From the tiny speaker Mr Ramsey's voice : 'Sir, news has just come from the press service below. The Reichs Chancellor is dead. Martin Bormann.' Ramsey's voice popped off. Silence.

Mr Tagomi thought, Cancel all business for today. He rose from his desk and paced rapidly back and forth, pressing his hands together. Let me see. Dispatch at once formal note to Reichs Consul. Minor item; subordinate can accomplish. Deep sorrow, etc. All Japan joins with German people in this sad hour. Then? Become vitally receptive. Must be in position to receive information from Tokyo instantly.

Pressing the intercom button he said, 'Mr Ramsey, be sure we are through to Tokyo. Tell the switchboard girls; be alert. Must not miss communication.'

'Yes, sir,' Mr Ramsey said.

'I will be in my office from now on. Thwart all routine matters. Turn back any and all callers whose business is customary.'

'Sir?'

'My hands must be free in case sudden activity is needed.'

'Yes, sir.'

Half an hour later, at nine, a message arrived from the highest-ranking Imperial Government official on the West Coast, the Japanese Ambassador to the Pacific States of America, the Honourable Baron L. B. Kaelemakule. The Foreign Office had called an extraordinary session at the embassy building on Sutter Street, and each Trade Mission was to send a highly placed personage to attend. In this case, it meant Mr Tagomi himself.

There was no time to change clothes. Mr Tagomi hurried to the express elevator, descended to the ground floor, and a moment later was on his way by Mission limousine, a black 1940 Cadillac driven by an experienced uniformed Chinese chauffeur.

At the embassy building he found other dignitaries' cars parked round about, a dozen in all. Highly placed worthies, some of whom he knew, some of whom were strangers to him, could be seen ascending the wide steps of the embassy building, filing on inside. Mr Tagomi's chauffeur held the door open, and he stepped out quickly, gripping his brief-case; it was empty, because he had no papers to bring – but it was essential to avoid appearance of being mere spectator. He strode up the steps in a manner suggesting a vital role in the happenings, although actually he had not even been told what this meeting would cover.

Small knots of personages had gathered; murmured discussions in the lobby. Mr Tagomi joined several individuals whom he knew, nodding his head and looking – with them – solemn.

An embassy employee appeared presently and directed them into a large hall. Chairs set up, folding type. All persons filed in, seated themselves silently except for coughing and shuffling. Talk had ceased.

Toward the front a gentleman with handful of papers, making way up to slightly raised table. Striped pants : representative from Foreign Office.

Bits of confusion. Other personages, discussing in low tones; heads bowed together.

'Sirs,' the Foreign Office person said in loud, commanding voice. All eyes fixed then on him. 'As you know, the Reichskanzler is now confirmed as dead. Official statement from Berlin. This meeting, which will not last long – you will soon be able to go back to your offices – is for purposes of informing you of our evaluation of several contending factions in German political life who can now be expected to step forth and engage in no-holds-barred disputation for spot evacuated by Herr Bormann.

'Briefly, the notables. The foremost, Hermann Göring. Bear with familiar details, please.

'The Fat One, so-called, due to body, originally courageous air ace in First World War, founded Gestapo and held post in Prussian Government of vast power. One of the most ruthless early Nazis, yet later sybaritic excesses gave rise to misguiding picture of amiable wine-tippling disposition which our government urges you to reject. This man although said to be unhealthy, possibly even morbidly so in terms of appetites, resembles more the self-gratifying ancient Roman Caesars whose power grew rather than abated as age progressed. Lurid picture of this person in toga with pet lions, owning immense castle filled with trophies and art objects, is no doubt accurate. Freight trains of stolen valuables made way to his private estates over military needs in wartime. Our evaluation : this man craves enormous power, and is capable of obtaining it. Most self-indulgent of all Nazis, and is in sharp contrast to late H. Himmler, who lived in personal want at low salary. Herr Göring representative of spoils mentality, using power as means of acquiring personal wealth. Primitive mentality, even vulgar, but quite intelligent man, possibly most intelligent of all Nazi chiefs. Object of his drives : self-glorification in ancient emperor fashion.

'Next, Herr J. Goebbels. Suffered polio in youth. Originally Catholic. Brilliant orator, writer, flexible and fanatic mind, witty, urbane, cosmopolitan. Much active with ladies. Elegant. Educated. Highly capable. Does much work; almost frenzied managerial drive. Is said never to rest. Much-respected personage. Can be charming, but is said to have rabid streak unmatched by other Nazis. Ideological orientation suggesting medieval Jesuitic viewpoint exacerbated by post-Romantic Germanic nihilism. Considered sole authentic intellectual of the Partei. Had ambitions to be playwright in youth. Few friends. Not liked by subordinates, but nevertheless highly polished product of many best elements in European culture. Not self-gratification is underlying ambition, but power for its use purely. Organizational attitude in classic Prussian State sense.

'Herr R. Heydrich.'

The Foreign Office official paused, glanced up and around at them all. Then resumed.

'Much younger individual than above, who helped original Revolution in 1932. Career man with elite S.S. Subordinate of H. Himmler, may have played role in Himmler's not yet fully explained death in 1948. Officially eliminated other contestants within police apparatus such as A. Eichmann, W. Schellenberg, et al. This man said to be feared by many Partei people. Responsible for controlling Wehrmacht elements after close of hostilities in famous clash between police and army which led to reorganization of governmental apparatus, out of all this the N.S.D.A.P. emerging victor. Supported M. Bormann throughout. Product of elite training and yet anterior to so-called S.S. Castle system. Said to be devoid of affective mentality in traditional sense. Enigmatic in terms of drive. Possibly may be said to have view of society which holds human struggle to be series of games; peculiar quasi-scientific detachment found also in certain technological circles. Not party to ideological disputes. Summation : can be called most modern in mentality; post-enlightenment type, dispensing with so-called necessary illusions such as belief in God, etc. Meaning of this so-called realistic mentality cannot be fathomed by social scientists in Tokyo, so this man must be considered a question mark. However, notice of resemblance to deterioration of affectivity in pathological schizophrenia should be made.'

Mr Tagomi felt ill as he listened.

'Baldur von Schirach. Former head of Hitler Youth. Considered idealist. Personally attractive in appearance, but considered not highly experienced or competent. Sincere believer in goals of Partei. Took responsibility for draining Mediterranean and reclaiming of huge areas of farmland. Also mitigated vicious policies of racial extermination in Slavic lands in early 'fifties. Pleaded case directly to German people for remnant of Slavic peoples to exist on reservation-like closed regions in Heartland area. Called for end of certain forms of mercy killings and medical experimentation, but failed here.

'Doctor Seyss-Inquart. Former Austrian Nazi, now in charge of Reich colonial areas, responsible for colonial policies. Possibly most hated man in Reich territory. Said to have instigated most if not all repressive measures dealing with conquered peoples. Worked with Rosenberg for ideological victories of most alarming grandiose type, such as attempt to sterilize entire Russian population remaining after close of hostilities. No facts for certain on this, but considered to be one of several responsible for decision to make holocaust of African continent thus creating genocide conditions for Negro population. Possibly closest in temperament to original Führer, A. Hitler.'

The Foreign Office spokesman ceased his dry, slow recitation.

Mr Tagomi thought, I think I am going mad.

I have to get out of here; I am having an attack. My body is throwing up things or spurting them out – I am dying. He scrambled to his feet, pushed down the aisle past other chairs and people. He could hardly see. Get to lavatory. He ran up the aisle.

Several heads turned. Saw him. Humiliation. Sick at important meeting. Lost place. He ran on, through the open door held by embassy employee.

At once the panic ceased. His gaze ceased to swim; he saw objects once more. Stable floor, walls.

Attack of vertigo. Middle-ear malfunction, no doubt.

He thought, Diencephalon, ancient brainstem, acting up. Some organic momentary breakdown.

Think along reassuring lines. Recall order of world. What to draw on? Religion? He thought, *Now a gavotte perform sedately. Capital both, capital both, you've caught it nicely. This is the style of thing precisely.* Small form of recognizable world, *Gondoliers.* G. & S. He shut his eyes, imagined the D'Oyly Carte Company as he had seen them on their tour after the war. The finite, finite world ...

An embassy employee, at his elbow, saying, 'Sir, can I give you assistance?'

Mr Tagomi bowed. 'I am recovered.'

The other's face, calm, considerate. No derision. They are all laughing at me, possibly? Mr Tagomi thought. Down underneath?

There is evil! It's actual, like cement.

I can't believe it. I can't stand it. Evil is not a view. He wandered about the lobby, hearing the traffic on Sutter Street, the Foreign Office spokesman addressing the meeting. All our religion is wrong. What'll I do? he asked himself. He went to the front door of the embassy; an employee opened it, and Mr Tagomi walked down the steps to the path. The parked cars. His own. Chauffeurs standing.

It's an ingredient in us. In the world. Poured over us, filtering into our bodies, minds, hearts, into the pavement itself.

Why?

We're blind moles. Creeping through the soil, feeling with our snouts. We know nothing. I perceived this . . . now I don't know where to go. Screech with fear, only. Run away.

Pitiful.

Laugh at me, he thought as he saw the chauffeurs regarding him as he walked to his car. Forgot my briefcase. Left it back there, by my chair. All eyes on him as he nodded to his chauffeur. Door held open; he crept into his car.

Take me to the hospital, he thought. No, take me back to the office. 'Nippon Times Building,' he said aloud. 'Drive slowly.' He watched the city, the cars, stores, tall building now, very modern. People. All the men and women, going on their separate businesses.

When he reached his office he instructed Mr Ramsey to contact one of the other Trade Missions, the Non-Ferrous Ores Mission, and to request that their representative to the Foreign Office meeting contact him on his return.

Shortly before noon, the call came through.

'Possibly you noticed my distress at meeting,' Mr Tagomi said into the phone. 'It was no doubt palpable to all, especially my hasty flight.'

'I saw nothing,' the Non-Ferrous man said. 'But after the

97

meeting I did not see you and wondered what had become of you.'

'You are tactful,' Mr Tagomi said bleakly.

'Not at all. I am sure everyone was too wrapped up in the Foreign Office lecture to pay heed to any other consideration. As to what occurred after your departure – did you stay through the rundown of aspirants in the power struggle? That came first.'

'I heard to the part about Doctor Seyss-Inquart.'

'Following that, the speaker dilated on the economic situation over there. The Home Islands take the view that Germany's scheme to reduce the populations of Europe and Northern Asia to the status of slaves – plus murdering all intellectuals, bourgeois elements, patriotic youth and what not – has been an economic catastrophe. Only the formidable technological achievements of German science and industry have saved them. Miracle weapons, so to speak.'

'Yes,' Mr Tagomi said. Seated at his desk, holding the phone with one hand, he poured himself a cup of hot tea. 'As did their miracle weapons V-one and V-two and their jet fighters in the war.'

'It is a sleight-of-hand business,' the Non-Ferrous Ores man said. 'Mainly, their uses of atomic energy have kept things together. And the diversion of their circus-like rocket travel to Mars and Venus. He pointed out that for all their thrilling import, such traffic have yielded nothing of economic worth.'

'But they are dramatic,' Mr Tagomi said.

'His prognosis was gloomy. He feels that most high-placed Nazis are refusing to face facts *vis-à-vis* their economic plight. By doing so, they accelerate the tendency towards greater tour de force adventures, less predictability, less stability in general. The cycle of manic enthusiasm, then fear, then Partei solutions of a desperate type – well, the point he got across was that all this tends to bring the most irresponsible and reckless aspirants to the top.'

Mr Tagomi nodded.

'So we must presume that the worst, rather than the best, choice will be made. The sober and responsible elements will be defeated in the present clash.'

'Who did he say was the worst?' Mr Tagomi said.

'R. Heydrich. Doctor Seyss-Inquart. H. Göring. In the Imperial Government's opinion.'

'And the best?'

'Possibly B. von Schirach and Doctor Goebbels. But on that he was less explicit.'

'Anything more?'

'He told us that we must have faith in the Emperor and the Cabinet at this time more than ever. That we can look towards the Palace with confidence.'

'Was there a moment of respectful silence?'

'Yes.'

Mr Tagomi thanked the Non-Ferrous Ores man and rang off.

As he sat drinking his tea, the intercom buzzed. Miss Ephreikian's voice came : 'Sir, you had wanted to send a message to the German consul.' A pause. 'Did you wish to dictate it to me at this time?'

That is so, Mr Tagomi realized. I had forgotten. 'Come into the office,' he said.

Presently she entered, smiling at him hopefully. 'You are feeling better, sir?'

'Yes. An injection of vitamins has helped.' He considered. 'Recall to me. What is the German consul's name?'

'I have that, sir. Freiherr Hugo Reiss.'

'Mein Herr,' Mr Tagomi began. 'Shocking news has arrived that your leader, Herr Martin Bormann, has succumbed. Tears rise to my eyes as I write these words. When I recall the bold deeds perpetrated by Herr Bormann in securing the salvation of the German people from her enemies both at home and abroad, as well as the soul-shaking measures of sternness meted out to the shirkers and traitors who would betray all mankind's vision of the cosmos, into which now the blond-haired blue-eyed Nordic races have after aeons plunged in their –' He stopped. There was no way to finish. Miss Ephreikian stopped her tape recorder, waiting.

'These are great times,' he said.

'Should I record that, sir? Is that the message?' Uncertainly she started up her machine.

'I was addressing you,' Mr Tagomi said.

She smiled.

'Play my utterances back,' Mr Tagomi said.

The tape transport spun. Then he heard his voice, tiny and metallic, issuing from the two-inch speaker. '. . . perpetrated by Herr Bormann in securing the salvation . . .' He listened to the insect-like squeak as it rambled on. Cortical flappings and scrapings, he thought.

'I have the conclusion,' he said, when the transport ceased turning. 'Determination to exhalt and immolate themselves and so obtain a niche in history from which no life form can cast them, no matter what may transpire.' He paused. 'We are all insects,' he said to Miss Ephreikian. 'Groping towards something terrible or divine. Do you not agree?' He bowed. Miss Ephreikian, seated with her tape recorder, made a slight bow back.

'Send that,' he told her. 'Sign it, et cetera. Work the sentences, if you wish, so that they will mean something.' As she started from the office he added, 'Or so that they mean nothing. Whichever you prefer.'

As she opened the office door she glanced at him curiously.

After she had left he began work on routine matters of the day. But almost at once Mr Ramsey was on the intercom. 'Sir, Mr Baynes is calling.'

Good, Mr Tagomi thought. Now we can begin important discussion. 'Put him on,' he said, picking up the phone.

'Mr Tagomi,' Mr Baynes's voice came.

'Good afternoon. Due to news of Chancellor Bormann's death I was unexpectedly out of my office this morning. However –'

'Did Mr Yatabe get in touch with you?'

'Not yet,' Mr Tagomi said.

'Did you tell your staff to keep an eye open for him?' Mr Baynes said. He sounded agitated.

'Yes,' Mr Tagomi said. 'They will usher him in directly he arrives.' He made a mental note to tell Mr Ramsey; as yet he had not gotten around to it. Are we not to begin discussions, then, until the old gentleman puts in his appearance? He felt dismay. 'Sir,' he began. 'I am anxious to begin. Are you about to present your injection moulds to us? Although we have been in confusion today—'

'There has been a change,' Mr Baynes said. 'We'll wait for Mr Yatabe. You're *sure* he hasn't arrived? I want you to give me your word that you'll notify me as soon as he calls you. Please exert yourself, Mr Tagomi,' Mr Baynes's voice sounded strained, jerky.

'I give you my word.' Now he, too, felt agitation. The Bormann death; that had caused the change. 'Meanwhile,' he said rapidly, 'I would enjoy your company, perhaps at lunch today. I not having had opportunity to have my lunch, yet.' Improvising, he continued, 'Although we will wait on specifics, perhaps we could ruminate on general world conditions, in particular—'

'No,' Mr Baynes said.

No? Mr Tagomi thought. 'Sir,' he said, 'I am not well today. I had a grievous incident; it was my hope to confide it to you.'

'I'm sorry,' Mr Baynes said. 'I'll ring you back later.' The phone clicked. He had abruptly hung up.

I offended him, Mr Tagomi thought. He must have gathered correctly that I tardily failed to inform my staff about the old gentleman. But it is a trifle; he pressed the intercom button and said, 'Mr Ramsey, please come into my office.' I can correct that immediately. More is involved, he decided. The Bormann death has shaken him.

A trifle – and yet indicative of my foolish and feckless attitude. Mr Tagomi felt guilt. This is not a good day. I should have consulted the oracle, discovered what Moment it is. I have drifted far from the Tao; that is obvious.

Which of the sixty-four hexagrams, he wondered, am I

labouring under? Opening his desk drawer he brought out the *I Ching* and laid the two volumes on the desk. So much to ask the sages. So many questions inside me which I can barely articulate...

When Mr Ramsey entered the office, he had already obtained the hexagram. 'Look, Mr Ramsey.' He showed him the book.

The hexagram was Forty-seven. Oppression – Exhaustion.

'A bad omen, generally,' Mr Ramsey said. 'What is your question, sir? If I'm not offending you to ask.'

'I inquired as to the Moment,' Mr Tagomi said. 'The Moment for us all. No moving lines. A static hexagram.' He shut the book.

At three o'clock that afternoon, Frank Frink, still waiting with his business partner for Wyndam-Matson's decision about the money, decided to consult the oracle. How are things going to turn out? he asked, and threw the coins.

The hexagram was Forty-seven. He obtained one moving line, Nine in the fifth place.

His nose and feet are cut off.
Oppression at the hands of the man with the purple knee bands. Joy comes softly.
It furthers one to make offerings and libations.

For a long time – at least half an hour – he studied the line and the material connected with it, trying to figure out what it might mean. The hexagram, and especially the moving line, disturbed him. At last he concluded reluctantly that the money would not be forthcoming.

'You rely on that thing too much,' Ed McCarthy said.

At four o'clock, a messenger from W.-M. Corporation appeared and handed Frink and McCarthy a manila envelope. When they opened it they found inside a certified check for two thousand dollars.

'So you were wrong,' McCarthy said.

Frink thought, Then the oracle must refer to some future consequence of this. That is the trouble; later on, when it has happened, you can look back and see exactly what it meant. But now –

'We can start setting up the shop,' McCarthy said.

'Today? Right now?' He felt weary.

'Why not? We've got our orders made out; all we have to do is stick them in the mail. The sooner the better. And the stuff we can get locally we'll pick up ourselves.' Putting on his jacket, Ed moved to the door of Frink's room.

They had talked Frink's landlord into renting them the basement of the building. Now it was used for storage. Once the cartons were out, they could build their bench, put in wiring, lights, begin to mount their motors and belts. They had drawn up sketches, specifications, parts lists. So they had actually already begun.

We're in business, Frank Frink realized. They had even agreed on a name.

EDFRANK CUSTOM JEWELLERS

'The most I can see today,' he said, 'is buying the wood for the bench, and maybe electrical parts. But no jewellery supplies.'

They went, then, to a lumber supply yard in south San Francisco. By the end of an hour they had their wood.

'What's bothering you?' Ed McCarthy said as they entered a hardware store that dealt on a wholesale basis.

'The money. It gets me down. To finance things that way.'

'Old W.-M. understands,' McCarthy said.

I know, Frink thought. That's why it gets me down. We have entered his world. We are like him. Is that a pleasant thought?

'Don't look back,' McCarthy said. 'Look ahead. To the business.'

I am looking ahead, Frink thought. He thought of the hexagram. What offerings and libations can I make? And – to whom?

7

The handsome young Japanese couple who had visited Robert Childan's store, the Kasouras, telephoned him towards the end of the week and requested that he come to their apartment for dinner. He had been waiting for some further word from them, and he was delighted.

A little early he shut up American Artistic Handcrafts Inc. and took a pedecab to the exclusive district where the Kasouras lived. He knew the district, although no white people lived there. As the pedecab carried him along the winding streets with their lawns and willow trees, Childan gazed up at the modern apartment buildings and marvelled at the grace of the designs. The wrought-iron balconies, the soaring yet modern columns, the pastel colours, the uses of varied textures . . . it all made up a work of art. He could remember when this had been nothing but rubble from the war.

The small Japanese children out playing watched him without comment, then returned to their football or baseball. But, he thought, not so the adults; the well-dressed young Japanese, parking their cars on entering the apartment buildings, noticed him with greater interest. Did he live here? they were perhaps wondering. Young Japanese businessmen coming home from their offices . . . even the heads of Trade Missions lived here. He noticed parked Cadillacs. As the pedecab took him closer to his destination, he became increasingly nervous.

Very shortly, as he ascended the stairs to the Kasouras' apartment, he thought, Here I am, not invited in a business context, but a dinner guest. He had of course taken special pains with his attire; at least he could be confident of his appearance. My appearance, he thought. Yes, that is it. How do I appear? There is no deceiving anyone; I do not belong here. On this land that white men cleared and built one of their finest cities. I am an outsider in my own country.

He came to the proper door along the carpeted hall, rang the bell. Presently the door opened. There stood young Mrs Kasoura, in a silk kimono and obi, her long black hair in shining tangle down her neck, smiling in welcome. Behind her in the living room, her husband, with drink in hand, nodding.

'Mr Childan. Enter.'

Bowing, he entered.

Tasteful in the extreme. And – so ascetic. Few pieces. A lamp here, table, bookcase, print on the wall. The incredible Japanese sense of *wabi.* It could not be thought in English. The ability to find in simple objects a beauty beyond that of the elaborate or ornate. Something to do with the arrangement.

'A drink?' Mr Kasoura asked. 'Scotch and soda?'

'Mr Kasoura –' he began.

'Paul,' the young Japanese said. Indicating his wife. 'Betty. And you are –'

Mr Childan murmured, 'Robert.'

Seated on the soft carpet with their drinks, they listened to a recording of koto, Japanese thirteen-string harp. It was newly released by Japanese H.M.V., and quite popular. Childan noticed that all parts of the phonograph were concealed, even the speaker. He could not tell where the sound came from.

'Not knowing your appetites in dining,' Betty said, 'we have played safe. In kitchen electric oven is broiling T-bone steak. Along with this, baked potato with sauce of sour cream and chives. Maxim utters : no one can err in serving steak to new-found guest first time.'

'Very gratifying,' Childan said. 'Quite fond of steak.' And that certainly was so. He rarely had it. The great stock-yards from the Middle West did not send out much to the West Coast any more. He could not recall when he had last had a good steak.

It was time for him to graft guest gift.

From his coat pocket he brought small tissue-paper-wrapped thing. He laid it discreetly on the low table. Both of them immediately noticed, and this required him to say, 'Bagatelle for you. To display fragment of the relaxation and enjoyment I feel in being here.'

His hand opened the tissue paper, showing them the gift. Bit of ivory carved a century ago by whalers from New England. Tiny ornamented art object, called a scrimshaw. Their faces illuminated with knowledge of the scrimshaws which the old sailors had made in their spare time. No single thing could have summed up old U.S. culture more. Silence.

'Thank you,' Paul said.

Robert Childan bowed.

There was peace, then, for a moment, in his heart. This offering, this – as the *I Ching* put it – libation. It had done what needed to be done. Some of the anxiety and oppression which he had felt lately began to lift from him.

From Ray Calvin he had received restitution for the Colt ·44, plus many written assurances of no second recurrence. And yet it had not eased his heart. Only now, in this unrelated situation, had he for a moment lost the sense that things were in the constant process of going askew. The *wabi* around him, radiations of harmony . . . that is it, he decided. The proportion. Balance. They are so close to the Tao, these two young Japanese. That is why I reacted to them before. I sensed the Tao through them. Saw a glimpse of it myself.

What would it be like, he wondered, to really know the Tao? *The Tao is that which first lets in the light, then the dark.* Occasions the interplay of the two primal forces so that there is always renewal. It is that which keeps it all from wearing down. The universe will never be extinguished because just when the darkness seems to have smothered all, to be truly transcendent, the new seeds of light are reborn in the very depths. That is the Way. When the seed falls, it falls into the earth, into the soil. And beneath, out of sight, it comes to life.

'An hors d'œuvre,' Betty said. She knelt to hold out a

plate on which lay small crackers of cheese, et cetera. He took two gratefully.

'International news much in notice these days,' Paul said as he sipped his drink. 'While I drove home tonight I heard direct broadcast of great pageant-like State Funeral at Munich, including rally of fifty thousand, flags and the like. Much "Ich hatte einen Kamerad" singing. Body now lying in state for all faithful to view.'

'Yes, it was distressing,' Robert Childan said. 'The sudden news earlier this week.'

'Nippon *Times* tonight saying reliable sources declare B. von Schirach under house arrest,' Betty said. 'By S.D. instruction.'

'Bad,' Paul said, shaking his head.

'No doubt the authorities desire to keep order,' Childan said. 'Von Schirach noted for hasty headstrong, even half-baked actions. Much similar to R. Hess in past. Recall mad flight to England.'

'What else reported by Nippon *Times*?' Paul asked his wife.

'Much confusion and intriguing. Army units moving from hither to yon. Leaves cancelled. Border stations closed. Reichstag in session. Speeches by all.'

'That recalls fine speech I heard by Doctor Goebbels,' Robert Childan said. 'On radio, year or so ago. Much witty invective. Had audience in palm of hand, as usual. Ranged throughout gamut of emotionality. No doubt; with original Adolf Hitler out of things, Doctor Goebbels A-one Nazi speaker.'

'True,' both Paul and Betty agreed, nodding.

'Doctor Goebbels also has fine children and wife,' Childan went on. 'Very high-type individuals.'

'True,' Paul and Betty agreed. 'Family man, in contrast to number of other grand moguls there,' Paul said. 'Of questionable sexual mores.'

'I wouldn't give rumours time of day,' Childan said. 'You refer to such as E. Roehm? Ancient history. Long since obliterated.'

'Thinking more of H. Göring,' Paul said, slowly sipping his drink and scrutinizing it. 'Tales of Rome-like orgies of assorted fantastic variety. Causes flesh to crawl even hearing about it.'

'Lies,' Childan said.

'Well, subject not worth discussing,' Betty said tactfully, with a glance at the two of them.

They had finished their drinks, and she went to refill.

'Lots of hot blood stirred up in political discussion,' Paul said. 'Everywhere you go. Essential to keep head.'

'Yes,' Childan agreed. 'Calmness and order. So things return to customary stability.'

'Period after death of Leader critical in totalitarian society,' Paul said. 'Lack of tradition and middle-class institutions combine –' He broke off. 'Perhaps better drop politics.' He smiled. 'Like old student days.'

Robert Childan felt his face flush, and he bent over his new drink to conceal himself from the eyes of his host. What a dreadful beginning he had made. In a foolish and loud manner he had argued politics; he had been rude in his disagreeing, and only the adroit tact of his host had sufficed to save the evening. How much I have to learn, Childan thought. They're so graceful and polite. And I – the white barbarian. It is true.

For a time he contented himself with sipping his drink and keeping on his face an artificial expression of enjoyment. I must follow their leads entirely, he told himself. Agree always.

Yet in a panic he thought, My wits scrambled by the drink. And fatigue and nervousness. Can I do it? I will never be invited back anyhow; it is already too late. He felt despair.

Betty, having returned from the kitchen, had once more seated herself on the carpet. How attractive, Robert Childan thought again. The slender body. Their figures are so superior; not fat, not bulbous. No bra or girdle needed. I must conceal my longing; that at all costs. And yet now and then he let himself steal a glance at her. Lovely dark colours of her skin, hair, and eyes. We are half-baked compared to them. Allowed out of the kiln before we were fully done. The old aboriginal myth; the truth, there.

I must divert my thoughts. Find social item, anything. His eyes strayed about, seeking some topic. The silence resigned heavily, making his tension sizzle. Unbearable. What the hell to say? Something safe. His eyes made out a book on a low black teak cabinet.

'I see you're reading *The Grasshopper Lies Heavy*,' he said. 'I hear it on many lips, but pressure of business prevents my own attention.' Rising, he went to pick it up, carefully consulting their expressions; they seemed to acknowledge this gesture of sociality, and so he proceeded. 'A mystery? Excuse my abysmal ignorance.' He turned the pages.

'Not a mystery,' Paul said. 'On contrary, interesting form of fiction possible within genre of science fiction.'

'Oh no,' Betty disagreed. 'No science in it. Not set in future. Science fiction deals with future, in particular future where science has advanced over now. Book fits neither premise.'

'But,' Paul said, 'it deals with alternate present. Many well-known science fiction novels of that sort.' To Robert he explained, 'Pardon my insistence in this, but as my wife knows, I was for a long time a science fiction enthusiast. I began that hobby early in my life; I was merely twelve. It was during the early days of the war.'

'I see,' Robert Childan said, with politeness.

'Care to borrow *Grasshopper*?' Paul asked. 'We will soon be through, no doubt within day or so. My office being downtown not far from your esteemed store, I could happily drop it off at lunch-time.' He was silent, and then – possibly, Childan thought, due to a signal from Betty – continued, 'You and I, Robert, could eat lunch together, on that occasion.'

'Thank you,' Robert said. It was all he could say. Lunch, in one of the downtown businessmen's fashionable restaurants. He and this stylish modern high-place young Japanese. It was too much; he felt his gaze blur. But he went on examining the book and nodding. 'Yes,' he said. 'this does look interesting. I would very much like to read it. I try to keep up with what's being discussed.' Was that proper to say? Admission that his interest lay in book's modishness. Perhaps that was low-place. He did not know, and yet he felt that it was. 'One cannot judge by book being best seller,' he said. 'We all know that. Many best sellers are terrible trash. This, however –' He faltered.

Betty said, 'Most true. Average taste really deplorable.'

'As in music,' Paul said. 'No interest in authentic American folk jazz, as example. Robert, are you fond of say Bunk Johnson and Kid Ory and the like? Early Dixieland jazz? I have record library of old such music, original Genet recordings.'

Robert said, 'Afraid I know little about Negro music.' They did not look exactly pleased at this remark. 'I prefer classical. Bach and Beethoven.' Surely that was acceptable. He felt now a bit of resentment. Was he supposed to deny the great masters of European music, the timeless classics in favour of New Orleans jazz from the honky-tonks and bistros of the Negro quarter?

'Perhaps if I play selection by New Orleans Rhythm Kings,' Paul began, starting from the room, but Betty gave him a warning look. He hesitated, shrugged.

'Dinner almost ready,' she said.

Returning, Paul once more seated himself. A little sulkily, Robert thought, he murmured, 'Jazz from New Orleans most authentic American folk music there is. Originated on this continent. All else came from Europe, such as corny English-style lute ballads.'

'This is perpetual argument between us,' Betty said, smiling at Robert. 'I do not share his love of original jazz.'

Still holding the copy of *The Grasshopper Lies Heavy*, Robert said, 'What sort of alternate present does this book describe?'

Betty, after a moment, said, 'One in which Germany and Japan lost the war.'

They were all silent.

'Time to eat,' Betty said, sliding to her feet. 'Please come, two hungry gentleman businessmen.' She cajoled Robert and Paul to the dining table, already set with white table-cloth, silver, china, huge rough napkins in what Robert recognized as Early American bone napkin rings. The silver, too, was sterling silver American. The cups and saucers were Royal Albert, deep blue and yellow. Very exceptional; he could not help glancing at them with professional admiration.

The plates were not American. They appeared to be Japanese; he could not tell, it being beyond his field.

'That is Imari porcelain,' Paul said, perceiving his interest. 'From Arita. Considered a first-place product, Japan.'

They seated themselves.

'Coffee?' Betty asked Robert.

'Yes,' he said. 'Thanks.'

'Toward end of meal,' she said, going to get the serving cart.

Soon they were all eating. Robert found the meal delicious. She was quite an exceptional cook. The salad in particular pleased him. Avocados, artichoke heart, some kind of blue cheese dressing . . . thank God they had not presented him with a Japanese meal, the dishes of mixed greens and meats of which he had eaten so much since the war.

And the unending seafoods. He had gotten so that he could no longer abide shrimp or any other shellfish.

'I would like to know,' Robert said, 'what he supposes it would be like in world where Germany and Japan lost the war.'

Neither Paul nor Betty answered for a time. Then Paul said at last, 'Very complicated differences. Better to read the book. It would spoil it for you, possibly, to hear.'

'I have strong convictions on the subject,' Robert said. 'I have frequently thought it over. The world would be much worse.' He heard his voice sound out firm, virtually harsh. 'Much worse.'

They seemed taken by surprise. Perhaps it was his tone. 'Communism would rule everywhere,' Robert continued.

Paul nodded. 'The author, Mr H. Abendsen, considers that point, as to unchecked spread of Soviet Russia. But same as in First World War, even on winning side, second-rate mostly peasant Russia naturally takes pratfall. Big laughing-stock, recalling Japan War with them, when –'

'We have had to suffer, to pay the cost,' Robert said. 'But we did it for a good cause. To stop Slavic world inundation.'

Betty said in a low voice, 'Personally, I do not believe any hysterical talk of "world inundation" by any people. Slavic or Chinese or Japanese.' She regarded Robert placidly. She was in complete control of herself, not carried away; but she intended to express her feeling. A spot of colour, deep red, had appeared in each of her cheeks.

They ate for a time without conversing.

I did it again, Robert Childan informed himself. Impossible to avoid the topic. Because it's everywhere, in a book I happen to pick up or a record collection, in these bone napkin rings – loot piled up by the conquerors. Pillage from my people.

Face facts. I'm trying to pretend that these Japanese and I are alike. But observe : even when I burst out as to my gratification that they won the war, that my nation lost – there's still no common ground. What words mean to me is sharp contrast vis-à-vis them. Their brains are different. Souls likewise. Witness them drinking from English bone china cups, eating with U.S. silver, listening to Negro style of music. It's all on the surface. Advantage of wealth and power makes this available to them, but it's ersatz as the day is long.

Even the *I Ching*, which they've forced down our throats; it's Chinese. Borrowed from way back when. Whom are they fooling? Themselves? Pilfer customs right and left, wear, eat, talk, walk, as for instance consuming with gusto baked potato served with sour cream and chives, old-fashioned American dish added to their haul. But nobody fooled, I can tell you; me least of all.

Only the white races endowed with creativity, he re-flected. And yet I, blood member of same, must bump head to floor for these two. Think how it would have been had we won! Would have crushed them out of existence. No Japan today, and the U.S.A. gleaming great sole power in entire wide world.

He thought : I must read that *Grasshopper* book. Patriotic duty, from the sound of it.

Betty said softly to him, 'Robert, you're not eating. Is the food misprepared?'

At once he took a forkful of salad. 'No,' he said. 'It is virtually the most delicious meal I have had in years.'

'Thank you,' she said, obviously pleased. 'Doing my best to be authentic . . . for instance, carefully shopping in teeny-tiny American markets down along Mission Street. Understand that's the real McCoy.'

You cook the native foods to perfection, Robert Childan thought. What they say is true : your powers of imitation are immense. Apple pie, Coca-Cola, stroll after the movie, Glenn Miller . . . you could paste together out of tin and rice paper a complete artificial America. Rice-paper Mom in the kitchen, rice-paper Dad reading the newspaper. Rice-paper pup at his feet. Everything.

Paul was watching him silently. Robert Childan, suddenly noticing the man's attention, ceased his line of thought and applied himself to his food. Can he read my mind? he wondered. See what I'm really thinking? I know I did not show it. I kept the proper expression; he could not possibly tell.

'Robert,' Paul said, 'since you were born and raised here, speaking the U.S. idiom, perhaps I could get your help with a book which has given me certain trouble. Novel from the 1930s by a U.S. author.'

Robert bowed slightly.

'The book,' Paul said, 'which is quite rare, and which I possess a copy of none the less, is by Nathanael West. Title is *Miss Lonelyhearts*. I have read it with enjoyment, but do not totally grasp N. West's meaning.' He looked hopefully at Robert.

Presently Robert Childan admitted, 'I – have never read that book, I fear.' Nor, he thought, even heard of it.

Disappointment showed in Paul's expression. 'Too bad. It is a tiny book. Tells about man who runs column in daily paper; receives heartache problems constantly, until evidently driven mad by pain and has delusion that he is J. Christ. Do you recall? Perhaps read long ago.'

'No,' Robert said.

'Gives strange view about suffering,' Paul said. 'Insight of most original kind into meaning of pain for no reason, problem which all religions cope with. Religions such as Christian often declare must be sin to account for suffering. N. West seems to add more compelling view of this, over older notions. N. West possibly saw could be suffering without cause due to his being a Jew.'

Robert said, 'If Germany and Japan had lost the war, the Jews would be running the world today. Through Moscow and Wall Street.'

The two Japanese, man and wife, seemed to shrink. They seemed to fade, grow cold, descend into themselves. The room itself grew cold. Robert Childan felt alone. Eating by himself, no longer in their company. What had he done now? What had they misunderstood? Stupid inability on their part to grasp alien tongue, the Western thought. Eluded them and so they took umbrage. What a tragedy, he thought as he continued eating. And yet – what could be done?

Former clarity – that of only a moment ago – had to be drawn on for all it was worth. Full extent not glimpsed until now. Robert Childan did not feel quite as badly as before, because the nonsensical dream had begun to lift from his mind. I showed up here with such anticipation, he recalled. Near-adolescent romantic haze befuddling me as I ascended stairs. But reality cannot be ignored; we must grow up.

And this is the straight dope, right here. *These people are not exactly human.* They don the dress but they're like monkeys dolled up in the circus. They're clever and can learn, *but that is all.*

Why do I cater to them, then? Due solely to their having won?

Big flaw in my character revealed through this encounter. But such is the way it goes. I have pathetic tendency to . . . well, shall we say, unerringly choose the easier of two evils. Like a cow catching sight of the trough; I gallop without premeditation.

What I've been doing is to go along with the exterior motions because it is safer; after all, these are the victors . . . they command. And I will go on doing it, I guess. Because why should I make myself unhappy? They read an American book and want me to explain it to them; they hope that I, a white man, can give them the answer. And I try! But in this case I can't, although had I read it, I no doubt could.

'Perhaps one day I'll have a look at that *Miss Lonelyhearts* book,' he said to Paul. 'And then I can convey to you its significance.'

Paul nodded slightly.

'However, at present I am too busy with my work,' Robert said. 'Later on, perhaps . . . I am sure it wouldn't take me very long.'

'No,' Paul murmured. 'Very short book.' Both he and Betty looked sad, Robert Childan thought. He wondered if they, too, sensed the unbridgeable gap between themselves and him. Hope so, he thought. They deserve to. A shame – just have to ferret out book's message on their own.

He ate with more enjoyment.

No further friction marred the evening. When he left the Kasouras' apartment at ten o'clock, Robert Childan still felt the sense of confidence which had overtaken him during the meal.

He meandered down the apartment house stairs with no genuine concern as to the occasional Japanese residents who, on their way to and from the communal baths, might notice him and stare. Out onto the dark evening sidewalk, then the hailing of a passing pedecab. And he was thereupon on his trip home.

I always wondered what it would be like to meet certain customers socially. Not so bad after all. And, he thought, this experience may well help me in my business.

It is therapeutic to meet these people who have intimidated you. And to discover what they are really like. Then the intimidation goes.

Thinking along those lines, he arrived at his own neighbourhood and finally at his own door. He paid the *chink* pedecab driver and ascended the familiar stairs.

There, in his front room, sat a man he did not know. A white man wearing an overcoat, sitting on the couch reading the newspaper. As Robert Childan stood astonished in the doorway, the man put down his newspaper, leisurely rose, and reached into his breast pocket. He brought out a wallet and displayed it.

'Kempeitai.'

He was a *pinoc*. Employee of Sacramento and its State Police installed by the Japanese occupation authorities. Frightening!

'You're R. Childan?'

'Yes, sir,' he said. His heart pounded.

'Recently,' the policeman said, consulting a clipboard of papers which he had taken from a briefcase on the couch, 'you were paid a visit by a man, a white, describing himself as representing an officer of the Imperial Navy. Subsequent investigation showed that this was not so. No such officer existed. No such ship.' He eyed Childan.

'That's correct,' Childan said.

'We have a report,' the policeman continued, 'of a racket being conducted in the Bay Area. This fellow evidently was involved. Would you describe him?'

'Small, rather dark-skinned,' Childan began.

'Jewish?'

'Yes!' Childan said. 'Now that I think about it. Although I overlooked it at the time.'

'Here's a photo.' The Kempeitai man passed it to him.

'That's him,' Childan said, experiencing recognition beyond any doubt. He was a little appalled by the Kempeitai's powers of detection. 'How'd you find him? I didn't report it, but I telephoned my jobber, Ray Calvin, and told him –'

The policeman waved him silent. 'I have a paper for you to sign, and that's all. You won't have to appear in court; this is a legal formality that ends your involvement.' He handed Childan the paper, plus pen. 'This states that you were approached by this man and that he tried to swindle you by misrepresenting himself and so forth. You read the paper.' The policeman rolled back his cuff and examined his watch as Robert Childan read the paper. 'Is that substantially correct?'

It was – substantially. Robert Childan did not have time to give the paper thorough attention, and anyhow he was a little confused as to what had happened that day. But he knew that the man had misrepresented himself, and that some racket was involved; and, as the Kempeitai man had said, the fellow was a Jew. Robert Childan glanced at the name beneath the photo of the man. Frank Frink, Born Frank Fink. Yes, he certainly was a Jew. Anybody could tell, with a name like Fink. And he had changed it.

Childan signed the paper.

'Thanks,' the policeman said. He gathered up his things, tipped his hat, wished Childan good night, and departed. The whole business had taken only a moment.

I guess they got him, Childan thought. Whatever he was up to.

Great relief. They work fast, all right.

We live in a society of law and order, where Jews can't pull their subtleties on the innocent. We're protected.

I don't know why I didn't recognize the racial characteristics when I saw him. Evidently I'm easily deceived.

He decided, I'm simply not capable of deceit and that renders me helpless. Without law, I'd be at their mercy. He could have convinced me of anything. It's a form of hypnosis. They can control an entire society.

Tomorrow I will have to go out and buy that *Grasshopper*

book, he told himself. It'll be interesting to see how the author depicts a world run by Jews and Communists, with the Reich in ruins, Japan no doubt a province of Russia; in fact, with Russia extending from the Atlantic to the Pacific. I wonder if he – whatever his name is – depicts a war between Russia and the U.S.A.? Interesting book, he thought. Odd nobody thought of writing it before.

He thought, It should help to bring home to us how lucky we are. In spite of the obvious disadvantages . . . we could be so much worse off. Great moral lesson pointed out by that book. Yes, there are Japs in power here, and we are a defeated nation. But we have to look ahead; we have to build. Out of this are coming great things, such as the colonization of the planets.

There should be a news broadcast on, he realized. Seating himself, he turned on the radio. Maybe the new Reichs Chancellor has been picked. He felt excitement and anticipation. To me, that Seyss-Inquart seems the most dynamic. The most likely to carry out bold programmes.

I wish I was there, he thought. Possibly some day I'll be well enough off to travel to Europe and see all that has been done. Shame to miss out. Stuck here on the West Coast, where nothing is happening. History is passing us by.

8

At eight o'clock in the morning Freiherr Hugo Reiss, the Reichs Consul in San Francisco, stepped from his Mercedes-Benz 220-E and walked briskly up the steps of the consulate. Behind him came two young male employees of the Foreign Office. The door had been unlocked by Reiss's staff, and he passed inside, raising his hand in greeting to the two switchboard girls, the vice-Consul Herr Frank, and then, in the inner office, Reiss's secretary, Herr Pferdehuf.

'Freiherr,' Pferdehuf said, 'there is a coded radiogram coming in just now from Berlin. Preface One.'

This meant the message was urgent. 'Thank you,' Reiss said, removing his overcoat and giving it to Pferdehuf to hang up.

'Ten minutes ago Herr Kreuz vom Meere called. He would like you to return his call.'

'Thank you,' Reiss said. He seated himself at the small table by the window of his office, removed the cover from his breakfast, saw on the plate the roll, scrambled eggs and sausage, poured himself hot black coffee from the silver pot, then unrolled his morning newspaper.

The caller, Kreuz vom Meere, was the chief of the Sicherheitsdienst in the P.S.A. area; his headquarters were located, under a cover name, at the air terminal. Relations between Reiss and Kreuz vom Meere were rather strained. Their jurisdiction overlapped in countless matters, a deliberate policy, no doubt, of the higher-ups in Berlin. Reiss held an honorary commission in the S.S., the rank of major, and this made him technically Kreuz vom Meere's subordinate. The commission had been bestowed several years ago, and at that time Reiss had discerned the purpose. But he could do nothing about it. None the less, he chafed still.

The newspaper, flown in by Lufthansa and arriving at six in the morning, was the *Frankfurter Zeitung*. Reiss read the front page carefully. Von Schirach under house arrest, possibly dead by now. Too bad. Göring residing at a Luftwaffe training base, surrounded by experienced veterans of the war, all loyal to the Fat One. No one would slip up on him. No S.D. hatchetmen. And what about Doctor Goebbels?

Probably in the heart of Berlin. Depending as always on his own wits, his ability to talk his way out of anything. If Heydrich sends a squad to do him in, Reiss reflected, the little Doctor will not only argue them out of it, he will probably persuade them to switch over. Make them employees of the Ministry of Propaganda and Public Enlightenment.

He could imagine Doctor Goebbels at this moment, in the apartment of some stunning movie actress, disdaining the Wehrmacht units bumping through the streets below. Nothing frightened that *Kerl*. Goebbels would smile his mocking smile . . . continue stroking the lovely lady's bosom with his left hand, while writing his article for the day's *Angriff* with –

Reiss's thoughts were interrupted by his secretary's knock. 'I'm sorry. Kreuz vom Meere is on the line again.'

Rising, Reiss went to his desk and took the receiver. 'Reiss here.'

The heavy Bavarian accents of the local S.D. chief. 'Any word on that Abwehr character?'

Puzzled, Reiss tried to make out what Kreuz vom Meere was referring to. 'Hmmm,' he murmured. 'To my knowledge, there are three or four Abwehr "characters" on the Pacific Coast at the moment.'

'The one travelling in by Lufthansa within the last week.'

'Oh,' Reiss said. Holding the receiver between his ear and shoulder, he took out his cigarette case. 'He never came in here.'

'What's he doing?'

'God, I don't know. Ask Canaris.'

'I'd like you to call the Foreign Office and have them call the Chancery and have whoever's on hand get hold of the Admiralty and demand that the Abwehr either take its people back out of here or give us an account of why they're here.'

'Can't you do that?'

'Everything's in confusion.'

They've completely lost the Abwehr man, Reiss decided. They – the local S.D. – were told by someone on Heydrich's staff to watch him, and they missed a connection. And now they want me to bail them out.

'If he comes in here,' Reiss said, 'I'll have somebody stay on him. You can rely on that.' Of course, there was little or no chance that the man would come in. And they both knew that.

'He undoubtedly uses a cover name,' Kreuz vom Meere plodded on. 'We don't know it, naturally. He's an aristocratic-looking fellow. About forty. A captain. Actual name Rudolf Wegener. One of those old monarchist families from East Prussia. Probably supported von Papen in the Systemzeit.' Reiss made himself comfortable at his desk as Kreuz vom Meere droned away. 'The only answer as I see it to these monarchist hangers-on is to cut the budget of the Navy so they can't afford...'

Finally Reiss managed to get off the phone. When he returned to his breakfast he found the roll cold. The coffee however was still hot; he drank it and resumed reading the newspaper.

No end to it, he thought. Those S.D. people keep a shift on duty at night. Call you at three in the morning.

His secretary, Pferdehuf, stuck his head into the office, saw that he was off the phone, and said, 'Sacramento called just now in great agitation. They claim there's a Jew running around the streets of San Francisco.' Both he and Reiss laughed.

'All right,' Reiss said. 'Tell them to calm down and send us the regular papers. Anything else?'

'You read the messages of condolence.'

'Are there more?'

'A few. I'll keep them on my desk, if you want them. I've already sent out answers.'

'I have to address that meeting today,' Reiss said. 'At one this afternoon. Those businessmen.'

'I won't let you forget,' Pferdehuf said.

Reiss leaned back in his chair. 'Care to make a bet?'

'Not on the Partei deliberations. If that's what you mean.'

'It'll be the Hangman.'

Lingering, Pferdehuf said, 'Heydrich has gone as far as he can. Those people never pass over to direct Partei control because everyone is scared of them. The Partei bigwigs would have a fit even at the idea. You'd get a coalition in twenty-five minutes, as soon as the first S.S. car took off from Prinzalbrechtstrasse. They'd have all those economic big shots like Krupp and Thyssen –' He broke off. One of the cryptographers had come up to him with an envelope.

Reiss held out his hand. His secretary brought the envelope to him.

It was the urgent coded radiogram, decoded and typed out.

When he had finished reading it he saw that Pferdehuf was waiting to hear. Reiss crumpled up the message in the big ceramic ashtray on his desk, lit it with his lighter. 'There's a Japanese general supposed to be travelling here incognito. Tedeki. You better go down to the public library and get one of those official Japanese military magazines that would have his picture. Do it discreetly, of course. I don't think we'd have anything on him here.' He started toward the locked filing cabinet, then changed his mind. 'Get what information you can. The statistics. They should all be available at the library.' He added, 'This General Tedeki was a chief of staff a few years ago. Do you recall anything about him?'

'Just a little,' Pferdehuf said. 'Quite a fire-eater. He should be about eighty, now. Seems to me he advocated some sort of crash programme to get Japan into space.'

'On that he failed,' Reiss said.

'I wouldn't be surprised if he's coming here for medical purposes,' Pferdehuf said. 'There've been a number of old Japanese military men here to use the big U.C. Hospital. That way they can make use of German surgical techniques they can't get at home. Naturally they keep it quiet. Patriotic reasons, you know. So perhaps we should have somebody at the U.C. Hospital watching, if Berlin wants to keep their eye on him.'

Reiss nodded. Or the old general might be involved in commercial speculations, a good deal of which went on in San Francisco. Connections he had made while in service would be of use to him now that he was retired. Or was he retired? The message called him *General*, not *Retired General*.

'As soon as you have a picture,' Reiss said, 'pass copies right on to our people at the airport and down at the harbour. He may have already come in. You know how long it takes them to get this sort of thing to us.' And of course if the general had already reached San Francisco, Berlin would be angry at the P.S.A. consulate. The consulate should have been able to intercept him – before the order from Berlin had even been sent.

Pferdehuf said, 'I'll stamp-date the coded radiogram from Berlin, so if any question comes up later on, we can show exactly when we received it. Right to the hour.'

'Thank you,' Reiss said. The people in Berlin were past masters at transferring responsibility, and he was weary of being stuck. It had happened too many times. 'Just to be on the safe side,' he said, 'I think I'd better have you answer that message. Say, "Your instructions abysmally tardy. Person already reported in area. Possibility of successful intercept remote at this stage." Put something along those lines into shape and send it. Keep it good and vague. You understand.'

Pferdehuf nodded. 'I'll send it right off. And keep a record of the exact date and moment it was sent.' He shut the door after him.

You have to watch out, Reiss reflected, or all at once you find yourself consul to a bunch of niggers on an island off the coast of South Africa. And the next you know, you have a black mammy for a mistress, and ten or eleven little pickaninnies calling you daddy.

Reseating himself at his breakfast table he lit an Egyptian Simon Artz cigarette Number 70, carefully reclosing the metal tin.

It did not appear that he would be interrupted for a little while now, so from his briefcase he took the book he had been reading, opened to his placemark, made himself comfortable, and resumed where he had last been forced to stop.

. . . Had he actually walked streets of quiet cars, Sunday morning peace of the Tiergarten, so far away? Another life. Ice cream, a taste that could never have existed. Now they boiled nettles and were glad to get them. God, he cried out. Won't they stop? The huge British tanks came on. Another building, it might have been an apartment house, or a store, a school or office; he could not tell – the ruins toppled, slid into fragments. Below in the rubble another handful of survivors buried, without even the sound of death. Death had spread out everywhere equally, over the living, the hurt, the corpses layer after layer that already had begun to smell. The stinking, quivering corpse of Berlin, the eyeless turrets still upraised, disappearing without protest like this one, this nameless edifice that man had once put up with pride.

His arms, the boy noticed, were covered with the film of gray, the ash, partly inorganic, partly the burned sifting final produce of life. All mixed now, the boy knew, and wiped it from him. He did not think much further; he had another thought that captured his mind if there was thinking to be done over the screams and the *hump hump* of the shells. Hunger. For six days he had eaten nothing but the nettles, and now they were gone. The pasture of weeds had disappeared into a single vast crater of earth. Other dim, gaunt figures had appeared at the rim, like the boy, had stood silent and then drifted away. An old mother with a *babushka* tied about her grey head, basket – empty – under her arm. A one-armed man, his eyes empty as the basket. A girl. Faded now back into the litter of slashed trees in which the boy Eric hid.

And still the snake came on.

Would it ever end? the boy asked, addressing no one. And if it did, what then? Would they fill their bellies, these –

'Freiherr,' Pferdehuf's voice came. 'Sorry to interrupt you. Just one word.'

Reiss jumped, shut his book. 'Certainly.'

How that man can write, he thought. Completely carried me away. Real. Fall of Berlin to the British, as vivid as if it had actually taken place. Brrr. He shivered.

Amazing, the power of fiction, even cheap popular fiction, to evoke. No wonder it's banned within Reich territory; I'd ban it myself. Sorry I started it. But too late; must finish, now.

His secretary said, 'Some seamen from a German ship. They're required to report to you.'

'Yes,' Reiss said. He hopped to the door and out to the front office. There were three seamen wearing heavy grey sweaters, all with thick blond hair, strong faces, a trifle nervous. Reiss raised his right hand. 'Heil Hitler.' He gave them a brief friendly smile.

'Heil Hitler,' they mumbled. They began showing him their papers.

As soon as he had certified their visit to the consulate, he hurried back into his private office.

Once more, alone, he reopened *The Grasshopper Lies Heavy.*

His eyes fell on a scene involving – Hitler. Now he found himself unable to stop; he began to read the scene out of sequence, the back of his neck burning.

The trial, he realized, of Hitler. After the close of the war. Hitler in the hands of the Allies, good God. Also Goebbels, Göring, all the rest of them. At Munich. Evidently Hitler was answering the American prosecutor.

. . . black, flaming, the spirit of old seemed for an instant once again to blaze up. The quivering, shambling body jerked taut; the head lifted. Out of the lips that ceaselessly drooled, a croaking half-bark, half-whisper. 'Deutsche, hier steh' Ich.' Shudders among those who watched and listened, the earphones pressed tightly, strained faces of Russian, American, British, and German alike. Yes, Karl thought. Here he stands once more . . . they have beaten us – and more. They have stripped this *superman*, shown him for what he is. Only – a

'Freiherr.'

Reiss realized that his secretary had entered the office. 'I'm busy,' he said angrily. He slammed the book shut. 'I'm trying to read this book, for God's sake !'

It was hopeless. He knew it.

'Another coded radiogram is coming in from Berlin,' Pferdehuf said. 'I caught a glimpse of it as they started decoding it. It deals with the political situation.'

'What did it say?' Reiss murmured, rubbing his forehead with his thumb and fingers.

'Doctor Goebbels has gone on the radio unexpectedly. A major speech.' The secretary was quite excited. 'We're supposed to take the text – they're transmitting it out of code – and make sure it's printed by the press, here.'

'Yes, yes,' Reiss said.

The moment his secretary had left once more, Reiss reopened the book. One more peek, despite my resolution . . . he thumbed the previous portion.

. . . in silence Karl contemplated the flag-draped casket. Here he lay, and now he was gone, really gone. Not even the demon-inspired powers could bring him back. The man – or was it after all *Uebermensch?* – whom Karl had blindly followed, worshipped . . . even to the brink of the grave. Adolf Hitler had passed beyond, but Karl clung to life. I will not follow him, Karl's mind whispered. I will go on, alive. And rebuild. And we will all rebuild. We must.

How far, how terribly far, the Leader's magic had carried him. And what was it, now that the last dot had been put on that incredible record, that journey from the isolated rustic town in Austria, up from rotting poverty in Vienna, from the nightmare ordeal of the trenches, through political intrigue, the founding of the Party, to the Chancellorship, to what for an instant had seemed near world domination?

Karl knew. Bluff. Adolf Hitler had lied to them. He had led them with empty words.

It is not too late. We see your bluff, Adolf Hitler. And we know you for what you are, at last. And the Nazi Party, the dreadful era of murder and megalomaniacal fantasy, for what it is. What it was.

Turning, Karl walked away from the silent casket . . .

Reiss shut the book and sat for a time. In spite of himself he was upset. More pressure should have been put on the Japs, he said to himself, to suppress this damn book. In fact, it's obviously deliberate on their part. They could have arrested this – whatever his name is. Abendsen. They have plenty of power in the Middle West.

What upset him was this. The *death* of Adolf Hitler, the defeat and destruction of Hitler, the Partei, and Germany itself, as depicted in Abendsen's book . . . it all was somehow grander, more in the old spirit than the actual world. The world of German hegemony.

How could that be? Reiss asked himself. Is it just this man's writing ability?

They know a million tricks, those novelists. Take Doctor Goebbels; that's how he started out, writing fiction. Appeals to the base lusts that hide in everyone no matter how respectable on the surface. Yes, the novelist knows humanity, how worthless they are, ruled by their testicles, swayed by cowardice, selling out every cause because of their greed – all he's got to do is thump on the drum, and there's his response. And he's laughing, of course, behind his hand at the effect he gets.

Look how he played on my sentiments, Herr Reiss reflected, not on my intellect; and naturally he's going to get paid for it – the money's there. Obviously somebody put the *Hundsfott* up to it, instructed him what to write. They'll write anything if they know they'll get paid. Tell any bunch of lies, and then the public actually takes the smelly brew seriously when it's dished out. Where was this published? Herr Reiss inspected the copy of the book. Omaha, Nebraska. Last outpost of the former plutocratic U.S. publishing industry, once located in downtown New York and supported by Jewish and Communist gold . . .

Maybe this Abendsen is a Jew.

They're still at it, trying to poison us. This *jüdisches Buch* – He slammed the covers of the *Grasshopper* violently together. Actual name probably Abendstein. No doubt the S.D. has looked into it by now.

Beyond doubt, we ought to send somebody across into the R.M.S. to pay Herr Abendstein a visit. I wonder if Kreuz vom Meere has gotten instructions to that effect. Probably hasn't, with all the confusion in Berlin. Everybody too busy with domestic matters.

But this book, Reiss thought, is dangerous.

If Abendstein should be found dangling from the ceiling

some fine morning, it would be a sobering notice to anyone who might be influenced by this book. We would have had the last word. Written the postscript.

It would take a white man, of course. I wonder what Skorzeny is doing these days.

Reiss pondered, reread the dust jacket of the book. The kike keeps himself barricaded. Up in this High Castle. Nobody's fool. Whoever gets in and gets him won't get back out.

Maybe it's foolish. The book after all is in print. Too late now. And that's Japanese-dominated territory . . . the little yellow men would raise a terrific fuss.

Nevertheless, if it was done adroitly . . . if it could be properly handled . . .

Freiherr Hugo Reiss made a notation on his pad. Broach subject with S.S. General Otto Skorzeny, or better yet Otto Ohlendorf at Amt III of the Reichssicherheitshauptamt. Didn't Ohlendorf head Einsatzgruppe D?

And then, all at once, without warning of any kind, he felt sick with rage. I thought this was over, he said to himself. Does it have to go on for ever? The war ended years ago. And we thought it was finished then. But that Africa fiasco, that crazy Seyss-Inquart carrying out Rosenberg's schemes.

That Herr Hope is right, he thought. With his joke about our contacts on Mars. Mars populated by Jews. We would see them there, too. Even with their two heads apiece, standing one foot high.

I have my routine duties, he decided. I don't have time for any of these harebrained adventures, this sending of Einsatzkommandos after Abendsen. My hands are full greeting German sailors and answering coded radiograms; let someone higher up initiate a project of that sort – it's their business.

Anyhow, he decided, if I instigated it and it backfired, one can imagine where I'd be : in Protective Custody in Eastern General Gouvernement, if not in a chamber being squirted with Zyklon B hydrogen cyanide gas.

Reaching out, he carefully scratched the notation on his

pad out of existence, then burned the paper itself in the ceramic ashtray.

There was a knock, and his office door opened. His secretary entered with a large handful of papers. 'Doctor Goebbels' speech. In its entirety.' Pferdehuf put the sheets down on the desk. 'You must read it. Quite good; one of his best.'

Lighting another Simon Artz Number 70 cigarette, Reiss began to read Doctor Goebbels' speech.

9

After two weeks of nearly constant work, Edfrank Custom Jewellery had produced its first finished batch. There the pieces lay, on two boards covered with black velvet, all of which went into a square wicker basket of Japanese origin. And Ed McCarthy and Frank Frink had made business cards. They had used an artgum eraser carved out to form their name; they printed in red from this, and then completed the cards with a children's toy rotary printing set. The effect – they had used a high-quality Christmas-card coloured heavy paper – was striking.

In every aspect of their work they had been professional. Surveying their jewellery, cards, and display, they could see no indication of the amateur. Why should there be? Frank Frink thought. We're both pros; not in jewellery making, but in shopwork in general.

The display boards held a good variety. Cuff bracelets made of brass, copper, bronze, and even hot-forged black iron. Pendants, mostly of brass, with a little silver ornamentation. Ear-rings of silver. Pins of silver or brass. The silver had cost them a good deal; even silver solder had set them back. They had bought a few semiprecious stones, too, for mounting in the pins : baroque pearls, spinels, jade, slivers of fire opal. And, if things went well, they would try gold and possibly five- or six-point diamonds.

It was gold that would make them a real profit. They had

already begun searching into sources of scrap gold, melted-down antique pieces of no artistic value – much cheaper to buy than new gold. But even so, an enormous expense was involved. And yet, one gold pin sold would bring more than forty brass pins. They could get almost any price on the retail market for a really well-designed and executed gold pin . . . assuming, as Frink had pointed out, that their stuff went over at all.

At this point they had not yet tried to sell. They had solved what seemed to be their basic technical problems; they had their bench with motors, flex-cable machine, arbor of grinding, and polishing wheels. They had in fact a complete range of finishing tools, ranging from the coarse wire brushes through brass brushes and Cratex wheels, to finer polishing buffs of cotton, linen, leather, chamois, which could be coated with compounds ranging from emery and pumice to the most delicate rouges. And of course they had their oxyacetylene welding outfit, their tanks, gauges, hoses, tips, masks.

And superb jewellers' tools. Pliers from Germany and France, micrometers, diamond drills, saws, tongs, tweezers, thirdhand structures for soldering, vices, polishing cloths, shears, hand-forged tiny hammers . . . rows of precision equipment. And their supplies of brazing rod of various gauge, sheet metal, pin backs, links, ear-ring clipbacks. Well over half the two thousand dollars had been spent; they had in their Edfrank bank account only two hundred and fifty dollars, now. But they were set up legally; they even had their P.S.A. permits. Nothing remained but to sell.

No retailer, Frink thought as he studied the displays, can give these a tougher inspection than we have. They certainly looked good, these few select pieces, each painstakingly gone over for bad welds, rough or sharp edges, spots of fire colour . . . their quality control was excellent. The slightest dullness or wire brush scratch had been enough reason to return a piece to the shop. We can't afford to show any crude or unfinished work; one unnoticed black speck on a silver necklace – and we're finished.

On their list, Robert Childan's store appeared first. But

only Ed could go there; Childan would certainly remember Frank Frink.

'You got to do most of the actual selling,' Ed said, but he was resigned to approaching Childan himself; he had bought a good suit, new tie, white shirt, to make the right impression. Nonetheless, he looked ill-at-ease. 'I know we're good,' he said for the millionth time. 'But – hell.'

Most of the pieces were abstract, whirls of wire, loops, designs which to some extent the molten metals had taken on their own. Some had a spider-web delicacy, an airiness; others had a massive, powerful, almost barbaric heaviness. There was an amazing range of shape, considering how few pieces lay on the velvet trays; and yet one store, Frink realized, could buy everything we have laid out here. We'll see each store once – if we fail. But if we succeed, if we get them to carry our line, we'll be going back to refill orders the rest of our lives.

Together, the two of them loaded the velvet board trays into the wicker basket. We could get back something on the metal, Frink said to himself, if worst comes to worst. And the tools and equipment; we can dispose of them at a loss, but at least we'll get something.

This is the moment to consult the oracle. Ask, How will Ed make out on this first selling trip? But he was too nervous to. It might give a bad omen, and he did not feel capable of facing it. In any case, the die was cast : the pieces were made, the shop set up – whatever the *I Ching* might blab out at this point.

It can't sell our jewellery for us . . . it can't *give* us luck.

'I'll tackle Childan's place first,' Ed said. 'We might as well get it over with. And then you can try a couple. You're coming along, aren't you? In the truck. I'll park around the corner.'

As they got into their pickup truck with their wicker hamper, Frink thought, God knows how good a salesman Ed is, or I am. Childan can be sold, but it's going to take a presentation, like they say.

If Juliana were here, he thought, she could stroll in there

and do it without batting an eye; she's pretty, she can talk to anybody on earth, and she's a woman. After all, this is women's jewellery. She could wear it into the store. Shutting his eyes, he tried to imagine how she would look with one of their bracelets on. Or one of their large silver necklaces. With her black hair and her pale skin, doleful, probing eyes ... wearing a grey jersey sweater, a little bit too tight, the silver resting against her bare flesh, metal rising and falling as she breathed ...

God, she was vivid in his mind, right now. Every piece they made, the strong, thin fingers picked up, examined; tossing her head back, holding the piece high. Juliana sorting, always a witness to what he had done.

Best for her, he decided, would be ear-rings. The bright dangly ones, especially the brass. With her hair held back by a clip or cut short so that her neck and ears could be seen. And we could take photos of her for advertising and display. He and Ed had discussed a catalogue, so they could sell by mail to stores in other parts of the world. She would look terrific . . . her skin is nice, very healthy, no sagging or wrinkles, and a fine colour. Would she do it, if I could locate her? No matter what she thinks of me; nothing to do with our personal life. This would be a strictly business matter.

Hell, I wouldn't even take the pictures. We'd get a professional photographer to do it. That would please her. Her vanity probably as great as always. She always liked people to look at her, admire her; anybody. I guess most women are like that. They crave attention all the time. They're very babyish that way.

He thought, Juliana could never stand being alone; she had to have me around all the time complimenting her. Little kids are that way; they feel if their parents aren't watching what they do then what they do isn't real. No doubt she's got some guy noticing her right now. Telling her how pretty she is. Her legs. Her smooth, flat stomach ...

'What's the matter?' Ed said, glancing at him. 'Losing your nerve?'

'No,' Frink said.

'I'm not just going to stand there,' Ed said. 'I've got a few ideas of my own. And I'll tell you something else : I'm not scared. I'm not intimidated just because it's a fancy place and I have to put on this fancy suit. I admit I don't like to dress up. I admit I'm not comfortable. But that doesn't matter a bit. I'm still going in there and really give it to that poop-head.'

Good for you, Frink thought.

'Hell, if you could go in there like you did,' Ed said, 'and give him that line about being a Jap admiral's gentleman, I ought to be able to tell him the truth, that this is really good creative original handmade jewellery, that –'

'Handwrought,' Frink said.

'Yeah. Hand*wrought*. I mean, I'll go in there and I won't come back out until I've given him a run for his money. He ought to buy this. If he doesn't he's really nuts. I've looked around; there isn't anything like ours for sale anywhere. God, when I think of him maybe looking at it and not buying it – it makes me so goddam mad I could start swinging.'

'Make sure you tell him it's not plated,' Frink said. 'That copper means solid copper and brass solid brass.'

'You let me work out my own approach,' Ed said. 'I got some really good ideas.'

Frink thought, What I can do is this. I can take a couple of pieces – Ed'll never care – and box them up and send them to Juliana. So she'll see what I'm doing. The postal authorities will trace her; I'll send it registered to her last known address. What'll she say when she opens the box? There'll have to be a note from me explaining that I made it myself; that I'm a partner in a little new creative jewellery business. I'll fire her imagination, give her an account that'll make her want to know more, that'll get her interested. I'll talk about the gems and the metals. The places we're selling to, the fancy stores . . .

'Isn't it along here?' Ed said, slowing the truck. They were in heavy downtown traffic; buildings blotted out the sky. 'I better park.'

'Another five blocks,' Frink said.

'Got one of those marijuana cigarettes?' Ed said. 'One would calm me right about now.'

Frink passed him his package of T'ien-lais, the 'Heavenly Music' brand he had learned to smoke at W.-M. Corporation.

I know she's living with some guy, Frink said to himself. Sleeping with him. As if she was his wife. I know Juliana. She couldn't survive any other way; I know how she gets around nightfall. When it gets cold and dark and everybody's home sitting around the living room. She was never made for a solitary life. Me neither, he realized.

Maybe the guy's a real nice guy. Some shy student she picked up. She'd be a good woman for some young guy who had never had the courage to approach a woman before. She's not hard or cynical. It would do him a lot of good. I hope to hell she's not with some older guy. That's what I couldn't stand. Some experienced mean guy with a toothpick sticking out of the side of his mouth, pushing her around.

He felt himself begin to breathe heavily. Image of some beefy hairy guy stepping down hard on Juliana, making her life miserable . . . I know she'd finally wind up killing herself, he thought. It's in the cards for her, if she doesn't find the right man – and that means a really gentle, sensitive, kindly student type who would be able to appreciate all those thoughts she has.

I was too rough for her, he thought. And I'm not so bad; there are a hell of a lot of guys worse than me. I could pretty well figure out what she was thinking, what she wanted, when she felt lonely or bad or depressed. I spent a lot of time worrying and fussing over her. But it wasn't enough. She deserved more. She deserves a lot, he thought.

'I'm parking,' Ed said. He had found a place and was backing the truck, peering over his shoulder.

'Listen,' Frink said. 'Can I send a couple of pieces to my wife?'

'I didn't know you were married.' Intent on parking, Ed answered him reflexively. 'Sure, as long as they're not silver.'

Ed shut off the truck motor.

'We're here,' he said. He puffed marijuana smoke, then stubbed the cigarette out on the dashboard, dropped the remains to the cab floor. 'Wish me luck.'

'Luck,' Frank Frink said.

'Hey, look. There's one of those Jap *waka* poems on the back of this cigarette package.' Ed read the poem aloud, over the traffic noises.

> 'Hearing a cuckoo cry,
> I looked up in the direction
> Whence the sound came:
> What did I see?
> Only the pale moon in the dawning sky.'

He handed the package of T'ien-lais back to Frink. 'Keeriiist!' he said, then slapped Frink on the back, grinned, opened the truck door, picked up the wicker hamper and stepped from the truck. 'I'll let you put the dime in the meter,' he said, starting off down the sidewalk.

In an instant he had disappeared among the other pedestrians.

Juliana, Frink thought. Are you as alone as I am?

He got out of the truck and put a dime in the parking meter.

Fear, he thought. This whole jewellery venture. *What if it should fail? What if it should fail?* That was how the oracle put it. Wailing, tears, beating the pot.

Man faces the darkening shadows of his life. His passage to the grave. If she were here it would not be so bad. Not bad at all.

I'm scared, he realized. Suppose Ed doesn't sell a thing. Suppose they laugh at us.

What then?

On a sheet on the floor of the front room of her apartment, Juliana lay holding Joe Cinnadella against her. The room

135

was warm and stuffy with mid-afternoon sunlight. Her body and the body of the man in her arms were damp with perspiration. A drop, rolling down Joe's forehead, clung a moment to his cheekbone, then fell to her throat.

'You're still dripping,' she murmured.

He said nothing. His breathing, long, slow, regular . . . like the ocean, she thought. We're nothing but water inside.

'How was it?' she asked.

He mumbled that it had been okay.

I thought so, Juliana thought. I can tell. Now we both have to get up, pull ourselves together. Or is that bad? Sign of subconscious disapproval?

He stirred.

'Are you getting up?' She gripped him tight with both her arms. 'Don't. Not yet.'

'Don't you have to get to the gym?'

I'm not going to the gym, Juliana said to herself. Don't you know that? We will go somewhere; we won't stay here too much longer. But it will be a place we haven't been before. It's time.

She felt him start to draw himself backwards and up onto his knees, felt her hands slide along his damp, slippery back. Then she could hear him walking away, his bare feet against the floor. To the bathroom, no doubt. For his shower.

It's over, she thought. Oh well. She sighed.

'I hear you,' Joe said from the bathroom. 'Groaning. Always downcast, aren't you? Worry, fear, and suspicion, about me and everything else in the world –' He emerged, briefly, dripping soapy water, face beaming. 'How would you like to take a trip?'

Her pulse quickened. 'Where?'

'To some big city. How about north, to Denver? I'll take you out; buy you ticket to a show, good restaurant, taxi, get you evening dress or what you need. Okay?'

She could hardly believe him, but she wanted to; she tried to.

'Will that Stude of yours make it?' Joe called.

'Sure,' she said.

136

'We'll both get some nice clothes,' he said. 'Enjoy ourselves, maybe for the first time in our lives. Keep you from cracking up.'

'Where'll we get the money?'

Joe said, 'I have it. Look in my suitcase.' He shut the bathroom door; the racket of water shut out any further words.

Opening the dresser, she got out his dented, stained little grip. Sure enough, in one corner she found an envelope; it contained Reichsbank bills, high value and good anywhere. Then we can go, she realized. Maybe he's not just stringing me along. I just wish I could get inside him and see what's there, she thought as she counted the money....

Beneath the envelope she found a huge, cylindrical fountain pen, or at least it appeared to be that; it had a clip, anyhow. But it weighed so much. Gingerly, she lifted it out, unscrewed the cap. Yes, it had a gold point. But ...

'What is this?' she asked Joe, when he reappeared from the shower.

He took it from her, returned it to the grip. How carefully he handled it ... she noticed that, reflected on it, perplexed.

'More morbidity?' Joe said. He seemed lighthearted, more so than at any time since she had met him; with a yell of enthusiasm, he clasped her around the waist, then hoisted her up into his arms, rocking her, swinging her back and forth, peering down into her face, breathing his warm breath over her, squeezing her until she bleated.

'No,' she said. 'I'm just – slow to change.' Still a little scared of you, she thought. So scared I can't even say it, tell you about it.

'Out the window,' Joe cried, stalking across the room with her in his arms. 'Here we go.'

'Please,' she said.

'Kidding. Listen – we're going on a march, like the March on Rome. You remember that. The Duce led them, my Uncle Carlo for example. Now we have a little march, less important, not noted in the history books. Right?' Inclining his head, he kissed her on the mouth, so hard that their teeth clashed. 'How nice we both'll look, in our new clothes. And you can explain to me exactly how to talk, deport myself; right? Teach me manners; right?'

'You talk okay,' Juliana said. 'Better than me, even.'

'No.' He became abruptly sombre. 'I talk very bad. A real wop accent. Didn't you notice it when you first met me in the café?'

'I guess so,' she said; it did not seem important to her.

'Only a woman knows the social conventions,' Joe said, carrying her back and dropping her to bounce frighteningly on the bed. 'Without a woman we'd discuss racing cars and horses and tell dirty jokes; no civilization.'

You're in a strange mood, Juliana thought. Restless and brooding, until you decide to move on; then you become hopped up. Do you really want me? You can ditch me, leave me here; it's happened before. I would ditch you, she thought, if I were going on.

'Is that your pay?' she asked as he dressed. 'You saved it up?' Is was so much. Of course, there was a good deal of money in the East. 'All the other truck drivers I've talked to never made so —'

'You say I'm a truck driver?' Joe broke in. 'Listen; I rode that rig not to drive but keep off hijackers. Look like a truck driver, snoozing in the cab.' Flopping in a chair in the corner of the room he lay back, pretending sleep, his mouth open, body limp. 'See?'

At first she did not see. And then she realized that in his hand was a knife, as thin as a kitchen potato skewer. Good grief, she thought. Where had it come from? Out of his sleeve; out of the air itself.

'That's why the Volkswagen people hired me. Service record. We protected ourselves against Haselden, those commandos; he led them.' The black eyes glinted; he grinned sideways at Juliana. 'Guess who got the Colonel, there at the end. When we caught them on the Nile — him and four of his Long Range Desert Group months after the Cairo campaign. They raided us for gasoline one night. I was on sentry duty.

Haselden sneaked up, rubbed with black all over his face and body, even his hands; they had no wire that time, only grenades and submachine guns. All too noisy. He tried to break my larynx. I got him.' From the chair, Joe sprang up at her, laughing. 'Let's pack. You tell them at the gym you're taking a few days off; phone them.'

His account simply did not convince her. Perhaps he had not been in North Africa at all, had not even fought in the war on the Axis side, had not even fought. What hijackers? she wondered. No truck that she knew of had come through Canon City from the East Coast with an armed professional ex-soldier as guard. Maybe he had not even lived in the U.S.A., had made everything up from the start; a line to snare her, to get her interested, to appear romantic.

Maybe he's insane, she thought. Ironic . . . I may actually do what I've pretended many times to have done; use my judo in self-defence. To save my – virginity? My life, she thought. But more likely he is just some poor low-class wop labouring slob with delusions of glory; he wants to go on a grand spree, spend all his money, live it up – and then go back to his monotonous existence. And he needs a girl to do it.

'Okay,' she said. 'I'll call the gym.' As she went towards the hall she thought, He'll buy me expensive clothes and then take me to some luxurious hotel. Every man yearns to have a really well-dressed woman before he dies, even if he has to buy her the clothes himself. This binge is probably Joe Cinnadella's lifelong ambition. And he is shrewd; I'll bet he's right in his analysis of me – I have a neurotic fear of the masculine. Frank knew it, too. That's why he and I broke up; that's why I feel this anxiety now, this mistrust.

When she returned from the pay phone, she found Joe once more engrossed in the *Grasshopper*, scowling as he read, unaware of everything else.

'Weren't you going to let me read that?' she asked.

'Maybe while I drive,' Joe said, without looking up.

'*You're* going to drive? But it's my car!'

He said nothing; he merely went on reading.

At the cash register, Robert Childan looked up to see a lean, tall, dark-haired man entering the store. The man wore a slightly less-than-fashion suit and carried a large wicker hamper. Salesman. Yet he did not have the cheerful smile; instead, he had a grim, morose look on his leathery face. More like a plumber or an electrician, Robert Childan thought.

When he had finished with his customer, Childan called to the man, 'Who do you represent?'

'Edfrank Jewellery,' the man mumbled back. He had set his hamper down on one of the counters.

'Never heard of them.' Childan sauntered over as the man unfastened the top of the hamper and with much wasted motion opened it.

'Handwrought. Each unique. Each an original. Brass, copper, silver. Even hot-forged black iron.'

Childan glanced into the hamper. Metal on black velvet, peculiar. 'No thanks. Not in my line.'

'This represents American artistry. Contemporary.'

Shaking his head no, Childan walked back to the cash register.

For a time the man stood fooling with his velvet display boards and hamper. He was neither taking the boards out nor putting them back; he seemed to have no idea what he was doing. His arms folded, Childan watched, thinking about various problems of the day. At two he had an appointment to show some early period cups. Then at three – another batch of items returning from the Cal labs, home from their authenticity test. He had been having more and more pieces examined, in the last couple of weeks. Ever since the nasty incident with the Colt ·44.

'These are not plated,' the man with the wicker hamper said, holding up a cuff bracelet. 'Solid copper.'

Childan nodded without answering. The man would hang around for a while, shuffle his samples about, but finally he would move on.

The telephone rang. Childan answered it. Customer inquiring about an ancient rocking chair, very valuable, which Childan was having mended for him. It had not been finished, and Childan had to tell a convincing story. Staring through the store window at the midday traffic, he soothed and reassured. At last the customer, somewhat appeased, rang off.

No doubt about it, he thought as he hung up the phone. The Colt ·44 affair had shaken him considerably. He no longer viewed his stock with the same reverence. Bit of knowledge like that goes a long way. Akin to primal childhood awakening; facts of life. Shows, he ruminated, the link with our early years : not merely U.S. history involved, but our own personal. As if, he thought, question might arise as to authenticity of our birth certificate. Or our impression of Dad.

Maybe I don't actually recall F.D.R. as example. Synthetic image distilled from hearing assorted talk. Myth implanted subtly in tissue of brain. Like, he thought, myth of Hepplewhite. Myth of Chippendale. Or rather more on lines of Abraham Lincoln ate here. Used this old silver knife, fork, spoon. You can't see it, but the fact remains.

At the other counter, still fumbling with his displays and wicker hamper, the salesman said, 'We can make pieces to order. Custom-made. If any of your customers have their own ideas.' His voice had a strangled quality; he cleared his throat, gazing at Childan and then down at a piece of jewellery which he held. He did not know how to leave, evidently.

Childan smiled and said nothing.

Not my responsibility. His, to get himself back out of here. Place saved or no.

Tough, such discomfort. But he doesn't have to be salesman. We all suffer in this life. Look at me. Taking it all day from Japs such as Mr Tagomi. By merest inflection manage to rub my nose in it, make my life miserable.

And then an idea occurred to him. Fellow's obviously not

experienced. Look at him. Maybe I can get some stuff on consignment. Worth a try.

'Hey,' Childan said.

The man glanced up swiftly, fastened his gaze.

Advancing towards him, his arms still folded, Childan said, 'Looks like a quiet half hour, here. No promises, but you can lay some of those things out. Clear back those racks of ties.' He pointed.

Nodding, the man began to clear himself a space on the top of the counter. He reopened his hamper, once more fumbled with the velvet trays.

He'll lay everything out, Childan knew. Arrange it painstakingly for the next hour. Fuss and adjust until he's got it all set up. Hoping. Praying. Watching me out of the corner of his eye every second. To see if I'm taking any interest. Any at all.

'When you have it out,' Childan said, 'If I'm not too busy I'll take a look.'

The man worked feverishly, as if he had been stung.

Several customers entered the store then, and Childan greeted them. He turned his attention to them and their wishes, and forgot the salesman labouring over his display. The salesman, recognizing the situation, became stealthy in his movements; he made himself inconspicuous. Childan sold a shaving mug, almost sold a hand-hooked rug, took a deposit on an afghan. Time passed. At last the customers left. Once more the store was empty except for himself and the salesman.

The salesman had finished. His entire selection of jewellery lay arranged on the black velvet on the surface of the counter.

Going leisurely over, Robert Childan lit a Land-O-Smiles and stood rocking back and forth on his heels, humming beneath his breath. The salesman stood silently. Neither spoke.

At last Childan reached out and pointed at a pin. 'I like that.'

The salesman said in a rapid voice, 'That's a good one.

You won't find any wire brush scratches. All rouge-finished. And it won't tarnish. We have a plastic lacquer sprayed on them that'll last for years. It's the best industrial lacquer available.'

Childan nodded slightly.

'What we've done here,' the salesman said, 'is to adapt tried and proven industrial techniques to jewellery making. As far as I know, nobody has ever done it before. No moulds. All metal to metal. Welding and brazing.' He paused. 'The backs are hard-soldered.'

Childan picked up two bracelets. Then a pin. Then another pin. He held them for a moment, then set them off to one side.

The salesman's face twitched. Hope.

Examining the price tag on a necklace, Childan said, 'Is this –'

'Retail. Your price is fifty per cent of that. And if you buy say around a hundred dollars or so, we give you an additional two per cent.'

One by one Childan laid several more pieces aside. With each additional one, the salesman became more agitated; he talked faster and faster, finally repeating himself, even saying meaningless foolish things, all in an undertone and very urgently. He really thinks he's going to sell, Childan knew. By his own expression he showed nothing; he went on with the game of picking pieces.

'That's an especially good one,' the salesman was rambling on, as Childan fished out a large pendant and then ceased. 'I think you got our best. All our best.' The man laughed. 'You really have good taste.' His eyes darted. He was adding in his mind what Childan had chosen. The total of the sale.

Childan said, 'Our policy, with untried merchandise, has to be consignment.'

For a few seconds the salesman did not understand. He stopped his talking, but he stared without comprehending. Childan smiled at him.

'Consignment,' the salesman echoed at last.

'Would you prefer not to leave it?' Childan said.

Stammering, the man finally said, 'You mean I leave it and you pay me later on when –'

'You get two-thirds of the proceeds. When the pieces sell. That way you make much more. You have to wait, of course, but –' Childan shrugged. 'It's up to you. I can give it some window display, possibly. And if it moves, then possibly later on, in a month or so, with the next order – well, we might see our way clear to buy some outright.'

The salesman had now spent well over an hour showing his wares, Childan realized. And he had everything out. All his displays disarranged and dismantled. Another hour's work to get it back ready to take somewhere else. There was silence. Neither man spoke.

'Those pieces you put to one side –' the salesman said in a low voice. 'They're the ones you want?'

'Yes. I'll let you leave them all.' Childan strolled over to his office in the rear of the store. 'I'll write up a tag. So you'll have a record of what you've left with me.' As he came back with his tag book he added, 'You understand that when merchandise is left on a consignment basis the store doesn't assume liability in case of theft or damage.' He had a little mimeographed release for the salesman to sign. The store would never have to account for the items left. When the unsold portion was returned, if some could not be located – they must have been stolen, Childan declared to himself. There's always theft going on in stores. Especially small items like jewellery.

There was no way that Robert Childan could lose. He did not have to pay for this man's jewellery; he had no investment in this kind of inventory. If any of it sold he made a profit, and if it did not, he simply returned it all – or as much as could be found – to the salesman at some vague later date.

Childan made out the tag, listing the items. He signed it and gave a copy to the salesman. 'You can give me a call,' he said, 'in a month or so. To find out how it's been doing.'

Taking the jewellery which he wanted he went off to the back of the store, leaving the salesman to gather up his remaining stuff.

I didn't think he'd go along with it, he thought. You never know. That's why it's always worth trying.

When he next looked up, he saw that the salesman was ready to leave. He had his wicker hamper under his arm and the counter was clear. The salesman was coming towards him, holding something out.

'Yes?' Childan said. He had been going over some correspondence.

'I want to leave our card.' The salesman put down an odd-looking little square of grey and red paper on Childan's desk. 'Edfrank Custom Jewellery. It has our address and phone number. In case you want to get in touch with us.'

Childan nodded, smiled silently, and returned to his work.

When next he paused and looked up the store was empty. The salesman had gone.

Putting a nickel into the wall dispenser, Childan obtained a cup of hot instant tea which he sipped contemplatively.

I wonder if it will sell, he wondered. Very unlikely. But it is well made. And one never sees anything like it. He examined one of the pins. Quite striking design. Certainly not amateurs.

I'll change the tags. Mark them up a lot higher. Push the hand-made angle. And the uniqueness. Custom originals. Small sculptures. Wear a work of art. Exclusive creation on your lapel or wrist.

And there was another notion circulating and growing in the back of Robert Childan's mind. *With these, there's no problem of authenticity.* And that problem may someday wreck the historic American artifacts industry. Not today or tomorrow – but after that, who knows.

Better not to have all irons in one fire. That visit by that Jewish crook; that might be the harbinger. If I quietly build up a stock of nonhistoric objects, contemporary work with no historicity either real or imagined, I might find I have the edge over the competition. And as long as it isn't costing me anything . . .

Leaning back his chair so that it rested against the wall he sipped his tea and pondered.

The Moment changes. One must be ready to change with it. Or otherwise left high and dry. *Adapt.*

The rule of survival, he thought. Keep eye peeled regarding situation around you. Learn its demands. And – meet them. Be there at the *right time* doing the *right thing.*

Be yinnish. The Oriental knows. The smart black yinnish eyes . . .

Suddenly he had a good idea; it made him sit upright instantly. Two birds, one stone. Ah. He hopped to his feet, excited. Carefully, wrap best of jewellery pieces (removing tag, of course). Pin, pendant, or bracelet. Something nice, anyhow. Then – since have to leave shop, close up at two as it is – saunter over to Kasouras' apartment building. Mr Kasoura, Paul, will be at work. However, Mrs Kasoura, Betty, *will very likely be home.*

Graft gift, this new original U.S. artwork. Compliments of myself personally, in order to obtain high-place reaction. This is how a new line is introduced. Isn't it lovely? Whole selection back at store; drop in, etc. This one for you, Betty.

He trembled. Just she and I, midday in the apartment. Husband off at work. All on up and up, however; brilliant pretext.

Airtight!

Getting a small box plus wrapping paper and ribbon, Robert Childan began preparing a gift for Mrs Kasoura. Dark, attractive woman, slender in her silk Oriental dress, high heels, and so on. Or maybe today blue cotton coolie-style lounging pyjamas, very light and comfortable and informal. Ah, he thought.

Or is this too bold? Husband Paul becoming irked. Scenting out and reacting badly. Perhaps go slower; take gift to *him*, to his office? Give much the same story, but to him. Then let him give gift to her; no suspicion. And, Robert

Childan thought, then I give Betty a call on the phone to-morrow or next day to get her reaction.

Even more airtight!

When Frank Frink saw his business partner coming back up the sidewalk he could tell that it had not gone well.

'What happened?' he said, taking the wicker hamper from Ed and putting it in the truck. 'Jesus Christ, you were gone an hour and a half. It took him that long to say no?'

Ed said, 'He didn't say no.' He looked tired. He got into the truck and sat.

'What'd he say, then?' Opening the hamper, Frink saw that a good many of the pieces were gone. Many of their best. 'He took a lot. What's the matter, then?'

'Consignment,' Ed said.

'You let him?' He could not believe it. 'We talked it over –'

'I don't know how come.'

'Christ,' Frink said.

'I'm sorry. He acted like he was going to buy it. He picked a lot out. I thought he was buying.'

They sat together silently in the truck for a long time.

10

It had been a terrible two weeks for Mr Baynes. From his hotel room he had called the Trade Mission every day at noon to ask if the old gentleman had put in an appearance. The answer had been an unvarying no. Mr Tagomi's voice had become colder and more formal each day. As Mr Baynes prepared to make his sixteenth call, he thought, Sooner or later they'll tell me that Mr Tagomi is out. That he isn't accepting any more calls from me. And that will be that.

What has happened? Where is Mr Yatabe?

He had a fairly good idea. The death of Martin Bormann had caused immediate consternation in Tokyo. Mr Yatabe no doubt had been en route to San Francisco, a day or so offshore, when new instructions had reached him. Return to the Home Islands for further consultation.

Bad luck, Mr Baynes realized. Possibly even fatal.

But he had to remain where he was, in San Francisco. Still trying to arrange the meeting for which he had come. Forty-five minutes by Lufthansa rocket from Berlin, and now this. A weird time in which we are alive. We can travel anywhere we want, even to other planets. And for what? To sit day after day, declining in morale and hope. Falling into an interminable ennui. And meanwhile, the others are busy. They are not sitting helplessly waiting.

Mr Baynes unfolded the midday edition of the Nippon *Times* and once more read the headlines.

Dr Goebbels named Reichs Chancellor

Surprise solution to leadership problem by Partei Committee. Radio speech viewed decisive. Berlin crowds cheer. Statement expected. Göring may be named Police Chief over Heydrich.

He reread the entire article. And then he put the paper once more away, took the phone, and gave the Trade Mission number.

'This is Mr Baynes. May I have Mr Tagomi?'

'A moment, sir.'

A very long moment.

'Mr Tagomi here.'

Mr Baynes took a deep breath and said, 'Forgive this situation depressing to us both, sir –'

'Ah. Mr Baynes.'

'Your hospitality to me, sir, could not be exceeded. Someday I know you will have understanding of the reasons which cause me to defer our conference until the old gentleman –'

'Regretfully, he has not arrived.'

Mr Baynes shut his eyes. 'I thought maybe since yesterday –'

'Afraid not, sir.' The barest politeness. 'If you will excuse me, Mr Baynes. Pressing business.'

'Good day, sir.'

The phone clicked. Today Mr Tagomi had rung off without even saying good-bye. Mr Baynes slowly hung the receiver.

I must take action. Can wait no longer.

It had been made very clear to him by his superiors that he was not to contact the Abwehr under any circumstances. He was simply to wait until he had managed to make connections with the Japanese military representative; he was to confer with the Japanese, and then he was to return to Berlin. But no one had foreseen that Bormann would die at this particular moment. Therefore –

The orders had to be superseded. By more practical advice. His own, in this case, since there was no one else to consult.

In the P.S.A. at least ten Abwehr persons were at work, but some of them – and possibly all – were known to the local S.D. and its competent senior regional chief, Bruno Kreuz vom Meere. Years ago he had met Bruno briefly at a Partei gathering. The man had had a certain infamous prestige in Police circles, inasmuch as it had been he, in 1943, who had uncovered the British–Czech plot on Reinhard Heydrich's life, and therefore who might be said to have saved the Hangman from assassination. In any case, Bruno Kreuz vom Meere was already then ascending in authority within the S.D. He was not a mere police bureaucrat.

He was, in fact, a rather dangerous man.

There was even a possibility that even with all the precautions taken, both on the part of the Abwehr in Berlin and the Tokkoka in Tokyo, the S.D. had learned of this attempted meeting in San Francisco in the offices of the Ranking Trade Mission. However, this was after all Japanese-administered land. The S.D. had no official authority to interfere. It could see to it that the German principal – himself in this case – was arrested as soon as he set foot again on Reich territory; but it could hardly take action against the Japanese principal, or against the existence of the meeting itself.

At least, so he hoped.

Was there any possibility that the S.D. had managed to

detain the old Japanese gentleman somewhere along the route? It was a long way from Tokyo to San Francisco, especially for a person so elderly and frail that he could not attempt air travel.

What I must do, Mr Baynes knew, is find out from those above me whether Mr Yatabe is still coming. They would know. If the S.D. has intercepted him or if the Tokyo Government has recalled him – they would know that.

And if they have managed to get to the old gentleman, he realized, they certainly are going to get to me.

Yet the situation even in those circumstances was not hopeless. An idea had come to Mr Baynes as he waited day after day alone in his room at the Abhirati Hotel.

It would be better to give my information to Mr Tagomi than to return to Berlin empty-handed. At least that way there would be a chance, even if it is rather slight, that ultimately the proper people will be informed. But Mr Tagomi could only listen; that was the fault in his idea. At best, he could hear, commit to memory, and as soon as possible take a business trip back to the Home Islands. Whereas Mr Yatabe stood at policy level. He could both hear – and speak.

Still, it was better than nothing. The time was growing too short. To begin all over, to arrange painstakingly, cautiously, over a period of months once again the delicate contact between a faction in Germany and a faction in Japan ...

It certainly would surprise Mr Tagomi, he thought acidly. To suddenly find knowledge of that kind resting on his shoulders. A long way from facts about injection moulds ...

Possibly he might have a nervous breakdown. Either blurt out the information to someone around him, or withdraw; pretend, even to himself, that he had not heard it. Simply refuse to believe me. Rise to his feet, bow and excuse himself from the room, the moment I begin.

Indiscreet. He could regard it that way. He is not supposed to hear such matters.

So easy, Mr Baynes thought. The way out is so immediate, so available, to him. He thought, I wish it was for me.

And yet in the final analysis it is not possible even for Mr

Tagomi. We are no different. He can close his ears to the news as it comes from me, comes in the form of words. But later. When it is not a matter of words. If I can make that clear to him now. Or to whomever I finally speak –

Leaving his hotel room, Mr Baynes descended by elevator to the lobby. Outside on the sidewalk, he had the doorman call a pedecab for him, and soon he was on his way up Market Street, the Chinese driver pumping away energetically.

'There,' he said to the driver, when he made out the sign which he was watching for. 'Pull over to the kerb.'

The pedecab stopped by a fire hydrant. Mr Baynes paid the driver and sent him off. No one seemed to have followed. Mr Baynes set off along the sidewalk on foot. A moment later, along with several other shoppers, he entered the big downtown Fuga Department Store.

There were shoppers everywhere. Counter after counter. Sales-girls, mostly white, with a sprinkling of Japanese as department managers. The din was terrific.

After some confusion Mr Baynes located the men's clothing department. He stopped at the racks of men's trousers and began to inspect them. Presently a clerk, a young white, came over, greeting him.

Mr Baynes said, 'I have returned for the pair of dark brown wool slacks which I was looking at yesterday.' Meeting the clerk's gaze he said, 'You're not the man I spoke to. He was taller. Red moustache. Rather thin. On his jacket he had the name Larry.'

The clerk said, 'He is presently out to lunch. But will return.'

'I'll go into a dressing room and try these on,' Mr Baynes said, taking a pair of slacks from the rack.

'Certainly, sir.' The clerk indicated a vacant dressing room, and then went off to wait on someone else.

Mr Baynes entered the dressing room and shut the door. He seated himself on one of the two chairs and waited.

After a few minutes there was a knock. The door of the dressing room opened and a short middle-aged Japanese

entered. 'You are from out of state, sir?' he said to Mr
Baynes. 'And I am to okay your credit? Let me see your
identification.' He shut the door behind him.

My Baynes got out his wallet. The Japanese seated himself
with the wallet and began inspecting the contents. He halted
at a photo of a girl. 'Very pretty.'

'My daughter. Martha.'

'I, too, have a daughter named Martha,' the Japanese
said. 'She at present is in Chicago studying piano.'

'My daughter,' Mr Baynes said, 'is about to be married.'

The Japanese returned the wallet and waited expectantly.

Mr Baynes said, 'I have been here two weeks and Mr
Yatabe has not shown up. I want to find out if he is still
coming. And if not, what I should do.'

'Return tomorrow afternoon,' the Japanese said. He rose,
and Mr Baynes also rose. 'Good day.'

'Good day,' Mr Baynes said. He left the dressing room,
hung the pair of slacks back up on the rack, and left the Fuga
Department Store.

That did not take very long, he thought as he moved along
the busy downtown sidewalk with the other pedestrians. Can
he actually get the information by then? Contact Berlin,
relay my questions, do all the coding and decoding – every
step involved?

Apparently so.

Now I wish I had approached the agent sooner. I would
have saved myself much worry and distress. And evidently
no major risk was involved; it all appeared to go off
smoothly. It took in fact only five or six minutes.

Mr Baynes wandered on, looking into store windows. He
felt much better now. Presently he found himself viewing
display photos of honky-tonk cabarets, grimy flyspecked
utterly white nudes whose breasts hung like half-inflated
volleyballs. That sight amused him and he loitered, people
pushing past him on their various errands up and down
Market Street.

At least he had done something, at last.

What a relief!

*

Propped comfortably against the car door, Juliana read. Beside her, his elbow out of the window, Joe drove with one hand lightly on the wheel, a cigarette stuck to his lower lip; he was a good driver, and they had covered a good deal of the distance from Canon City already.

The car radio played mushy beer-garden folk music, an accordion band doing one of the countless polkas or schottisches; she had never been able to tell them one from another.

'Kitsch,' Joe said, when the music ended. 'Listen, I know a lot about music; I'll tell you who a great conductor was. You probably don't remember him. Arturo Toscanini.'

'No,' she said, still reading.

'He was Italian. But the Nazis wouldn't let him conduct after the war, because of his politics. He's dead, now. I don't like that von Karajan, permanent conductor of the New York Philharmonic. We had to go to concerts by him, our work dorm. What I like, being a wop – you can guess.' He glanced at her. 'You like that book?' he said.

'It's engrossing.'

'I like Verdi and Puccini. All we get in New York is heavy German bombastic Wagner and Orff, and we have to go every week to one of those corny U.S. Nazi Party dramatic spectacles at Madison Square Garden, with the flags and drums and trumpets and the flickering flame. History of the Gothic tribes or other educational crap, chanted instead of spoken, so as to be called "art". Did you ever see New York before the war?'

'Yes,' she said, trying to read.

'Didn't they have swell theatre in those days? That's what I heard. Now it's the same as the movie industry; it's all a cartel in Berlin. In the thirteen years I've been in New York not one good new musical or play ever opened, only those –'

'Let me read,' Juliana said.

'And the same with the book business,' Joe said, unperturbed. 'It's all a cartel operating out of Munich. All they do in New York is print; just big printing presses – but before the war, New York was the centre of the world's publishing industry, or so they say.'

Putting her fingers in her ears, she concentrated on the page open in her lap, shutting his voice out. She had arrived at a section in *The Grasshopper* which described the fabulous television, and it enthralled her; especially the part about the inexpensive little sets for backward people in Africa and Asia.

. . . Only Yankee know-how and the mass-production system – Detroit, Chicago, Cleveland, the magic names! – could have done the trick, sent that ceaseless and almost witlessly noble flood of cheap one-dollar (the China Dollar, the trade dollar) television kits to every village and backwater of the Orient. And when the kit had been assembled by some gaunt, feverish-minded youth in the village, starved for a chance, for that which the generous Americans held out to him, that tinny little instrument with its built-in power supply no larger than a marble began to receive. And what did it receive? Crouching before the screen, the youths of the village – and often the elders as well – saw words. Instructions. How to read, first. Then the rest. How to dig a deeper well. Plough a deeper furrow. How to purify their water, heal their sick. Overhead, the American artificial moon wheeled, distributing the signal, carrying it everywhere . . . to all the waiting, avid masses of the East.

'Are you reading straight through?' Joe asked. 'Or skipping around in it?'

She said, 'This is wonderful; he has us sending food and education to all the Asiatics, millions of them.'

'Welfare work on a worldwide scale,' Joe said.

'Yes. The New Deal under Tugwell; they raise the level of the masses – listen.' She read aloud to Joe :

. . . What had China been? Yearning, one needful commingled entity looking towards the West, its great democratic President, Chiang Kai-shek, who had led the Chinese people through the years of war, now into the years of peace, into the Decade of Rebuilding. But for China it was not a rebuilding, for that almost supernaturally vast flat land had never been built, lay still slumbering in the ancient dream. Arousing; yes, the entity, the giant, had to partake at last of full consciousness, had to waken into the modern world with its jet airplanes and atomic power, its autobahns and factories, and medicines. And from whence would come the crack of thunder which would rouse the giant? Chiang had known that, even during the struggle to defeat Japan. It would come from the United States. And, by 1950, American technicians and engineers, teachers, doctors, agronomists, swarming like some new life form into each province, each –

Interrupting, Joe said, 'You know what he's done, don't you? He's taken the best about Nazism, the socialist part, the Todt Organization and the economic advances we got through Speer, and who's he giving the credit to? The New Deal. And he's left out the bad part, the S.S. part, the racial extermination and segregation. It's a utopia! You imagine if the Allies had won, the New Deal would have been able to revive the economy and make those socialist welfare improvements, like he says? Hell no; he's talking about a form of state syndicalism, the corporate state, like we developed under the Duce. He's saying, You would have had all the good and none of –'

'Let me read,' she said fiercely.

He shrugged. But he did cease babbling. She read on at once, but to herself.

. . . And these markets, the countless millions of China, set the factories in Detroit and Chicago to humming; that vast mouth could never be filled, those people could not in a hundred years be given enough trucks or bricks or steel ingots or clothing or typewriters or canned peas or clocks or radios or nosedrops. The American workman, by 1960, had the highest standard of living in the world, and all due to what they genteelly called 'the most favoured nation' clause in every commercial transaction with the East. The U.S. no longer occupied Japan, and she had never occupied China; and yet the fact could not be disputed: Canton and Tokyo, and Shanghai did not buy from the British; they bought American. And with each sale, the working man in Baltimore or Los Angeles or Atlanta saw a little more prosperity.

It seemed to the planners, the men of vision in the White House, that they had almost achieved their goal. The exploring rocket ships would soon nose cautiously out into the void from a world that had at last seen an end to its age-old griefs: hunger, plague, war, ignorance. In the British Empire, equal measures towards social and economic progress had brought similar relief to the masses in India, Burma, Africa, the Middle East. The factories of the Ruhr, Manchester, of the Saar, the oil of Baku, all flowed and interacted in intricate but effective harmony; the populations of Europe basked in what appeared . . .

'I think they should be the rulers,' Juliana said, pausing. 'They always were the best. The British.'

Joe said nothing to that, although she waited. At last she went on reading.

. . . Realization of Napoleon's vision: rational homogeneity of the diverse ethnic strains which had squabbled and balkanized Europe since the collapse of Rome. Vision, too, of Charlemagne: united Christendom, totally at peace not only with itself but with the balance of the world. And yet – there still remained one annoying sore.

Singapore.

The Malay States held a large Chinese population, mostly of the enterprising business class, and these thrifty, industrious bourgeois saw in American administration of China a more equitable treatment of what was called 'the native'. Under British rule, the darker races were excluded from the country clubs, the hotels, the better restaurants; they found themselves, as in archaic times, confined to particular sections of the train and bus and – perhaps worst of all – limited to their choice of residence within each city. These 'natives' discerned, and noted in their table conversations and newspapers, that in the U.S.A. the colour problem had by 1950 been solved. Whites and Negroes lived and worked and ate shoulder by shoulder, even in the Deep South; World War Two had ended discrimination . . .

'Is there trouble?' Juliana asked Joe.

He grunted, keeping his eyes on the road.

'Tell me what happens,' she said. 'I know I won't get to finish it; we'll be in Denver pretty soon. Do America and Britain get into a war, and one emerges as ruler of the world?'

Presently Joe said, 'In some ways it's not a bad book. He works all the details out; the U.S. has the Pacific, about like our East Asia Co-Prosperity Sphere. They divide Russia. It works for around ten years. Then there's trouble – naturally.'

'Why naturally?'

'Human nature.' Joe added, 'Nature of states. Suspicion, fear, greed. Churchill thinks the U.S.A. is undermining British rule in South Asia by appealing to the large Chinese populations, who naturally are pro-U.S.A., due to Chiang Kai-shek. The British start setting up' – he grinned at her briefly – 'what are called "detention preserves". Concentration camps, in other words. For thousands of maybe disloyal Chinese. They're accused of sabotage and propaganda. Churchill is so –'

'You mean he's *still* in power? Wouldn't he be around ninety?'

Joe said, 'That's where the British system has it over the American. Every eight years the U.S. boots out its leaders, no matter how qualified – but Churchill just stays on. The U.S. doesn't have any leadership like him, after Tugwell. Just nonentities. And the older he gets, the more autocratic and rigid he gets – Churchill, I mean. Until by 1960, he's like some old warlord out of Central Asia; nobody can cross him. He's been in power twenty years.'

'Good God,' she said, leafing through the last part of the book, searching for verification of what Joe was saying.

'On that I agree,' Joe said. 'Churchill was the one good leader the British had during the war; if they'd retained him they'd have been better off. I tell you; a state is no better than its leader. *Führerprinzip* – Principle of Leadership, like the Nazis say. They're right. Even this Abendsen has to face that. Sure, the U.S.A. expands economically after winning the war over Japan, because it's got that huge market in Asia that it's wrested from the Japs. But that's not enough; that's got no spirituality. Not that the British have. They're both plutocracies, ruled by the rich. If they had won, all they'd have thought about was making more money, that upper class. Abendsen, he's wrong; there would be no social reform, no welfare public works plans – the Anglo-Saxon plutocrats wouldn't have permitted it.'

Juliana thought, Spoken like a devout Fascist.

Evidently Joe perceived by her expression what she was thinking; he turned towards her, slowing the car, one eye on her, one on the cars ahead. 'Listen, I'm not an intellectual – Fascism has no need of that. What is wanted is the *deed*. Theory derives from action. What our corporate state demands from us is comprehension of the social forces – of history. You see? I tell you; I know, Juliana.' His tone was earnest, almost beseeching. 'Those old rotten money-run empires, Britain and France and U.S.A., although the latter actually a sort of bastard sideshoot, not strictly empire, but money-oriented even so. They had no soul, so naturally no future. No growth. Nazis a bunch of street thugs; I agree. You agree? Right?'

She had to smile; his Italian mannerisms had overpowered him in his attempt to drive and make his speech simultaneously.

'Abendsen talks like it's big issue as to whether U.S. or Britain ultimately wins out. Bull! Has no merit, no history to it. Six of one, dozen of other. You ever read what the Duce wrote? Inspired. Beautiful man. Beautiful writing. Explains the underlying actuality of every event. Real issue in war was: old versus new. Money – that's why Nazis dragged Jewish question mistakenly into it – versus communal mass spirit, what Nazis call *Gemeinschaft* – folkness. Like Soviet. Commune. Right? Only, Communists sneaked in Pan-Slavic Peter the Great empire ambitions along with it, made social reform means for imperial ambitions.'

Juliana thought, Like Mussolini did. Exactly.

'Nazi thuggery a tragedy,' Joe stuttered away as he passed a slow-moving truck. 'But change's always harsh on the loser. Nothing new. Look at previous revolutions such as French. Or Cromwell against Irish. Too much philosophy in Germanic temperament; too much theatre, too. All those rallies. You never find true Fascist talking, only doing – like me. Right?'

Laughing, she said, 'God, you've been talking a mile a minute.'

He shouted excitedly, 'I'm explaining Fascist theory of action!'

She couldn't answer; it was too funny.

But the man beside her did not think it was funny; he glowered at her, his face red. Veins in his forehead became distended and he began once more to shake. And again he passed his fingers clutchingly along his scalp, forward and back, not speaking, only staring at her.

'Don't get sore at me,' she said.

For a moment she thought he was going to hit her; he drew his arm back . . . but then he grunted, reached and turned up the car radio.

They drove on. Band music from the radio, static. Once more she tried to concentrate on the book.

'You're right,' Joe said after a long time.

'About what?'

'Two-bit empire. Clown for a leader. No wonder we got nothing out of the war.'

She patted his arm.

'Juliana, it's all darkness,' Joe said. 'Nothing is true or certain. Right?'

'Maybe so,' she said absently, continuing to try to read.

'Britain wins,' Joe said, indicating the book. 'I save you the trouble. U.S. dwindles, Britain keeps needling and poking and expanding, keeps the initiative. So put it away.'

'I hope we have fun in Denver,' she said, closing the book. 'You need to relax. I want you to.' If you don't, she thought, you're going to fly apart in a million pieces. Like a bursting spring. And what happens to me, then? How do I get back? And – do I just leave you?

I want the good time you promised me, she thought. I don't want to be cheated; I've been cheated too much in my life before, by too many people.

'We'll have it,' Joe said. 'Listen.' He studied her with a queer, introspective expression. 'You take to that *Grasshopper* book so much; I wonder – do you suppose a man who writes a best seller, an author like that Abendsen . . . do people write letters to him? I bet lots of people praise his book by letters to him, maybe even visit.'

All at once she understood. 'Joe – it's only another hundred miles!'

His eyes shone; he smiled at her, happy again, no longer flushed or troubled.

'We could!' she said. 'You drive so good – it'd be nothing to go on up there, would it?'

Slowly, Joe said, 'Well, I doubt a famous man lets visitors drop in. Probably so many of them.'

'Why not try Joe –' She grabbed his shoulder, squeezed him excitedly. 'All he could do is send us away. *Please.*'

With great deliberation, Joe said, 'When we've gone shopping and got new clothes, all spruced up . . . that's important, to make a good impression. And maybe even rent a new car up in Cheyenne. Bet you can do that.'

'Yes,' she said. 'And you need a haircut. And let me pick your clothes; please, Joe. I used to pick Frank's clothes for him; a man can never buy his own clothes.'

'You got good taste in clothes,' Joe said, once more turning towards the road ahead, gazing out sombrely. 'In other ways, too. Better if *you* call him. Contact him.'

'I'll get my hair done,' she said.

'Good.'

'I'm not scared at all to walk up and ring the bell,' Juliana said. 'I mean, you live only once. Why should we be intimidated? He's just a man like the rest of us. In fact, he probably would be pleased to know somebody drove so far just to tell him how much they liked his book. We can get an autograph on the book, on the inside where they do that. Isn't that so? We better buy a new copy; this one is all stained. It wouldn't look good.'

'Anything you want,' Joe said. 'I'll let you decide all the details; I know you can do it. Pretty girl always gets everyone; when he sees what a knockout you are he'll open the door wide. But listen; no monkey business.'

'What do you mean?'

'You say we're married. I don't want you getting mixed

up with him – you know. That would be dreadful. Wreck everyone's existence; some reward for him to let visitors in, some irony. So watch it, Juliana.'

'You can argue with him,' Juliana said. 'That part about Italy losing the war by betraying them; tell him what you told me.'

Joe nodded. 'That's so. We can discuss the whole subject.'

They drove swiftly on.

At seven o'clock the following morning, P.S.A. reckoning, Mr Nobusuke Tagomi rose from bed, started towards the bathroom, then changed his mind and went directly to the oracle.

Seated cross-legged on the floor of his living room he began manipulating the forty-nine yarrow stalks. He had a deep sense of the urgency of his questioning, and he worked at a feverish pace until at last he had the six lines before him.

Shock! Hexagram Fifty-one!

God appears in the sign of the Arousing. Thunder and lightning. Sounds – he involuntarily put his fingers up to cover his ears. Ha-ha! ho-ho! Great burst that made him wince and blink. Lizard scurries and tiger roars, and out comes God himself!

What does it mean? He peered about his living room. Arrival of – what? He hopped to his feet and stood panting, waiting.

Nothing. Heart pounding. Respiration and all somatic processes, including all manner of diencephalic-controlled autonomic responses to crises : adrenalin, greater heartbeat, pulse rate, glands pouring, throat paralysed, eyes staring, bowels loose, et al. Stomach queasy and sex instinct suppressed.

And yet, nothing to see; nothing for body to do. Run? All in preparation for panic flight. But where to and why? Mr Tagomi asked himself. No clue. Therefore impossible. Dilemma of civilized man; body mobilized, but danger obscure.

He went to the bathroom and began lathering his face to shave.

The telephone rang.

'Shock,' he said aloud, putting down his razor. 'Be prepared.' He walked rapidly from the bathroom, back into the living room. 'I am prepared,' he said, and lifted the receiver. 'Tagomi, here.' His voice squeaked and he cleared his throat.

A pause. And then a faint, dry, rustling voice, almost like old leaves far off, said, 'Sir. This is Shinjiro Yatabe. I have arrived in San Fancisco.'

'Greetings from the Ranking Trade Mission,' Mr Tagomi said. 'How glad I am. You are in good health and relaxed?'

'Yes, Mr Tagomi. When may I meet you?'

'Quite soon. In half an hour.' Mr Tagomi peered at the bedroom clock, trying to read it. 'A third party: Mr Baynes. I must contact him. Possible delay, but –'

'Shall we say two hours, sir?' Mr Yatabe said.

'Yes,' Mr Tagomi said, bowing.

'At your office in the Nippon Times Building.'

Mr Tagomi bowed once more.

Click. Mr Yatabe had rung off.

Pleased Mr Baynes, Mr Tagomi thought. Delight in order of cat tossed piece of salmon, for instance fatty nice tail. He jiggled the hook, then dialled speedily the Abhirati Hotel.

'Ordeal concluded,' he said, when Mr Baynes' sleepy voice came on the wire.

At once the voice ceased to be sleepy. 'He's here?'

'My office,' Mr Tagomi said. 'Ten-twenty. Good-bye.' He hung up and ran back to the bathroom to finish shaving. No time for breakfast; have Mr Ramsey scuttle about after office arrival completed. All three of us perhaps can indulge simultaneously – in his mind as he shaved he planned a fine breakfast for them all.

In his pyjamas, Mr Baynes stood at the phone, rubbing his forehead and thinking. A shame I broke down and made contact with that agent, he thought. If I had waited only one day more . . .

But probably no harm's been done. Yet he was supposed to return to the department store today. Suppose I don't show up? It may start a chain reaction; they'll think I've been murdered or some such thing. An attempt will be made to trace me.

It doesn't matter. *Because he's here. At last.* The waiting is over.

Mr Baynes hurried to the bathroom and prepared to shave.

I have no doubt that Mr Tagomi will recognize him the moment he meets him, he decided. We can drop the 'Mr Yatabe' cover, now. In fact, we can drop all covers, all pretences.

As soon as he had shaved, Mr Baynes hopped into the shower. As water roared around him he sang at the top of his lungs:

> 'Wer reitet so spät,
> Durch Nacht und Wind?
> Es ist der Vater
> Mit seinem Kind.'

It is probably too late now for the S.D. to do anything, he thought. Even if they find out. So perhaps I can cease worrying; at least, the trivial worry. The finite, private worry about my own particular skin.

But as to the rest – we can just begin.

I I

For the Reichs Consul in San Francisco, Freiherr Hugo Reiss, the first business of this particular day was unexpected and distressing. When he arrived at his office he found a visitor waiting already, a large, heavy-jawed, middle-aged man with pocked skin and disapproving scowl that drew his black, tangled eyebrows together. The man rose and made a Partei salute, at the same time murmuring, 'Heil.'

Reiss said, 'Heil.' He groaned inwardly, but maintained a businesslike formal smile. 'Herr Kreuz vom Meere. I am surprised. Won't you come in?' He unlocked his inner office, wondering where his vice-consul was, and who had let the S.D. chief in. Anyhow, here the man was. There was nothing to be done.

Following along after him, his hands in the pockets of his dark wool overcoat, Kreuz vom Meere said, 'Listen, Freiherr. We located this Abwehr fellow. This Rudolf Wegener. He showed up at an old Abwehr drop we have under surveillance.' Kreuz vom Meere chuckled, showing enormous gold teeth. 'And we trailed him back to his hotel.'

'Fine,' Reiss said, noticing that his mail was on his desk. So Pferdehuf was around somewhere. No doubt he had left the office locked to keep the S.D. chief from a little informal snooping.

'This is important,' Kreuz vom Meere said. 'I notified Kaltenbrunner about it. Top priority. You'll probably be getting word from Berlin any time now. Unless those *Unratfressers* back home get it all mixed up.' He seated himself on the consul's desk, took a wad of folded paper from his coat pocket, unfolded the paper laboriously, his lips moving. 'Cover name is Baynes. Posing as a Swedish industrialist or salesman or something connected with manufacturing. Received phone call this morning at eight-ten from Japanese official regarding appointment at ten-twenty in the Jap's office. We're presently trying to trace the call. Probably will have it traced in another half hour. They'll notify me here.'

'I see,' Reiss said.

'Now, we may pick up this fellow,' Kreuz vom Meere continued. 'If we do, we'll naturally send him back to the Reich aboard the next Lufthansa plane. However, the Japs or Sacramento may protest and try to block it. They'll protest to you, if they do. In fact, they may bring enormous pressure to bear. And they'll run a truckload of those Tokkoka toughs to the airport.'

'You can't keep them from finding out?'

'Too late. He's on his way to this appointment. We may have to pick him up right there on the spot. Run in, grab him, run out.'

'I don't like that,' Reiss said. 'Suppose his appointment is with some extremely high-place Jap officials? There may be an Emperor's personal representative in San Francisco, right now. I heard a rumour the other day –'

Kreuz vom Meere interrupted. 'It doesn't matter. He's a German national. Subject to Reichs law.'

And we know what Reichs law is, Reiss thought.

'I have a Kommando squad ready,' Kreuz vom Meere went on. 'Five good men.' He chuckled. 'They look like violinists. Nice ascetic faces. Soulful. Maybe like divinity students. They'll get in. The Japs'll think they're a string quartet –'

'Quintet,' Reiss said.

'Yes. They'll walk right up to the door – they're dressed just right.' He surveyed the consul. 'Pretty much as you are.'

Thank you, Reiss thought.

'Right in plain sight. Broad daylight. Up to this Wegener. Gather around him. Appear to be conferring. Message of importance.' Kreuz vom Meere droned on, while the consul began opening his mail. 'No violence. Just, "Herr Wegener. Come with us, please. You understand." And between the vertebrae of his spine a little shaft. Pump. Upper ganglia paralysed.'

Reiss nodded.

'Are you listening?'

'Ganz bestimmt.'

'Then out again. To the car. Back to my office. Japs make a lot of racket. But polite to the last.' Kreuz vom Meere lumbered from the desk to pantomime a Japanese bowing. ' "Most vulgar to deceive us, Herr Kreuz vom Meere. However, good-bye, Herr Wegener –" '

'Baynes,' Reiss said. 'Isn't he using his cover name?'

'Baynes. "So sorry to see you go. Plenty more talk maybe next time." ' The phone on Reiss's desk rang, and Kreuz vom Meere ceased his prank. 'That may be for me.' He started to answer it, but Reiss stepped to it and took it himself.

'Reiss, here.'

An unfamiliar voice said, 'Consul, this is the Ausland Fernsprechamt at Nova Scotia. Transatlantic telephone call for you from Berlin, urgent.'

'All right,' Reiss said.

'Just a moment, Consul.' Faint static, crackles. Then another voice, a woman operator. 'Kanzlei.'

'Yes, this is Ausland Fernsprechamt at Nova Scotia. Call for the Reichs Consul H. Reiss, San Francisco; I have the consul on the line.'

'Hold on.' A long pause, during which Reiss continued, with one hand, to inspect his mail. Kreuz vom Meere watched slackly. 'Herr Konsul, sorry to take your time.' A man's voice. The blood in Reiss's veins instantly stopped its motion. Baritone, cultivated, rolling-out-smooth voice familiar to Reiss. 'This is Doktor Goebbels.'

'Yes, Kanzler.' Across from Reiss, Kreuz vom Meere slowly showed a smile. The slack jaw ceased to hang.

'General Heydrich has just asked me to call you. There is an agent of the Abwehr here in San Francisco. His name is Rudolf Wegener. You are to co-operate fully with the police regarding him. There isn't time to give you details. Simply put your office at their disposal. Ich danke Ihnen sehr dabei.'

'I understand, Herr Kanzler,' Reiss said.

'Good day, Konsul.' The Reichskanzler rang off.

Kreuz vom Meere watched intently as Reiss hung up the phone. 'Was I right?'

Reiss shrugged. 'No dispute, there.'

'Write out an authorization for us to return this Wegener to Germany forcibly.'

Picking up his pen, Reiss wrote out the authorization, signed it, handed it to the S.D. chief.

'Thank you,' Kreuz vom Meere said. 'Now, when the Jap authorities call you and complain –'

'If they do.'

Kreuz vom Meere eyed him. 'They will. They'll be here within fifteen minutes of the time we pick this Wegener up.' He had lost his joking, clowning manner.

'No string quintet violinists,' Reiss said.

Kreuz vom Meere did not answer. 'We'll have him some time this morning, so be ready. You can tell the Japs that he's a homosexual or a forger, or something like that. Wanted for a major crime back home. Don't tell them he's wanted for political crimes. You know they don't recognize ninety per cent of National Socialist law.'

'I know that,' Reiss said. 'I know what to do.' He felt irritable and put upon. Went over my head, he said to himself. As usual. Contacted the Chancery. The bastards.

His hands were shaking. Call from Doctor Goebbels; did that do it? Awed by the mighty? Or is it resentment, feeling of being hemmed in . . . goddam these police, he thought. They get stronger all the time. They've got Goebbels working for them already; they're running the Reich.

But what can I do? What can anybody do?

Resignedly he thought, Better co-operate. No time to be on the wrong side of this man; he can probably get whatever he wants back home, and that might include the dismissal of everybody hostile to him.

'I can see,' he said aloud, 'that you did not exaggerate the importance of this matter, Herr Polizeiführer. Obviously, the security of Germany herself hangs on your quick detection of this spy or traitor or whatever he is.' Inwardly, he cringed to hear his choice of words.

However, Kreuz vom Meere looked pleased. 'Thank you, Consul.'

'You may have saved us all.'

Gloomily Kreuz vom Meere said, 'Well, we haven't picked him up. Let's wait for that. I wish that call would come.'

'I'll handle the Japanese,' Reiss said. 'I've had a good deal of experience, as you know. Their complaints –'

'Don't ramble on,' Kreuz vom Meere interrupted. 'I have

to think.' Evidently the call from the Chancery had bothered him; he, too, felt under pressure now.

Possibly this fellow will get away, and it will cost you your job, Consul Hugo Reiss thought. My job, your job – we both could find ourselves out on the street any time. No more security for you than for me.

In fact, he thought, it might be worth seeing how a little foot-dragging here and there could possibly stall your activities, Herr Polizeiführer. Something negative that could never be pinned down. For instance, when the Japanese come in here to complain, I might manage to drop a hint as to the Lufthansa flight on which this fellow is to be dragged away ... or barring that, needle them into a bit more outrage by, say, just the trace of a contemptuous smirk -- suggesting that the Reich is amused by them, doesn't take little yellow men seriously. It's easy to sting them. And if they get angry enough, they might carry it directly to Goebbels.

All sorts of possibilities. The S.D. can't really get this fellow out of the P.S.A. without my active co-operation. If I can only hit on precisely the right twist ...

I hate people who go over my head, Freiherr Reiss said to himself. It makes me too damn uncomfortable. It makes me so nervous that I can't sleep, and when I can't sleep I can't do my job. So I owe it to Germany to correct this problem. I'd be a lot more comfortable at night and in the daytime, too, for that matter, if this low-class Bavarian thug were back home writing up reports in some obscure Gau police station.

The trouble is, *there's not the time.* While I'm trying to decide how to –

The phone rang.

This time Kreuz vom Meere reached out to take it and Consul Reiss did not bar the way. 'Hello,' Kreuz vom Meere said into the receiver. A moment of silence as he listened.

Already? Reiss thought.

But the S.D. chief was holding out the phone. 'For you.'

Secretly relaxing with relief, Reiss took the phone.

'It's some schoolteacher,' Kreuz vom Meere said. 'Wants

to know if you can give them scenic posters of Austria for their class.'

Towards eleven o'clock in the morning, Robert Childan shut up his store and set off, on foot, for Mr Paul Kasoura's business office.

Fortunately, Paul was not busy. He greeted Childan politely and offered him tea.

'I will not bother you long,' Childan said after they had both begun sipping. Paul's office, although small, was modern and simply furnished. On the wall one single superb print : Mokkei's Tiger, a late-thirteenth-century masterpiece.

'I'm always happy to see you, Robert,' Paul said, in a tone that held – Childan thought – perhaps a trace of aloofness.

Or perhaps it was his imagination. Childan glanced cautiously over his teacup. The man certainly looked friendly. And yet – Childan sensed a change.

'Your wife,' Childan said, 'was disappointed by my crude gift. I possibly insulted. However, with something new and untried, as I explained to you when I grafted it to you, no proper or final evaluation can be made – at least not by someone in the purely business end. Certainly, you and Betty are in a better position to judge than I.'

Paul said, 'She was not disappointed, Robert. I did not give the piece of jewellery to her.' Reaching into his desk, he brought out the small white box. 'It has not left this office.'

He knows, Childan thought. Smart man. Never even told her. So that's that. Now, Childan realized, let's hope he's not going to rave at me. Some kind of accusation about my trying to seduce his wife.

He could ruin me, Childan said to himself. Carefully he continued sipping his tea, his face impassive.

'Oh?' he said mildly. 'Interesting.'

Paul opened the box, brought out the pin and began inspecting it. He held it to the light, turned it over and around.

'I took the liberty of showing this to a number of business acquaintances,' Paul said, 'individuals who share my taste for American historic objects or for artifacts of general artistic, aesthetic merit.' He eyed Robert Childan. 'None of course had even seen such as this before. As you explained, no such contemporary work hithertofore has been known. I think, too, you informed that you are sole representative.'

'Yes, that is so,' Childan said.

'You wish to hear their reaction?'

Childan bowed.

'These persons laughed,' Paul said, 'laughed.'

Childan was silent.

'Yet I, too, laughed behind my hand, invisible to you,' Paul said, 'the other day when you appeared and showed me this thing. Naturally to protect your sang-froid, I concealed that amusement; as you no doubt recall, I remained more or less noncommittal in my apparent reaction.'

Childan nodded.

Studying the pin, Paul went on. 'One can easily understand this reaction. Here is a piece of metal which has been melted until it has become shapeless. It represents nothing. Nor does it have design, of any intentional sort. It is merely amorphous. One might say, it is mere content, deprived of form.'

Childan nodded.

'Yet,' Paul said, 'I have for several days now inspected it, and for no logical reason *I feel a certain emotional fondness.* Why is that? I may ask. I do not even now project into this blob, as in psychological German tests, my own psyche. I still see no shapes or forms. But it somehow partakes of Tao. You see?' He motioned Childan over. 'It is balanced. The forces within this piece are stabilized. At rest. So to speak, this object has made its peace with the universe. It has separated from it and hence has managed to come to homeostasis.'

Childan nodded, studied the piece. But Paul had lost him.

'It does not have *wabi,*' Paul said, 'nor could it ever. But –' He touched the pin with his nail. 'Robert, this object has *wu.*'

'I believe you are right,' Childan said, trying to recall

what *wu* was; it was not a Japanese word – it was Chinese. Wisdom, he decided. Or comprehension. Anyhow, it was highly good.

'The hands of the artificer,' Paul said, 'had wu, and allowed that wu to flow into this piece. Possibly he himself knows only that this piece satisfies. It is complete, Robert. By contemplating it, we gain more wu ourselves. We experience the tranquillity associated not with art but with holy things. I recall a shrine in Hiroshima wherein a shinbone of some medieval saint could be examined. However, this is an artifact and that was a relic. This is alive in the now, whereas that merely *remained*. By this meditation, conducted by myself at great length since you were last here, I have come to identify the value which this has in opposition to historicity. I am deeply moved, as you may see.'

'Yes,' Childan said.

'To have no historicity, and also no artistic, aesthetic worth, and yet to partake of some ethereal value – that is a marvel. Just precisely because this is a miserable, small, worthless-looking blob; that, Robert, contributes to its possessing wu. For it is a fact that wu is customarily found in least imposing places, as in the Christian aphorism, "stones rejected by the builder". One experiences awareness of wu in such trash as an old stick, or a rusty beer can by the side of the road. However, in those cases, the wu is within the viewer. It is a religious experience. Here, an artificer has put wu into the object, rather than merely witnessed the wu inherent in it.' He glanced up. 'Am I making myself clear?'

'Yes,' Childan said.

'In other words, an entire new world is pointed to, by this. The name for it is neither art, for it has no form, nor religion. What is it? I have pondered this pin unceasingly, yet cannot fathom it. We evidently lack the word for an object like this. So you are right, Robert. It is authentically a new thing on the face of the world.'

Authentic, Childan thought. Yes, it certainly is. I catch ...at notion. But as to the rest –

'Having meditated to this avail,' Paul continued, 'I next

called back in here the selfsame business acquaintances. I took it upon myself, as I have done with you just now, to deliver an expostulation devoid of tact. This subject carries authority which compels an abandonment of propriety, so great is the necessity of delivering the awareness itself. I required that these individuals listen.'

Childan knew that for a Japanese such as Paul to force his ideas on other persons was an almost incredible situation.

'The result,' Paul said, 'was sanguine. They were able to adopt under such duress my viewpoint; they perceived what I had delineated. So it was worth it. Having done that, I rested. Nothing more, Robert. I am exhausted.' He laid the pin back in the box. 'Responsibility with me has ended. Discharged.' He pushed the box to Childan.

'Sir, it's yours,' Childan said, feeling apprehensive; the situation did not fit any model he had ever experienced. A high-placed Japanese lauding to the skies a gift grafted to him – and then returning it. Childan felt his knees wobble. He did not have any idea what to do; he stood plucking at his sleeve, his face flushing.

Calmly, even harshly, Paul said, 'Robert, you must face reality with more courage.'

Blanching, Childan stammered, 'I'm confused by –'

Paul stood up, facing him. 'Take heed. The task is yours. You are the sole agent for this piece and others of its ilk. Also you are a professional. Withdraw for a period into isolation. Meditate, possibly consult the *Book of Changes*. Then study your window displays, your ads, your system of merchandising.'

Childan gaped at him.

'You will see your way,' Paul said. 'How you must go about putting these objects over in a big fashion.'

Childan felt stunned. The man's telling me I'm *obliged* to assume moral responsibility for the Edfrank jewellery! Crackpot neurotic Japanese world view : nothing less than number-one spiritual and business relationship with the jewellery tolerable in the eyes of Paul Kasoura.

And the worst part of it was that Paul certainly spoke with

authority, right out of dead centre of Japanese culture and tradition.

Obligation, he thought bitterly. It could stick with him the rest of his life, once incurred. Right to the grave itself. Paul had – to his own satisfaction, anyhow – discharged his. But Childan's; ah, that regrettably had the earmark of being unending.

They're out of their minds, Childan said to himself. Example : they won't help a hurt man up from the gutter due to the obligation it imposes. What do you call that? I say that's typical; just what you'd expect from a race that when told to duplicate a British destroyer managed even to copy the patches on the boiler as well as –

Paul was eyeing him intently. Fortunately, long habit had caused Childan to suppress any show of authentic feelings automatically. He had assumed a bland, sober expression, persona that correctly matched the nature of the situation. He could sense it there, the mask.

This is dreadful, Childan realized. A catastrophe. Better Paul had thought I was trying to seduce his wife.

Betty. There was no chance now that she would see the piece, that his original plan would come off. Wu was incompatible with sexuality; it was, as Paul said, solemn and holy, like a relic.

'I gave each of these individuals one of your cards,' Paul said.

'Pardon?' Childan said, preoccupied.

'Your business cards. So that they could come in and inspect other examples.'

'I see,' Childan said.

'There is one more thing,' Paul said. 'One of these individuals wishes to discuss this entire subject with you at his location. I have written out his name and address.' Paul handed Childan a folded square of paper. 'He wants his business colleagues to hear.' Paul added, 'He is an importer. He imports and exports on a mass basis. Especially to South America. Radios, cameras, binoculars, tape recorders, the like.'

Childan gazed down at the paper.

'He deals, of course, in immense quantlty,' Paul said. 'Perhaps tens of thousands of each item. His company controls various enterprises that manufacture for him at low overhead, all located in the Orient where there is cheaper labour.'

'Why is he —' Childan began.

Paul said, 'Pieces such as this . . .' He picked up the pin once more, briefly. Closing the lid, he returned the box to Childan. '. . . can be mass-produced. Either in base metal or plastic. From a mould. In any quantity desired.'

After a time Childan said, 'What about wu? Will that remain in the pieces?'

Paul said nothing.

'You advise me to see him?' Childan said.

'Yes,' Paul said.

'Why?'

'Charms,' Paul said.

Childan stared.

'Good-luck charms. To be worn. By relatively poor people. A line of amulets to be peddled all over Latin America and the Orient. Most of the masses still believe in magic, you know. Spells. Potions. It's a big business, I am told.' Paul's face was wooden, his voice toneless.

'It sounds,' Childan said slowly, 'as if there would be a good deal of money in it.'

Paul nodded.

'Was this your idea?' Childan said.

'No,' Paul said. He was silent, then.

Your employer, Childan thought. You showed the piece to your superior, who knows this importer. Your superior — or some influential person over your head, someone who has power over you, someone rich and big — contacted this importer.

That's why you're giving it back to me, Childan realized. You want no part of this. But you know what I know: that I will go to this address and see this man. I have to. I have no choice. I will lease the designs, or sell them on a percentage basis; some deal will be made between me and this party.

Clearly out of your hands. Entirely. Bad taste on your part to presume to stop me or argue with me.

'There is a chance for you,' Paul said, 'to become extremely wealthy.' He continued to gaze stoically ahead.

'The idea strikes me as bizarre,' Childan said. 'Making good-luck charms out of such art objects; I can't imagine it.'

'For it is not your natural line of business. You are devoted to the savoured esoteric. Myself, I am the same. And so are those individuals who will shortly visit your store, those whom I mentioned.'

Childan said, 'What would you do if you were me?'

'Don't underevaluate the possibility suggested by the esteemed importer. He is a shrewd personage. You and I – we have no awareness of the vast number of uneducated. They can obtain from mould-produced identical objects a joy which would be denied to us. We must suppose that we have the only one of a kind, or at least something rare, possessed by a very few. And, of course, something truly authentic. Not a model or replica.' He continued to gaze past Childan at empty space. 'Not something cast by the tens of thousands.'

Has he stumbled onto correct notion, Childan wondered, that certain of the historic objects in stores such as mine (not to mention many items in his own personal collection) are imitations? There seems a trace of hint in his words. As if in ironic undertone he is telling me a message quite different from what appears. Ambiguity, as one trips over in the oracle . . . quality, as they say, of the Oriental mind.

Childan thought, He's actually saying : Which are you, Robert? He whom the oracle calls 'the inferior man', or that other for whom all the good advice is meant? Must decide, here. You may trot on one way or the other, but not both. Moment of choice now.

And which way *will* the superior man go? Robert Childan inquired of himself. At least according to Paul Kasoura. And what we have before us here isn't a many-thousand-year-old compilation of divinely inspired wisdom; this is merely the opinion of one mortal – one young Japanese businessman.

Yet, there's a kernel to it. Wu, as Paul would say. The wu of this situation is this : whatever our personal dislikes, there can be no doubt, the reality lies in the importer's direction. Too bad for what we had intended; we must adapt, as the oracle states.

And after all, the originals can still be sold in my shop. To connoisseurs, as for example Paul's friends.

'You wrestle with yourself,' Paul observed. 'No doubt it is in such a situation that one prefers to be alone.' He had started towards the office door.

'I have already decided.'

Paul's eyes flickered.

Bowing, Childan said, 'I will follow your advice. Now I will leave to visit the importer.' He held up the folded slip of paper.

Oddly, Paul did not seem pleased; he merely grunted and returned to his desk. They contain their emotions to the last, Childan reflected.

'Many thanks for your business help,' Childan said as he made ready to depart. 'Some day I will if possible reciprocate. I will remember.'

But still the young Japanese showed no reaction. Too true, Childan thought, what we used to say : they are inscrutable.

Accompanying him to the door, Paul seemed deep in thought. All at once he blurted, 'American artisans made this piece hand by hand, correct? Labour of their personal bodies?'

'Yes, from initial design to final polish.'

'Sir ! Will these artisans play along? I would imagine they dreamed otherwise for their work.'

'I'd hazard they could be persuaded,' Childan said; the problem, to him, appeared minor.

'Yes,' Paul said. 'I suppose so.'

Something in his tone made Robert Childan take sudden note. A nebulous and peculiar emphasis, there. And then it swept over Childan. Without a doubt he had split the ambiguity – he *saw*.

Of course. Whole affair a cruel dismissal of American efforts, taking place before his eyes. Cynicism, but God forbid, he had swallowed hook, line, and sinker. Got me to agree, step by step, led me along the garden path to this conclusion : products of American hands good for nothing but to be models for junky good-luck charms.

This was how the Japanese ruled, not crudely but with subtlety, ingenuity, timeless cunning.

Christ! We're barbarians compared to them, Childan realized. We're no more than boobs against such pitiless reasoning. Paul did not say – did not tell me – that our art was worthless; he got me to say it for him. And, as a final irony, he regretted my utterance. Faint, civilized gesture of sorrow as he heard the truth out of me.

He's broken me, Childan almost said aloud – fortunately, however, he managed to keep it only a thought; as before, he held it in his interior world, apart and secret, for himself alone. Humiliated me and my race. And I'm helpless. There's no avenging this; we are defeated and our defeats are like this, so tenuous, so delicate, that we're hardly able to perceive them. In fact, we have to rise a notch in our evolution to know it ever happened.

What more proof could be presented, as to the Japanese fitness to rule? He felt like laughing, possibly with appreciation. Yes, he thought, that's what it is, as when one hears a choice anecdote. I've got to recall it, savour it later on, even relate it. But to whom? Problem, there. Too personal for narration.

In the corner of Paul's office a wastebasket. Into it ! Robert Childan said to himself, with this blob, this wu-ridden piece of jewellery.

Could I do it? Toss it away? End the situation before Paul's eyes?

Can't even toss it away, he discovered as he gripped the piece. Must not – if you anticipate facing your Japanese fellowman again.

Damn them, I can't free myself of their influence, can't give in to impulse. All spontaneity crushed ... Paul scrutinized him, needing to say nothing; the man's very presence enough. Got my conscience snared, has run an invisible string from this blob in my hands up my arm to my soul.

Guess I've lived around them too long. Too late now to flee, to get back among whites and white ways.

Robert Childan said, 'Paul –' His voice, he noted, croaked in sickly escape; no control, no modulation.

'Yes, Robert.'

'Paul, I ... am ... humiliated.'

The room reeled.

'Why so, Robert?' Tones of concern, but detached. Above involvement.

'Paul. One moment.' He fingered the bit of jewellery; it had become slimy with sweat. 'I – am proud of this work. There can be no consideration of trashy good-luck charms. I reject.'

Once more he could not make out the young Japanese man's reaction, only the listening ear, the mere awareness.

'Thank you, however,' Robert Childan said.

Paul bowed.

Robert Childan bowed.

'The men who made this,' Childan said, 'are American proud artists. Myself included. To suggest trashy good-luck charms therefore insults us and I ask for apology.'

Incredible prolonged silence.

Paul surveyed him. One eyebrow lifted slightly and his thin lips twitched. A smile?

'I demand,' Childan said. That was all; he could carry it no further. He now merely waited.

Nothing occurred.

Please, he thought. Help me.

Paul said, 'Forgive my arrogant imposition.' He held out his hand.

'All right,' Robert Childan said.

They shook hands.

Calmness descended in Childan's heart. I have lived through and out, he knew. All over. Grace of God; it existed at the exact moment for me. Another time – otherwise. Could I ever dare once more, press my luck? Probably not.

He felt melancholy. Brief instant, as if I rose to the surface and saw unencumbered.

Life is short, he thought. Art, or something not life, is long, stretching out endless, like concrete worm. Flat, white, un-smoothed by any passage over or across it. Here I stand. But no longer. Taking the small box, he put the Edfrank jewellery piece away in his coat pocket.

12

Mr Ramsey said, 'Mr Tagomi, this is Mr Yatabe.' He retired to a corner of the office, and the slender elderly gentleman came forward.

Holding out his hand, Mr Tagomi said, 'I am glad to meet you in person, sir.' The light, fragile old hand slipped into his own; he shook without pressing and released at once. Nothing broken I hope, he thought. He examined the old gentleman's features, finding himself pleased. Such a stern, coherent spirit there. No fogging of wits. Certainly lucid transmission of all the stable ancient traditions. Best quality which the old could represent . . . and then he dis-covered that he was facing General Tedeki, the former Imperial Chief of Staff.

Mr Tagomi bowed low.

'General,' he said.

'Where is the third party?' General Tedeki said.

'On the double, he nears,' Mr Tagomi said. 'Informed by self at hotel room.' His mind utterly rattled, he retreated several steps in the bowing position, scarcely able to regain an erect posture.

The general seated himself. Mr Ramsey, no doubt still ignorant of the old man's identity, assisted with the chair but showed no particular deference. Mr Tagomi hesitantly took a chair facing.

'We loiter,' the general said. 'Regrettably but unavoidably.'

'True,' Mr Tagomi said.

Ten minutes passed. Neither man spoke.

'Excuse me, sir,' Mr Ramsey said at last, fidgeting. 'I will depart unless needed.'

Mr Tagomi nodded, and Mr Ramsey departed.

'Tea, General?' Mr Tagomi said.

'No, sir.'

'Sir,' Mr Tagomi said, 'I admit to fear. I sense in this encounter something terrible.'

The general inclined his head.

'Mr Baynes, whom I have met,' Mr Tagomi said, 'and entertained in my home, declares himself a Swede. Yet perusal persuades one that he is in fact a highly placed German of some sort. I say this because –'

'Please continue.'

'Thank you. General, his agitation regarding this meeting causes me to infer a connection with the political upheavals in the Reich.' Mr Tagomi did not mention another fact : his awareness of the general's failure to appear at the time anticipated.

The general said, 'Sir, now you are fishing. Not informing.' His grey eyes twinkled in fatherly manner. No malice, there.

Mr Tagomi accepted the rebuke. 'Sir, is my presence in this meeting merely a formality to baffle the Nazi snoops?'

'Naturally,' the general said, 'we are interested in maintaining a certain fiction. Mr Baynes is representative for Tor-Am Industries of Stockholm, purely businessman. And I am Shinjiro Yatabe.'

Mr Tagomi thought, And I am Tagomi. That part is so.

'No doubt the Nazis have scrutinized Mr Baynes's comings and goings,' the general said. He rested his hands on his knees, sitting bolt upright . . . as if, Mr Tagomi thought, he were sniffing far-off beef tea odour. 'But to demolish the fiction they must resort to legalities. That is the genuine purpose; not to deceive, but to require the formalities in case of exposure. You see for instance that to apprehend Mr Baynes they must do more than merely shoot him down . . . which they could do, were he to travel as – well, travel without this verbal umbrella.'

'I see,' Mr Tagomi said. Sounds like a game, he decided. But they know the Nazi mentality. So I suppose it is of use.

The desk intercom buzzed. Mr Ramsey's voice. 'Sir, Mr Baynes is here. Shall I send him on in?'

'Yes!' Mr Tagomi cried.

The door opened and Mr Baynes, sleekly dressed, his clothes all quite pressed and masterfully tailored, his features composed, appeared.

General Tedeki rose to face him. Mr Tagomi also rose. All three men bowed.

'Sir,' Mr Baynes said to the general, 'I am Captain R. Wegener of the Reichs Naval Counter-Intelligence. As understood, I represent no one but myself and certain private unnamed individuals, no departments or bureaux of the Reich Government of any sort.'

The general said, 'Herr Wegener, I understand that you in no way officially allege representation of any branch of the Reich Government. I am here as an unofficial private party who by virtue of former position with the Imperial Army can be said to have access to circles in Tokyo who desire to hear whatever you have to say.'

Weird discourse, Mr Tagomi thought. But not unpleasant. Certain near-musical quality to it. Refreshing relief, in fact.

They sat down.

'Without preamble,' Mr Baynes said, 'I would like to inform you and those you have access to that there is in advance stage in the Reich a programme called Löwenzahn. Dandelion.'

'Yes,' the general said, nodding as if he had heard this before; but, Mr Tagomi thought, he seemed quite eager for Mr Baynes to go on.

'Dandelion,' Mr Baynes said, 'consists of an incident on the border between the Rocky Mountain States and the United States.'

The general nodded, smiling slightly.

'U.S. troops will be attacked and will retaliate by crossing the border and engaging the regular R.M.S. troops stationed near by. The U.S. troops have detailed maps showing Midwest army installations. This is step one. Step two consists of a declaration by Germany regarding the conflict. A volunteer detachment of Wehrmacht paratroopers will be sent to aid the U.S. However, this is further camouflage.'

'Yes,' the general said, listening.

'The basic purpose of Operation Dandelion,' Mr Baynes said, 'is an enormous nuclear attack on the Home Islands, without advance warning of any kind.' He was silent then.

'With purpose of wiping out Royal Family, Home Defence Army, most of Imperial Navy, civil population, industries, resources,' General Tedeki said. 'Leaving overseas possessions for absorption by the Reich.'

Mr Baynes said nothing.

The general said, 'What else?'

Mr Baynes seemed at a loss.

'The date, sir,' the general said.

'All changed,' Mr Baynes said. 'Due to the death of M. Bormann. At least, I presume. I am not in contact with the Abwehr now.'

Presently the general said, 'Go on, Herr Wegener.'

'What we recommend is that the Japanese Government enter into the Reich's domestic situation. Or at least, that was what I came here to recommend. Certain groups in the Reich favour Operation Dandelion; certain others do not. It was hoped that those opposing it could come to power upon the death of Chancellor Bormann.'

'But while you were here,' the general said, 'Herr Bormann died and the political situation took its own solution. Doctor Goebbels is now Reichs Chancellor. The upheaval is over.' He paused. 'How does that faction view Operation Dandelion?'

Mr Baynes said, 'Doctor Goebbels is an advocate of Dandelion.'

Unnoticed by them, Mr Tagomi closed his eyes.

'Who stands opposed?' General Tedeki asked.

Mr Baynes's voice came to Mr Tagomi. 'S.S. General Heydrich.'

'I am taken by surprise,' General Tedeki said. 'I am dubious. Is this legitimate information or only a viewpoint which you and your colleagues hold?'

Mr Baynes said, 'Administration of the East – that is, the area now held by Japan – would be by the Foreign Office, Rosenberg's people, working directly with the Chancery. This was a bitterly disputed issue in many sessions between the principals last year. I have photostats of notes made. The police demanded authority but were turned down. They are to manage the space colonization, Mars, Luna, Venus. That's to be their domain. Once this division of authority was settled the police put all their weight behind the space programme and against Dandelion.'

'Rivalry,' General Tedeki said. 'One group played against another. By the Leader. So he is never challenged.'

'True,' Mr Baynes said. 'That is why I was sent here, to plead for your intervention. It would still be possible to intervene; the situation is still fluid. It will be months before Doctor Goebbels can consolidate his position. He will have to break the police, possibly have Heydrich and other top S.S. and S.D. leaders executed. Once that is done –'

'We are to give support to the Sicherheitsdienst?' General Tedeki interrupted. 'The most malignant portion of German society?'

Mr Baynes said, 'That is right.'

'The Emperor,' General Tedeki said, 'would never tolerate that policy. He regards the Reichs elite corps, wherever the black uniform is worn, the death's head, the Castle System – all, to him, is evil.'

Evil, Mr Tagomi thought. Yes, it is. Are we to assist it in gaining power, in order to save our lives? Is that the paradox of our earthly situation?

I cannot face this dilemma, Mr Tagomi said to himself. That man should have to act in such moral ambiguity. There is no Way in this; all is muddled. All chaos of light and dark, shadow and substance.

'The Wehrmacht,' Mr Baynes said, 'the military, is sole possessor in the Reich of the hydrogen bomb. Where the blackshirts have used it, they have done so only under Army supervision. The Chancery under Bormann never allowed any nuclear armament to go to the police. In Operation Dandelion, all will be carried out by O.K.W. The Army High Command.'

'I am aware of that,' General Tedeki said.

'The moral practices of the blackshirts exceed in ferocity that of the Wehrmacht. But their power is less. We should reflect solely on reality, on actual power. Not on ethical intentions.'

'Yes, we must be realists,' Mr Tagomi said aloud.

Both Mr Baynes and General Tedeki glanced at him.

To Mr Baynes the general said, 'What specifically do you suggest? That we establish contact with the S.D. here in the Pacific States? Directly negotiate with – I do not know who is S.D. chief here. Some repellent character, I imagine.'

'The local S.D. knows nothing,' Mr Baynes said. 'Their chief here, Bruno Kreuz vom Meere, is an old-time Partei hack. Ein Altparteigenosse. An imbecile. No one in Berlin would think of telling him anything; he merely carries out routine assignments.'

'What, then?' The general sounded angry. 'The consul, here, or the Reichs Ambassador in Tokyo?'

This talk will fail, Mr Tagomi thought. No matter what is at stake. We cannot enter the monstrous schizophrenic morass of Nazi internecine intrigue; our minds cannot adapt.

'It must be handled delicately,' Mr Baynes said. 'Through a series of intermediaries. Someone close to Heydrich who is stationed outside of the Reich, in a neutral country. Or someone who travels back and forth between Tokyo and Berlin.'

'Do you have someone in mind?'

'The Italian Foreign Minister, Count Ciano. An intelligent, reliable, very brave man, completely devoted to international understanding. However – his contact with the S.D. apparatus is nonexistent. But he might work through someone else in Germany, economic interests such as the Krupps or through General Speidel or possibly even through Waffen-S.S. personages. The Waffen-S.S. is less fanatic, more in the mainstream of German society.'

'Your establishment, the Abwehr – it would be futile to attempt to reach Heydrich through you.'

'The blackshirts utterly revile us. They've been trying for twenty years to get Partei approval for liquidating us in toto.'

'Aren't you in excessive personal danger from them?' General Tedeki said. 'They are active here on the Pacific Coast, I understand.'

'Active but inept,' Mr Baynes said. 'The Foreign Office man, Reiss, is skilful, but opposed to the S.D.' He shrugged.

General Tedeki said, 'I would like your photostats. To turn over to my government. Any material you have pertaining to these discussions in Germany. And –' He pondered. 'Proof. Of objective nature.'

'Certainly,' Mr Baynes said. He reached into his coat and took out a flat silver cigarette case. 'You will find each cigarette to be a hollow container for microfilm.' He passed the case to General Tedeki.

'What about the case itself?' the general said, examining it. 'It seems too valuable an object to give away.' He started to remove the cigarettes from it.

Smiling, Mr Baynes said, 'The case, too.'

'Thank you.' Also smiling, the general put the case away in his topcoat pocket.

The desk intercom buzzed. Mr Tagomi pressed the button.

Mr Ramsey's voice came: 'Sir, there is a group of S.D. men in the downstairs lobby; they are attempting to take over the building. The *Times* guards are scuffling with them.' In the distance, noise of a siren; outside the building from the street below Mr Tagomi's window. 'Army M.P.s are on the way, plus San Francisco Kempeitai.'

'Thank you, Mr Ramsey,' Mr Tagomi said. 'You have done an honourable thing, to report placidly.' Mr Baynes and General Tedeki were listening, both rigid. 'Sirs,' Mr Tagomi said to them, 'we will no doubt kill the S.D. thugs before they reach this floor.' To Mr Ramsey he said, 'Turn off the power to the elevators.'

'Yes, Mr Tagomi.' Mr Ramsey broke the connection.

Mr Tagomi said, 'We will wait.' He opened his desk drawer and lifted out a teakwood box; unlocking it, he brought forth a perfectly preserved U.S. 1860 Civil War Colt ·44, a treasured collector's item. Taking out a box of loose powder, ball and cap ammunition, he began loading the re-volver. Mr Baynes and General Tedeki watched wide-eyed.

'Part of personal collection,' Mr Tagomi said. 'Much fooled around in vainglorious swift-draw practising and firing, in spare hours. Admit to compare favourably with other enthusiasts in contest-timing. But mature use hereto-fore delayed.' Holding the gun in correct fashion he pointed it at the office door. And sat waiting.

At the bench in their basement workshop, Frank Frink sat at the arbor. He held a half-finished silver ear-ring against the noisily turning cotton buff; bits of rouge spattered his glasses and blackened his nails and hands. The ear-ring, shaped in a snail-shell spiral, became hot from friction, but Frink grimly bore down even more.

'Don't get it too shiny,' Ed McCarthy said. 'Just hit the high spots; you can even leave the lows completely.'

Frank Frink grunted.

'There's a better market for silver if it's not polished up too much,' Ed said. 'Silverwork should have that old look.'

Market, Frink thought.

They had sold nothing. Except for the consignment at American Artistic Handcrafts, no one had taken anything, and they had visited five retail shops in all.

We're not making any money, Frink said to himself.

We're making more and more jewellery and it's just piling up around us.

The screw-back of the ear-ring caught in the wheel; the piece whipped out of Frink's hands and flew to the polish shield, then fell to the floor. He shut off the motor.

'Don't let those pieces go,' McCarthy said, at the welding torch.

'Christ, it's the size of a pea. No way to get a grip.'

'Well, pick it up anyhow.'

The hell with the whole thing, Frink thought.

'What's the matter?' McCarthy said, seeing him make no move to fish up the ear-ring.

Frink said. 'We're pouring money in for nothing.'

'We can't sell what we haven't made.'

'We can't sell anything,' Frink said. 'Made or unmade.'

'Five stores. Drop in the bucket.'

'But the trend,' Frink said. 'It's enough to know.'

'Don't kid yourself.'

Frink said, 'I'm not kidding myself.'

'Meaning what?'

'Meaning it's time to start looking for market for scrap.'

'All right,' McCarthy said, 'quit, then.'

'I have.'

'I'll go on by myself.' McCarthy lit the torch again.

'How are we going to split the stuff?'

'I don't know. But we'll find a way.'

'Buy me out,' Frink said.

'Hell no.'

Frink computed. 'Pay me six hundred dollars.'

'No, you take half of everything.'

'Half the motor?'

They were both silent then.

'Three more stores,' McCarthy said. 'Then we'll talk about it.' Lowering his mask he began brazing a section of brass rod into a cuff bracelet.

Frank Frink stepped down from the bench. He located the snail-shell ear-ring and replaced it in the carton of incomplete pieces. 'I'm going outside for a smoke,' he said, and walked across the basement to the stairs.

A moment later he stood outdoors on the sidewalk, a T'ien-lai between his fingers.

It's all over, he said to himself. I don't need the oracle to tell me; I recognize what the Moment is. The smell is there. Defeat.

And it is hard really to say why. Maybe, theoretically, we could go on. Store to store, other cities. But – something is wrong. And all the effort and ingenuity won't change it.

I want to know why, he thought.

But I never will.

What should we have done? Made what instead?

We bucked the moment. Bucked the Tao. Upstream, in the wrong direction. And now – dissolution. Decay.

Yin has us. The light showed us its ass, went elsewhere. We can only knuckle under.

While he stood there under the eaves of the building, taking quick drags on his marijuana cigarette and dully watching traffic go by, an ordinary-looking, middle-aged white man sauntered up to him.

'Mr Frink? Frank Frink?'

'You got it,' Frink said.

The man produced a folded document and identification. 'I'm with the San Francisco Police Department. I've a warrant for your arrest.' He held Frink's arm already; it had already been done.

'What for?' Frink demanded.

'Bunco. Mr Childan, American Artistic Handcrafts.' The cop forcibly led Frink along the sidewalk; another plain-clothes cop joined them, one now on each side of Frink. They hustled him towards a parked unmarked Toyopet.

This is what the time requires of us, Frink thought as he was dumped onto the car seat between the two cops. The door slammed shut; the car, driven by a third cop, this one in uniform, shot out into traffic. These are the sons-of-bitches we must submit to.

'You got an attorney?' one of the cops asked him.

188

'No,' he said.

'They'll give you a list of names at the station.'

'Thanks,' Frink said.

'What'd you do with the money?' one of the cops asked later on, as they were parking in the Kearny Street police station garage.

Frink said, 'Spent it.'

'All?'

He did not answer.

One of the cops shook his head and laughed.

As they got out of the car, one of them said to Frink, 'Is your real name Fink?'

Frink felt terror.

'Fink,' the cop repeated. 'You're a kike.' He exhibited a large grey folder. 'Refugee from Europe.'

'I was born in New York,' Frank Frink said.

'You're an escapee from the Nazis,' the cop said. 'You know what that means?'

Frank Frink broke away and ran across the garage. The three cops shouted, and at the doorway he found himself facing a police car with uniformed armed police blocking his path. The police smiled at him, and one of them, holding a gun, stepped out and smacked a handcuff into place over his wrist.

Jerking him by the wrist – the thin metal cut into his flesh, to the bone – the cop led him back the way he had come.

'Back to Germany,' one of the cops said, surveying him.

'I'm an American,' Frank Frink said.

'You're a Jew,' the cop said.

As he was taken upstairs, one of the cops said, 'Will he be booked here?'

'No,' another said. 'We'll hold him for the German consul. They want to try him under German law.'

There was no list of attorneys, after all.

For twenty minutes Mr Tagomi had remained motionless at his desk, holding the revolver pointed at the door, while Mr Baynes paced about the office. The old general had, after some thought, lifted the phone and put through a call to the Japanese embassy in San Francisco. However, he had not been able to get through to Baron Kaelemakule; the ambassador, a bureaucrat had told him, was out of the city.

Now General Tedeki was in the process of placing a transpacific call to Tokyo.

'I will consult with the War College,' he explained to Mr Baynes. 'They will contact Imperial military forces stationed near by us.' He did not seem perturbed.

So we will be relieved in a number of hours, Mr Tagomi said to himself. Possibly by Japanese Marines from a carrier, armed with machine guns and mortars.

Operating through official channels is highly efficient in terms of final result . . . but there is regrettable time lag. Down below us, blackshirt hooligans are busy clubbing secretaries and clerks.

However, there was little more that he personally could do.

'I wonder if it would be worth trying to reach the German consul,' Mr Baynes said.

Mr Tagomi had a vision of himself summoning Miss Ephreikian in with her tape recorder, to take dictation of urgent protest to Herr H. Reiss.

'I can call Herr Reiss,' Mr Tagomi said. 'On another line.'

'Please,' Mr Baynes said.

Still holding his Colt ·44 collector's item, Mr Tagomi pressed a button on his desk. Out came a nonlisted phone line, especially installed for esoteric communication.

He dialled the number of the German consulate.

'Good day, who is calling?' Accented brisk male functionary voice. Undoubtedly underling.

Mr Tagomi said, 'His Excellency Herr Reiss, please. Urgent. This is Mr Tagomi, here. Ranking Imperial Trade Mission, Top Place.' He used his hard, no-nonsense voice.

'Yes sir. A moment, if you will.' A long moment, then. No sound at all on the phone, not even clicks. He is merely standing there with it, Mr Tagomi decided. Stalling through typical Nordic wile.

To General Tedeki, waiting on the other phone, and Mr Baynes, pacing, he said, 'I am naturally being put off.'

At last the functionary's voice once again. 'Sorry to keep you waiting, Mr Tagomi.'

'Not at all.'

'The consul is in conference. However —'

Mr Tagomi hung up.

'Waste of effort, to say the least,' he said, feeling discomfited. Whom else to call? Tokkoka already informed, also M.P. units down on waterfront; no use to phone them. Direct call to Berlin? To Reichs Chancellor Goebbels? To Imperial Military airfield at Napa, asking for air-rescue assistance?

'I will call S.D. chief Herr B. Kreuz vom Meere,' he decided aloud. 'And bitterly complain. Rant and scream invective.' He began to dial the number formally – euphemistically – listed in the San Francisco phone book as the 'Lufthansa Airport Terminal Precious-Shipment Guard Detail'. As the phone buzzed he said, 'Vituperate in high-pitched hysteria.'

'Put on good performance,' General Tedeki said, smiling.

In Mr Tagomi's ear a Germanic voice said, 'Who is it?' More no-nonsense-than-myself voice, Mr Tagomi thought. But he intended to go on. 'Hurry up,' the voice demanded.

Mr Tagomi shouted, 'I am ordering the arrest and trial of your band of cut-throats and degenerates who run amok like blond berserk beasts, unfit even to describe! Do you know me, *Kerl*? This is Tagomi, Imperial Government Consultant. Five seconds or waive legality and have Marines' shock troop unit begin massacre with flame-throwing phosphorus bombs. Disgrace to civilization.'

On the other end the S.D. flunky was sputtering anxiously. Mr Tagomi winked at Mr Baynes.

'. . . we know nothing about it,' the flunky was saying.

'Liar!' Mr Tagomi shouted. 'Then we have no choice.' He slammed the receiver down. 'It is no doubt mere gesture,' he said to Mr Baynes and General Tedeki. 'But it can do no harm, anyhow. Always faint possibility certain nervous element even in S.D.'

General Tedeki started to speak. But then a tremendous clatter at the office door; he ceased. The door swung open.

Two burly white men appeared, both armed with pistols equipped with silencers. They made out Mr Baynes.

'Da ist er,' one said. They started for Mr Baynes.

At his desk, Mr Tagomi pointed his Colt ·44 ancient collector's item and compressed the trigger. One of the S.D. men fell to the floor. The other whipped his silencer-equipped gun towards Mr Tagomi and returned fire. Mr Tagomi heard no report, saw only a tiny wisp of smoke from the gun, heard the whistle of a slug passing near. With record-eclipsing speed he fanned the hammer of the single-action Colt, firing it again and again.

The S.D. man's jaw burst. Bits of bone, flesh, shreds of tooth, flew in the air. Hit in the mouth, Mr Tagomi realized. Dreadful spot, especially if ball ascending. The jawless S.D. man's eyes still contained life, of a kind. He still perceives me, Mr Tagomi thought. Then the eyes lost their lustre and the S.D. man collapsed, dropping his gun and making un-human gargling noises.

'Sickening,' Mr Tagomi said.

No more S.D. men appeared in the open doorway.

'Possibly it is over,' General Tedeki said after a pause.

Mr Tagomi, engaged in tedious three-minute task of re-loading, paused to press the button of the desk intercom. 'Bring medical emergency aid,' he instructed. 'Hideously injured thug, here.'

No answer, only a hum.

Stooping, Mr Baynes had picked up both the Germans' guns; he passed one to the general, keeping the other him-self.

'Now we will mow them down,' Mr Tagomi said, re-seating himself with his Colt ·44, as before. 'Formidable triumvirate, in this office.'

From the hall a voice called. 'German hoodlums surrender!'

'Already taken care of,' Mr Tagomi called back. 'Lying either dead or dying. Advance and verify empirically.'

A party of Nippon *Times* employees gingerly appeared, several of them carrying building riot equipment such as axes and rifles, and tear-gas grenades.

'*Cause célèbre,*' Mr Tagomi said. 'P.S.A. Government in Sacramento could declare war on Reich without hesitation.' He broke open his gun. 'Anyhow, over with.'

'They will deny complicity,' Mr Baynes said. 'Standard technique. Used countless times.' He laid the silencer-equipped pistol on Mr Tagomi's desk. 'Made in Japan.'

He was not joking. It was true. Excellent quality Japanese target pistol. Mr Tagomi examined it.

'And not German nationals,' Mr Baynes said. He had taken the wallet of one of the whites, the dead one. 'P.S.A. citizen. Lives in San José. Nothing to connect him with the S.D. Name is Jack Sanders.' He tossed the wallet down.

'A holdup,' Mr Tagomi said. 'Motive : our locked vault. No political aspects.' He arose shakily to his feet.

In any case, the assassination or kidnapping attempt by the S.D. had failed. At least, this first one had. But clearly they knew who Mr Baynes was, and no doubt what he had come for.

'The prognosis,' Mr Tagomi said, 'is gloomy.'

He wondered if in this instance the oracle would be of any use. Perhaps it could protect them. Warn them, shield them, with its advice.

Still quite shaky, he began taking out the forty-nine yarrow stalks. Whole situation confusing and anomalous, he decided. No human intelligence could decipher it; only five-thousand-year-old joint mind applicable. German totalitarian society resembles some faulty form of life, worse than natural thing. Worse in all its admixtures, its potpourri of pointlessness.

Here, he thought, local S.D. acts as instrument of policy totally at odds with head in Berlin. Where in this composite being is the sense? Who really is Germany? Who ever was? Almost like decomposing nightmare parody of problems customarily faced in course of existence.

The oracle will cut through it. Even weird breed of cat like Nazi Germany comprehensible to *I Ching*.

Mr Baynes, seeing Mr Tagomi distractedly manipulating the handful of vegetable stalks, recognized how deep the man's distress was. For him, Mr Baynes thought, this event, his having had to kill and mutilate these two men, is not only dreadful; it is inexplicable.

What can I say that might console him? He fired on my behalf; the moral responsibility for these two lives is therefore mine, and I accept it. I view it that way.

Coming over beside Mr Baynes, General Tedeki said in a soft voice, 'You witness the man's despair. He, you see, was no doubt raised as a Buddhist. Even if not formally, the influence was there. A culture in which no life is to be taken; all lives holy.'

Mr Baynes nodded.

'He will recover his equilibrium,' General Tedeki continued. 'In time. Right now he has no standpoint by which he can view and comprehend his act. That book will help him, for it provides an external frame of reference.'

'I see,' Mr Baynes said. He thought, Another frame of reference which might help him would be the Doctrine of Original Sin. I wonder if he has ever heard of it. We are all doomed to commit acts of cruelty or violence or evil; that is our destiny, due to ancient factors. Our karma.

To save one life, Mr Tagomi had to take two. The logical, balanced mind cannot make sense of that. A kindly man like Mr Tagomi could be driven insane by the implications of such reality.

Nevertheless, Mr Baynes thought, the crucial point lies not in the present, not in either my death or the death of the two S.D. men; it lies – hypothetically – in the future. What has happened here is justified, or not justified, by what happens later. Can we perhaps save the lives of millions, all Japan in fact?

But the man manipulating the vegetable stalks could not think of that; the present, the actuality, was too tangible, the dead and dying Germans on the floor of his office.

General Tedeki was right; time would give Mr Tagomi perspective. Either that, or he would perhaps retreat into the shadow of mental illness, avert his gaze for ever, due to a hopeless perplexity.

And we are not really different from him, Mr Baynes thought. We are faced with the same confusions. Therefore unfortunately we can give Mr Tagomi no help. We can only wait, hoping that finally he will recover and not succumb.

13

In Denver they found chic, modern stores. The clothes, Juliana thought, were numbingly expensive, but Joe did not seem to care or even to notice; he simply paid for what she picked out, and then they hurried on to the next store.

Her major acquisition – after much trying on of dresses and much prolonged deliberating and rejecting – occurred late in the day: a light blue Italian original with short, fluffy sleeves and a wildly low neckline. In a European fashion magazine she had seen a model wearing such a dress; it was considered the finest style of the year, and it cost Joe almost two hundred dollars.

To go with it, she needed three pairs of shoes, more nylon stockings, several hats, and a new handmade black leather purse. And, she discovered, the neckline of the Italian dress demanded the new brassieres which covered only the lower part of each breast. Viewing herself in the full-length mirror of the dress shop, she felt overexposed and a little insecure about bending over. But the sales girl assured her that the new half-bras remained firmly in place, despite their lack of straps.

Just up to the nipple, Juliana thought as she peered at herself in the privacy of the dressing room, and not one millimetre more. The bras, too, cost quite a bit; also imported, the salesgirl explained, and handmade. The salesgirl showed her sportswear, too, shorts and bathing suits and a terrycloth beach robe; but all at once Joe became restless. So they went on.

As Joe loaded the parcels and bags into the car she said, 'Don't you think I'm going to look terrific?'

'Yes,' he said in a preoccupied voice. 'Especially that blue dress. You wear that when we go there, to Abendsen's; understand?' He spoke the last word sharply as if it was an order; the tone surprised her.

'I'm a size twelve or fourteen,' she said as they entered the next dress shop. The salesgirl smiled graciously and accompanied them to the racks of dresses. What else did she need? Juliana wondered. Better to get as much as possible while she could; her eyes took in everything at once, the blouses, skirts, sweaters, slacks, coats. Yes, a coat. 'Joe,' she said, 'I have to have a long coat. But not a cloth coat.'

They compromised with one of the synthetic fibre coats from Germany; it was more durable than natural fur, and less expensive. But she felt disappointed. To cheer herself up she began examining jewellery. But it was dreary costume junk, without imagination or originality.

'I have to get *some* jewellery,' she explained to Joe. 'Earrings, at least. Or a pin – to go with the blue dress.' She led him along the sidewalk to a jewellery store. 'And your clothes,' she remembered, with guilt. 'We have to stop for you, too.'

While she looked for jewellery, Joe stopped at a barbershop for his haircut. When he appeared a half hour later, she was amazed; he had not only gotten his hair cut as short as possible, but he had had it dyed. She would hardly have recognized him; he was now blond. Good God, she thought, staring at him. Why?

Shrugging, Joe said, 'I'm tired of being a wop.' That was all he would say; he refused to discuss it as they entered a men's clothing store and began shopping for him.

They bought him a nicely tailored suit of one of Du

Pont's new synthetic fibres, Dacron. And new socks, underwear, and a pair of stylish sharp-toed shoes. What now? Juliana thought. Shirts. And ties. She and the clerk picked out two white shirts with French cuffs, several ties made in France, and a pair of silver cuff links. It took only forty minutes to do all the shopping for him; she was astonished to find it so easy, compared to her own.

His suit, she thought, should be altered. But again Joe had become restless; he paid the bill with the Reichsbank notes which he carried. I know something else, Juliana realized. A new billfold. So she and the clerk picked out a black alligator billfold for him, and that was that. They left the store and returned to the car; it was four-thirty and the shopping – at least as far as Joe was concerned – was over.

'You don't want the waistline taken in a little?' she asked Joe as he drove out into downtown Denver traffic. 'On your suit –'

'No.' His voice, brusque and impersonal, startled her.

'What's wrong? Did I buy too much?' I know that's it, she said to herself; I spent much too much. 'I could take some of the skirts back.'

'Let's eat dinner,' he said.

'Oh God,' she explained. 'I know what I didn't get. Nightgowns.'

He glared at her ferociously.

'Don't you want me to get some nice new pyjamas?' she said. 'So I'll be all fresh and –'

'No.' He shook his head. 'Forget it. Look for a place to eat.'

Juliana said in a steady voice, 'We'll go and register at the hotel first. So we can change. Then we'll eat.' And it better be a really fine hotel, she thought, or it's all off. Even this late. And we'll ask them at the hotel what's the best place in Denver to eat. And the name of a good nightclub where we can see a once-in-a-lifetime act, not some local talent but some big names from Europe, like Eleanor Perez or Willie Beck. I know great U.F.A. stars like that come out to Denver, because I've seen the ads. And I won't settle for anything less.

As they searched for a good hotel, Juliana kept glancing at the man beside her. With his hair short and blond, and in his new clothes, he doesn't look like the same person, she thought. Do I like him better this way? It was hard to tell. And me – when I've been able to arrange for my hair being done, we'll be two different persons, almost. Created out of nothing or, rather, out of money. But I just must get my hair done, she told herself.

They found a large stately hotel in downtown Denver with a uniformed doorman who arranged for the car to be parked. That was what she wanted. And a bellboy – actually a grown man, but wearing the maroon uniform – came quickly and carried all their parcels and luggage, leaving them with nothing to do but climb the wide carpeted steps, under the awning, pass through the glass and mahogany doors and into the lobby.

Small shops on each side of the lobby, flower shops, gifts, candy, place to telegraph, desk to reserve plane flights, the bustle of guests at the desk and the elevators, the huge potted plants, and under their feet the carpeting, thick and soft . . . she could smell the hotel, the many people, the activity. Neon signs indicated in which direction the hotel restaurant, cocktail lounge, snack bar, lay. She could barely take it all in as they crossed the lobby and at last reached the reservation desk.

There was even a bookstore.

While Joe signed the register, she excused herself and hurried over to the bookstore to see if they had *The Grass-hopper*. Yes, there it was, a bright stack of copies in fact, with a display sign saying how popular and important it was, and of course that it was verboten in German-run regions. A smiling middle-aged woman, very grandmotherly, waited on her; the book cost almost four dollars, which seemed to Juliana a great deal, but she paid for it with a Reichsbank note from her new purse and then skipped back to join Joe.

Leading the way with their luggage, the bellboy conducted them to the elevator and then up to the second floor, along the corridor – silent and warm and carpeted – to their superb, breathtaking room. The bellboy unlocked the door for them, carried everything inside, adjusted the window and lights; Joe tipped him and he departed, shutting the door after him.

All was unfolding exactly as she wanted.

'How long will we stay in Denver?' she asked Joe, who had begun opening packages on the bed. 'Before we go on up to Cheyenne?'

He did not answer; he had become involved in the contents of his suitcase.

'One day or two?' she asked as she took off her new coat. 'Do you think we could stay *three*?'

Lifting his head Joe answered, 'We're going on tonight.'

At first she did not understand; and when she did, she could not believe him. She stared at him and he stared back with a grim, almost taunting expression, his face constricted with enormous tension, more than she had seen in any human in her life before. He did not move; he seemed paralysed there, with his hands full of his own clothing from the suitcase, his body bent.

'After we eat,' he added.

She could not think of anything to say.

'So wear that blue dress that cost so much,' he said. 'The one you like; the really good one – you understand?' Now he began unbuttoning his shirt. 'I'm going to shave and take a good hot shower.' His voice had a mechanical quality as if he were speaking from miles away through some sort of instrument; turning, he walked towards the bathroom with stiff, jerky steps.

With difficulty she managed to say, 'It's too late tonight.'

'No. We'll be through dinner around five-thirty, six at the latest. We can get up to Cheyenne in two, two and a half hours. That's only eight-thirty. Say nine at the latest. We can phone from here, tell Abendsen we're coming; explain the situation. That'll make an impression, a long-distance call. Say this – we're flying to the West Coast; we're in Denver only tonight. But we're so enthusiastic about his book we're going to drive up to Cheyenne and drive back again tonight, just for a chance to –'

She broke in, 'Why?'

Tears began to surge up into her eyes, and she found herself doubling up her fists, with the thumbs inside, as she had done as a child; she felt her jaw wobble, and when she spoke her voice could hardly be heard. 'I don't want to go and see him tonight; I'm not going. I don't want to at all, even tomorrow. I just want to see the sights here. Like you promised me.' And as she spoke, the dread once more reappeared and settled on her chest, the peculiar blind panic that had scarcely gone away, even in the brightest of moments with him. It rose to the top and commanded her; she felt it quivering in her face, shining out so that he could easily take note of it.

Joe said, 'We'll buzz up there and then afterwards when we come back – we'll take in the sights here.' He spoke reasonably, and yet still with the stark deadness as if he were reciting.

'No,' she said.

'Put on that blue dress.' He rummaged around among the parcels until he found it in the largest box. He carefully removed the cord, got out the dress, laid it on the bed with precision; he did not hurry. 'Okay? You'll be a knockout. Listen, we'll buy a bottle of high-price Scotch and take it along. That Vat 69.'

Frank, she thought. Help me. I'm in something I don't understand.

'It's much farther,' she answered, 'than you realize. I looked on the map. It'll be real late when we get there, more like eleven or past midnight.'

He said, 'Put on the dress or I'll kill you.'

Closing her eyes, she began to giggle. My training, she thought. It was true, after all; now we'll see. Can he kill me or can't I pinch a nerve in his back and cripple him for life? But he fought those British commandos; he's gone through this already, many years ago.

'I know you maybe can throw me,' Joe said. 'Or maybe not.'

'Not throw you,' she said. 'Maim you permanently. I actually can. I lived out on the West Coast. The Japs taught me, up in Seattle. You go on to Cheyenne if you want to and leave me here. Don't try to force me. I'm scared of you and I'll try.' Her voice broke. 'I'll try to get you so bad, if you come at me.'

'Oh come on – put on the goddam dress! What's this all about? You must be nuts, talking like that about killing and maiming, just because I want you to hop in the car after dinner and drive up the autobahn with me and see this fellow whose book you –'

A knock at the door.

Joe stalked to it and opened it. A uniformed boy in the corridor said, 'Valet service. You inquired at the desk, sir.'

'Oh yes,' Joe said, striding to the bed; he gathered up the new white shirts which he had bought and carried them to the bellboy. 'Can you get them back in half an hour?'

'Just ironing out the folds,' the boy said, examining them. 'Not cleaning. Yes, I'm sure they can, sir.'

As Joe shut the door, Juliana said, 'How did you know a new white shirt can't be worn until it's pressed?'

He said nothing; he shrugged.

'I had forgotten,' Juliana said. 'And a woman ought to know . . . when you take them out of the cellophane they're all wrinkled.'

'When I was younger I used to dress up and go out a lot.'

'How did you know the hotel had valet service? I didn't know it. Did you really have your hair cut and dyed? I think your hair always was blond, and you were wearing a hairpiece. Isn't that so?'

Again he shrugged.

'You must be an S.D. man,' she said. 'Posing as a wop truck driver. You never fought in North Africa, did you? You're supposed to come up here to kill Abendsen; isn't that so? I know it is. I guess I'm pretty dumb.' She felt dried-up, withered.

After an interval, Joe said, 'Sure I fought in North Africa. Maybe not with Pardi's artillery battery. With the Brandenburgers.' He added, 'Wehrmacht kommando. Infiltrated British H.Qs. I don't see what difference it makes; we saw plenty of action. And I was at Cairo; I earned the medal and a battlefield citation. Corporal.'

'Is that fountain pen a weapon?'

He did not answer.

'A bomb,' she realized suddenly, saying it aloud. 'A booby-trap kind of bomb, that's wired so it'll explode when someone touches it.'

'No,' he said. 'What you saw is a two-watt transmitter and receiver. So I can keep in radio contact. In case there's a change of plan, what with the day-by-day political situation in Berlin.'

'You check in with them just before you do it. To be sure.'

He nodded.

'You're not Italian; you're a German.'

'Swiss.'

She said, 'My husband is a Jew.'

'I don't care what your husband is. All I want is for you to put on that dress and fix yourself up so we can go to dinner. Fix your hair somehow; I wish you could have gotten to the hairdresser's. Possibly the hotel beauty salon is still open. You could do that while I wait for my shirts and take my shower.'

'How are you going to kill him?'

Joe said, 'Please put on the new dress, Juliana. I'll phone down and ask about the hairdresser.' He walked over to the room phone.

'Why do you need me along?'

Dialling, Joe said, 'We have a folder on Abendsen and it seems he is attracted to a certain type of dark, libidinous girl. A specific Middle-Eastern or Mediterranean type.'

As he talked to the hotel people, Juliana went over to the bed and lay down. She shut her eyes and put her arm across her face.

'They do have a hairdresser,' Joe said when he had hung

up the phone. 'And she can take care of you right away. You go down to the salon; it's on the mezzanine.' He handed her something; opening her eyes she saw that it was more Reichsbank notes. 'To pay her.'

She said, 'Let me lie here. Will you please?'

He regarded her with a look of acute curiosity and concern.

'Seattle is like San Francisco would have been,' she said, 'if there had been no Great Fire. Real old wooden buildings and some brick ones, and hilly like S.F. The Japs there go back to a long time before the war. They have a whole business section and houses, stores and everything, very old. It's a port. This little old Jap who taught me – I had gone up there with a Merchant Marine guy, and while I was there I started taking these lessons. Minoru Ichoyasu; he wore a vest and tie. He was as round as a yo-yo. He taught upstairs in a Jap office building; he had that old-fashioned gold lettering on his door, and a waiting room like a dentist's office. With *National Geographics.*'

Bending over her, Joe took hold of her arm and lifted her to a sitting position; he supported her, propped her up. 'What's the matter? You act like you're sick.' He peered into her face, searching her features.

'I'm dying,' she said.

'It's just an anxiety attack. Don't you have them all the time? I can get you a sedative from the hotel pharmacy. What about phenobarbital? And we haven't eaten since ten this morning. You'll be all right. When we get to Abendsen's, you don't have to do a thing, only stand there with me; I'll do the talking. Just smile and be companionable with me and him; stay with him and make conversation with him, so that he stays with us and doesn't go off somewhere. When he sees you I'm certain he'll let us in, especially with that Italian dress cut as it is. I'd let you in, myself, if I were he.'

'Let me go into the bathroom,' she said. 'I'm sick. Please.' She struggled loose from him. 'I'm being sick – let me go.'

He let her go, and she made her way across the room and into the bathroom; she shut the door behind her.

I can do it, she thought. She snapped the light on; it dazzled her. She squinted. I can find it. In the medicine cabinet, a courtesy pack of razor blades, soap, toothpaste. She opened the fresh little pack of blades. Single edge, yes. Unwrapped the new greasy blue-black blade.

Water ran in the shower. She stepped in – good God; she had on her clothes. Ruined. Her dress clung. Hair streaming. Horrified, she stumbled, half fell, groping her way out. Water drizzling from her stockings ... she began to cry.

Joe found her standing by the bowl. She had taken her wet ruined suit off; she stood naked, supporting herself on one arm, leaning and resting. 'Jesus Christ,' she said to him when she realized he was there. 'I don't know what to do. My jersey suit is ruined. It's wool.' She pointed; he turned to see the heap of sodden clothes.

Very calmly – but his face was stricken – he said, 'Well, you weren't going to wear that anyhow.' With a fluffy white hotel towel he dried her off, led her from the bathroom back to the warm carpeted main room. 'Put on your underwear – get something on. I'll have the hairdresser come up here; she has to, that's all there is.' Again he picked up the phone and dialled.

'What did you get me in the way of pills?' she asked, when he had finished phoning.

'I forgot. I'll call down to the pharmacy. No, wait; I have something. Nembutal or some damn thing.' Hurrying to his suitcase, he began rummaging.

When he held out two yellow capsules to her she said, 'Will they destroy me?' She accepted them clumsily.

'What?' he said, his face twitching.

Rot my lower body, she thought. Groin to dry. 'I mean,' she said cautiously, 'weaken my concentration?'

'No – it's some A.G. Chemie product they give back home. I use them when I can't sleep. I'll get you a glass of water.' He ran off.

Blade, she thought. I swallowed it; now cuts my loins for ever. Punishment. Married to a Jew and shacking up with a Gestapo assassin. She felt tears again in her eyes, boiling. For all I have committed. Wrecked. 'Let's go,' she said, rising to her feet. 'The hairdresser.'

'You're not dressed!' He led her, sat her down, tried to get her underpants onto her without success. 'I have to get your hair fixed,' he said in a despairing voice. 'Where is that *Hur*, that woman?'

She said, speaking slowly and painstakingly, 'Hair creates bear who removes spots in nakedness. Hiding, no hide to be hung with a hook. The hook from God. Hair, hear, *Hur*.' Pills eating. Probably turpentine acid. They all met, decided dangerous most corrosive solvent to eat me for ever.

Staring down at her, Joe blanched. Must read into me, she thought. Reads my mind with his machine, although I can't find it.

'Those pills,' she said. 'Confuse and bewilder.'

He said, 'You didn't take them.' He pointed to her clenched fist; she discovered that she still had them there. 'You're mentally ill,' he said. He had become heavy, slow, like some inert mass. 'You're very sick. We can't go.'

'No doctor,' she said. 'I'll be okay.' She tried to smile; she watched his face to see if she had. Reflection from his brain, caught my thoughts in rots.

'I can't take you to the Abendsens',' he said. 'Not now, anyway. Tomorrow. Maybe you'll be better. We'll try tomorrow. We have to.'

'May I go to the bathroom again?'

He nodded, his face working, barely hearing her. So she returned to the bathroom; again she shut the door. In the cabinet another blade, which she took in her right hand. She came out once more.

'Bye-bye,' she said.

As she opened the corridor door he exclaimed, grabbed wildly at her.

Whisk. 'It is awful,' she said. 'They violate. I ought to know.' Ready for purse snatcher; the various night prowlers, I can certainly handle. Where had this one gone? Slapping his neck, doing a dance. 'Let me by,' she said. 'Don't bar my way unless you want a lesson. However, only women.'

Holding the blade up she went on opening the door. Joe sat on the floor, hands pressed to the side of his throat. Sunburn posture. 'Good-bye,' she said, and shut the door behind her. The warm carpeted corridor.

A woman in a white smock, humming or singing, wheeled a cart along, head down. Gawked at door numbers, arrived in front of Juliana; the woman lifted her head, and her eyes popped and her mouth fell.

'Oh sweetie,' she said, 'you really are tight; you need a lot more than a hairdresser – you go right back inside your room and get your clothes on before they throw you out of this hotel. My good lord.' She opened the door behind Juliana. 'Have your man sober you up; I'll have room service send up hot coffee. Please now, get into your room.' Pushing Juliana back into the room, the woman slammed the door after her and the sound of her cart diminished.

Hairdresser lady, Juliana realized. Looking down, she saw that she did have nothing on; the woman had been correct.

'Joe,' she said. 'They won't let me.' She found the bed, found her suitcase, opened it, spilled out clothes. Underwear, then blouse and skirt . . . pair of low-heeled shoes. 'Made me come back,' she said. Finding a comb, she rapidly combed her hair, then brushed it. 'What an experience. That woman was right outside, about to knock.' Rising, she went to find the mirror. 'Is this better?' Mirror in the closet door; turning, she surveyed herself, twisting, standing on tiptoe. 'I'm so embarrassed,' she said, glancing around for him. 'I hardly know what I'm doing. You must have given me something; whatever it was it just made me sick, instead of helping me.'

Still sitting on the floor, clasping the side of his neck, Joe said, 'Listen. You're very good. You cut my aorta. Artery in my neck.'

Giggling, she clapped her hand to her mouth. 'Oh God – you're such a freak. I mean, you get words all wrong. The aorta's in your chest; you mean the carotid.'

'If I let go,' he said, 'I'll bleed out in two minutes. You

know that. So get me some kind of help, get a doctor or an ambulance. You understand me? Did you mean to? Evidently. Okay – you'll call or go get someone?'

After pondering, she said, 'I meant to.'

'Well,' he said, 'anyhow, get them for me. For my sake.'

'Go yourself.'

'I don't have it completely closed.' Blood had seeped through his fingers, she saw, down his wrist. Pool on the floor. 'I don't dare move. I have to stay here.'

She put on her new coat, closed her new handmade leather purse, picked up her suitcase and as many of the parcels which were hers as she could manage; in particular she made sure she took the big box and the blue Italian dress tucked carefully in it. As she opened the corridor door she looked back at him. 'Maybe I can tell them at the desk,' she said. 'Downstairs.'

'Yes,' he said.

'All right,' she said. 'I'll tell them. Don't look for me back at the apartment in Canon City because I'm not going back there. And I have most of those Reichsbank notes, so I'm in good shape, in spite of everything. Good-bye. I'm sorry.' She shut the door and hurried along the hall as fast as she could manage, lugging the suitcase and parcels.

At the elevator, an elderly well-dressed businessman and his wife helped her; they took the parcels for her, and downstairs in the lobby they gave them to a bellboy for her.

'Thank you,' Juliana said to them.

After the bellboy had carried her suitcase and parcels across the lobby and out onto the front sidewalk, she found a hotel employee who could explain to her how to get back her car. Soon she was standing in the cold concrete garage beneath the hotel, waiting while the attendant brought the Studebaker around. In her purse she found all kinds of change; she tipped the attendant and the next she knew she was driving up a yellow-lit ramp and onto the dark street with its headlights, cars, advertising neon signs.

The uniformed doorman of the hotel personally loaded

her luggage and parcels into the trunk for her, smiling with such hearty encouragement that she gave him an enormous tip before she drove away. No one tried to stop her, and that amazed her; they did not even raise an eyebrow. I guess they know he'll pay, she decided. Or maybe he already did when he registered for us.

While she waited with other cars for a streetlight to change, she remembered that she had not told them at the desk about Joe sitting on the floor of the room needing the doctor. Still waiting up there, waiting from now on until the end of the world or until the cleaning women showed up tomorrow some time. I better go back, she decided, or telephone. Stop at a pay booth.

It's so silly, she thought as she drove along searching for a place to park and telephone. Who would have thought an hour ago? When we signed in, when we stopped . . . we almost went on, got dressed up and went out to dinner; we might even have gotten out to the nightclub. Again she had begun to cry, she discovered; tears dripped from her nose, onto her blouse, as she drove. Too bad I didn't consult the oracle; it would have known and warned me. Why didn't I? Any time I could have asked, any place along the trip or even before we left. She began to moan involuntarily; the noise, a howling she had never heard issue out of her before, horrified her, but she could not suppress it even though she clamped her teeth together. A ghastly chanting, singing, wailing, rising up through her nose.

When she had parked she sat with the motor running, shivering, hands in her coat pockets. Christ, she said to herself miserably. Well, I guess that's the sort of thing that happens. She got out of the car and dragged her suitcase from the trunk; in the back seat she opened it and dug around among the clothes and shoes until she had hold of the two black volumes of the oracle. There, in the back seat of the car, with the motor running, she began tossing three R.M.S. dimes, using the glare of a department store window to see by. What'll I do? she asked it. Tell me what to do; *please*.

Hexagram Forty-two, Increase, with moving lines in the second, third, fourth and top places; therefore changing to Hexagram Forty-three, Breakthrough. She scanned the text ravenously, catching up the successive stages of meaning in her mind, gathering it and comprehending; Jesus, it depicted the situation exactly – a miracle once more. All that had happened, there before her eyes, blueprint, schematic:

> It furthers one
> To undertake something.
> It furthers one to cross the great water.

Trip, to go and do something important, not stay here. Now the lines. Her lips moved, seeking . . .

> Ten pairs of tortoises cannot oppose him.
> Constant perseverance brings good fortune.
> The king presents him before God.

Now six in the third. Reading, she became dizzy;

> One is enriched through unfortunate events.
> No blame, if you are sincere
> And walk in the middle,
> And report with a seal to the prince.

The prince . . . it meant Abendsen. The seal, the new copy of his book. Unfortunate events – the oracle knew what had happened to her, the dreadfulness with Joe or whatever he was. She read six in the fourth place:

> If you walk in the middle
> And report to the prince,
> He will follow.

I must go there, she realized, even if Joe comes after me. She devoured the last moving line, nine at the top:

> He brings increase to no one.
> Indeed, someone even strikes him.
> He does not keep his heart constantly steady,
> Misfortune.

Oh God, she thought; it means the killer, the Gestapo people – it's telling me that Joe or someone like him, someone else, will get there and kill Abendsen. Quickly, she turned to Hexagram Forty-three. The judgement:

> One must resolutely make the matter known
> At the court of the king.
> It must be announced truthfully. Danger.
> It is necessary to notify one's own city.
> It does not further to resort to arms.
> It furthers one to undertake something.

So it's no use to go back to the hotel and make sure about him; it's hopeless, because there will be others sent out. Again the oracle says, even more emphatically: Get up to Cheyenne and warn Abendsen, however dangerous it is to me. I must bring him the truth.

She shut the volume.

Getting back behind the wheel of the car, she backed out into traffic. In a short time she had found her way out of downtown Denver and onto the main autobahn going north; she drove as fast as the car would go, the engine making a strange throbbing noise that shook the wheel and the seat and made everything in the glove compartment rattle.

Thank God for Doctor Todt and his autobahns, she said to herself as she hurtled along through the darkness, seeing only her own headlights and the lines marking the lanes.

At ten o'clock that night because of tyre trouble she had still not reached Cheyenne, so there was nothing to do but pull off the road and search for a place to spend the night.

An autobahn exit sign ahead of her read GREELEY FIVE MILES. I'll start out again tomorrow morning, she told herself as she drove slowly along the main street of Greeley a few minutes later. She saw several motels with vacancy signs lit, so there was no problem. What I must do, she decided, is call Abendsen tonight and say I'm coming.

When she had parked she got wearily from the car, relieved to be able to stretch her legs. All day on the road, from eight in the morning on. An all-night drugstore could be made out not far down the sidewalk; hands in the pockets of her coat, she walked that way, and soon she was shut up in the privacy of the phone booth, asking the operator for Cheyenne information.

Their phone – thank God – was listed. She put in the quarters and the operator rang.

'Hello,' a woman's voice sounded presently, a vigorous, rather pleasant younger-woman's voice; a woman no doubt about her own age.

'Mrs Abendsen?' Juliana said. 'May I talk to Mr Abendsen?'

'Who is this, please?'

Juliana said, 'I read his book and I drove all day up from Canon City, Colorado. I'm in Greeley now. I thought I could make it to your place tonight, but I can't, so I want to know if I can see him some time tomorrow.'

After a pause, Mrs Abendsen said in a still-pleasant voice, 'Yes, it's too late, now; we go to bed quite early. Was there any – special reason why you wanted to see my husband? He's working very hard right now.'

'I wanted to speak to him,' she said. Her own voice in her ears sounded drab and wooden; she stared at the wall of the booth, unable to find anything further to say – her body ached and her mouth felt dry and full of foul tastes. Beyond the phone booth she could see the druggist at the soda counter serving milk shakes to four teen-agers. She longed to be there; she scarcely paid attention as Mrs Abendsen answered. She longed for some fresh, cold drink, and something like a chicken salad sandwich to go with it.

'Hawthorne works erratically,' Mrs Abendsen was saying in her merry, brisk voice. 'If you drive up here tomorrow I can't promise you anything, because he might be involved all day long. But if you understand that before you make the trip –'

'Yes,' she broke in.

'I know he'll be glad to chat with you for a few minutes if he can,' Mrs Abendsen continued. 'But please don't be disappointed if by chance he can't break off long enough to talk to you or even see you.'

'We read his book and liked it,' Juliana said. 'I have it with me.'

'I see,' Mrs Abendsen said good-naturedly.

'We stopped off at Denver and shopped, so we lost a lot of time.' No, she thought; it's all changed, all different. 'Listen,' she said, 'the oracle told me to come to Cheyenne.'

'Oh my,' Mrs Abendsen said, sounding as if she knew about the oracle, and yet not taking the situation seriously.

'I'll give you the lines.' She had brought the oracle with her into the phone booth; propping the volumes up on the shelf beneath the phone, she laboriously turned the pages. 'Just a second.' She located the page and read first the judgement and then the lines to Mrs Abendsen. When she got to the nine at the top – she heard Mrs Abendsen exclaim. 'Pardon?' Juliana said, pausing.

'Go ahead,' Mrs Abendsen said. Her tone, Juliana thought, had a more alert, sharpened quality now.

After Juliana had read the judgement of the Forty-third hexagram, with the word danger in it, there was silence. Mrs Abendsen said nothing and Juliana said nothing.

'Well, we'll look forward to seeing you tomorrow, then,' Mrs Abendsen said finally. 'And would you give me your name, please?'

'Juliana Frink,' she said. 'Thank you very much, Mrs Abendsen.' The operator, now, had broken in to clamour about the time being up, so Juliana hung up the phone, collected her purse and the volumes of the oracle, left the phone booth and walked over to the drugstore fountain.

After she had ordered a sandwich and a Coke, and was sitting smoking a cigarette and resting, she realized with a rush of unbelieving horror that she had said nothing to Mrs Abendsen about the Gestapo man or the S.D. man or whatever he was, that Joe Cinnadella she had left in the hotel room in Denver. She simply could not believe it. I forgot! she said to herself. It dropped completely out of my mind. How could that be? I must be nuts; I must be terribly sick and stupid and nuts.

For a moment she fumbled with her purse, trying to find

change for another call. No, she decided as she started up from the stool. I can't call them again tonight; I'll let it go – it's just too goddam late. I'm tired and they're probably asleep by now.

She ate her chicken salad sandwich, drank her Coke, and then she drove to the nearest motel, rented a room and crept tremblingly into bed.

14

Mr Nobusuke Tagomi thought, There is no answer. No understanding. Even in the oracle. Yet I must go on living day to day anyhow.

I will go and find the small. Live unseen, at any rate. Until some later time when –

In any case he said good-bye to his wife and left his house. But today he did not go to the Nippon Times Building as usual. What about relaxation? Drive to Golden Gate Park with its zoo and fish? Visit where things who cannot think nonetheless enjoy.

Time. It is a long trip for the pedecab, and it gives me more time to perceive. If that can be said.

But trees and zoos are not personal. I must clutch at human life. This had made me into a child, although that could be good. I could make it good.

The pedecab driver pumped along Kearny Street, towards downtown San Francisco. Ride cable car, Mr Tagomi thought suddenly. Happiness in clearest, almost tear-jerking voyage, object that should have vanished in 1900 but is oddly yet extant.

He dismissed the pedecab, walked along the sidewalk towards the nearest cable tracks.

Perhaps, he thought, I can never go back to the Nippon Times Building, with its stink of Death. My career over, but just as well. A replacement can be found by the Board of

Trade Mission Activities. But Tagomi still walks, exists, recalling every detail. So nothing is accomplished.

In any case the war, Operation Dandelion, will sweep us all away. No matter what we are doing at the time. Our enemy, alongside whom we fought in the last war. What good did it do us? We should have fought them, possibly. Or permitted them to lose, assisted their enemies, the United States, Britain, Russia.

Hopeless wherever one looks.

The oracle enigmatic. Perhaps it has withdrawn from the world of man in sorrow. The sages leaving.

We have entered a Moment when we are alone. We cannot get assistance, as before. Well, Mr Tagomi thought, perhaps that too is good. Or can be made good. One must still try to find the Way.

He boarded the California Street cable car, rode all the way to the end of the line. He even hopped out and assisted in turning the cable car around on its wooden turntable. That, of all experiences in the city, had the most meaning for him, customarily. Now the effect languished; he felt the void even more acutely, due to vitiation here of all places.

Naturally he rode back. But . . . a formality, he realized as he watched the streets, buildings, traffic pass in reverse of before.

Near Stockton he rose to get off. But at the stop, when he started to descend, the conductor hailed him. 'Your briefcase, sir.'

'Thank you.' He had left it on the cable car. Reaching up he accepted it, then bowed as the cable car clanged into motion. Very valuable briefcase contents, he thought. Priceless Colt ·44 collector's item carried within. Now kept within easy reach constantly, in case vengeful hooligans of S.D. should try to repay me as individual. One never knows. And yet – Mr Tagomi felt that this new procedure, despite all that had occurred, was neurotic. I should not yield to it, he told himself once again as he walked along carrying the briefcase. Compulsion-obsession-phobia. But he could not free himself.

It in my grip, I in its, he thought.

Have I then lost my delighted attitude? he asked himself. Is *all* instinct perverted from the memory of what I did? All collecting damaged, not merely attitude towards this one item? Mainstay of my life . . . area, alas, where I dwelt with such relish.

Hailing a pedecab, he directed the driver to Montgomery Street and Robert Childan's shop. Let us find out. One thread left, connecting me with the voluntary. I possibly could manage my anxious proclivities by a ruse : trade the gun in on more historicity sanctioned item. This gun, for me, has too much subjective history . . . all of the wrong kind. But that ends with me; no one else can experience it from the gun. Within my psyche only.

Free myself, he decided with excitement. When the gun goes, it all leaves, the cloud of the past. For it is not merely in my psyche; it is – as has always been said in the theory of historicity – within the gun as well. An equation between us !

He reached the store. Where I have dealt so much, he observed as he paid the driver. Both business and private. Carrying the briefcase he quickly entered.

There, at the cash register, Mr Childan. Polishing with cloth some artifact.

'Mr Tagomi,' Childan said, with a bow.

'Mr Childan.' He, too, bowed.

'What a surprise. I am overcome.' Childan put down the object and cloth. Around the corner of the counter he came. Usual ritual, the greeting, et cetera. Yet, Mr Tagomi felt the man today somehow different. Rather – muted. An improvement, he decided. Always a trifle loud, shrill. Skipping about with agitation. But this might well be a bad omen.

'Mr Childan,' Mr Tagomi said, placing his briefcase on the counter and unzipping it, 'I wish to trade in an item bought several years ago. You do that, I recollect.'

'Yes,' Mr Childan said. 'Depending on condition, for instance.' He watched alertly.

'Colt ·44 revolver,' Mr Tagomi said.

They were both silent, regarding the gun as it lay in its open teakwood box with its carton of partly consumed ammunition.

Shade colder by Mr Childan. Ah, Mr Tagomi realized. Well, so be it. 'You are not interested,' Mr Tagomi said.

'No, sir,' Mr Childan said in a stiff voice.

'I will not press it.' He did not feel any strength. I yield. Yin, the adaptive, receptive, holds sway in me, I fear . . .

'Forgive me, Mr Tagomi.'

Mr Tagomi bowed, replaced the gun, ammunition, box, in his briefcase. Destiny. I must keep this thing.

'You seem – quite disappointed,' Mr Childan said.

'You notice.' He was perturbed; had he let his inner world out for all to view? He shrugged. Certainly it was so.

'Was there a special reason why you wanted to trade that item in?' Mr Childan said.

'No,' he said, once more concealing his personal world – as should be.

Mr Childan hesitated, then said, 'I – wonder if that did emanate from my store. I do not carry that item.'

'I am sure,' Mr Tagomi said. 'But it does not matter. I accept your decision; I am not offended.'

'Sir,' Childan said, 'allow me to show you what has come in. Are you free for a moment?'

Mr Tagomi felt within him the old stirring. 'Something of unusual interest?'

'Come, sir.' Childan led the way across the store; Mr Tagomi followed.

Within a locked glass case, on trays of black velvet, lay small metal swirls, shapes that merely hinted rather than were. They gave Mr Tagomi a queer feeling as he stopped to study.

'I show these ruthlessly to each of my customers,' Robert Childan said. 'Sir, do you know what these are?'

'Jewellery, it appears,' Mr Tagomi said, noticing a pin.

'These are American-made. Yes of course. But, sir. These are not the old.'

Mr Tagomi glanced up.

'Sir, these are the new.' Robert Childan's white, somewhat drab features were disturbed by passion. 'This is the new life of my country, sir. The beginning in the form of tiny imperishable seeds. Of beauty.'

With due interest, Mr Tagomi took time to examine in his own hands several of the pieces. Yes, there is something new which animates these, he decided. The Law of Tao is borne out, here; when yin lies everywhere, the first stirring of light is suddenly alive in the darkest depths ... we are all familiar; we have seen it happen before, as I see it here now. And yet for me they are just scraps. I cannot become rapt, as Mr R. Childan, here. Unfortunately, for both of us. But that is the case.

'Quite lovely,' he murmured, laying down the pieces.

Mr Childan said in a forceful voice, 'Sir, it does not occur at once.'

'Pardon?'

'The new view in your heart.'

'You are converted,' Mr Tagomi said. 'I wish I could be. I am not.' He bowed.

'Another time,' Mr Childan said, accompanying him to the entrance of the store; he made no move to display any alternative items, Mr Tagomi noticed.

'Your certitude is in questionable taste,' Mr Tagomi said. 'It seems to press untowardly.'

Mr Childan did not cringe. 'Forgive me,' he said. 'But I am correct. I sense accurately in these the contracted germ of the future.'

'So be it,' Mr Tagomi said. 'But your Anglo-Saxon fanaticism does not appeal to me.' Nonetheless, he felt a certain renewal of hope. His own hope, in himself. 'Good day.' He bowed. 'I will see you again one of these days. We can perhaps examine your prophecy.'

Mr Childan bowed, saying nothing.

Carrying his briefcase, with the Colt .44 within, Mr Tagomi departed. I go out as I came in, he reflected. Still seeking. Still without what I need if I am to return to the world.

What if I had bought one of those odd, indistinct items? Kept it, re-examined, contemplated . . . would I have subsequently, through it, found my way back? I doubt it.

Those are for him, not me.

And yet, even if one person finds his way . . , that means there is a Way. Even if I personally fail to reach it.

I envy him.

Turning, Mr Tagomi started back toward the store. There, in the doorway, stood Mr Childan regarding him. He had not gone back in.

'Sir,' Mr Tagomi said, 'I will buy one of those, whichever you select. I have no faith, but I am currently grasping at straws.' He followed Mr Childan through the store once more, to the glass case. 'I do not believe. I will carry it about with me, looking at it at regular intervals. Once every other day, for instance. After two months if I do not see –'

'You may return it for full credit,' Mr Childan said.

'Thank you,' Mr Tagomi said. He felt better. Sometimes one must try anything, he decided. It is no disgrace. On the contrary, it is a sign of wisdom, of recognizing the situation.

'This will calm you,' Mr Childan said. He laid out a single small silver triangle ornamented with hollow drops. Black beneath, bright and light-filled above.

'Thank you,' Mr Tagomi said.

By pedecab Mr Tagomi journeyed to Portsmouth Square, a little open park on the slope above Kearny Street overlooking the police station. He seated himself on a bench in the sun. Pigeons walked along the paved paths in search of food. On other benches shabby men read the newspaper or dozed. Here and there others lay on the grass, nearly asleep.

Bringing from his pocket the paper bag marked with the name of Mr Childan's store, Mr Tagomi sat holding the paper bag with both hands, warming himself. Then he opened the bag and lifted out his new possession for inspection in solitude, here in this little grass and path park of old men.

He held the squiggle of silver. Reflection of the midday

sun, like boxtop cereal trinket, sent-away acquired Jack Armstrong magnifying mirror. Or – he gazed down into it. *Om*, as the Brahmins say. Shrunk spot in which all is captured. Both, at least in hint. The size, the shape. He continued to inspect dutifully.

Will it come, as Mr R. Childan prophesied? Five minutes. Ten minutes. I sit as long as I can. Time, alas, will make us sell it short. What is it I hold, while there is still time?

Forgive me, Mr Tagomi thought in the direction of the squiggle. Pressure on us always to rise and act. Regretfully, he began to put the thing away back in its bag. One final hopeful glance – he again scrutinized with all that he had. Like child, he told himself. Imitate the innocence and faith. On seashore, pressing randomly found shell to head. Hearing in its blabber the wisdom of the sea.

This, with eye replacing ear. Enter me and inform what has been done, what it means, why. Compression of understanding into one finite squiggle.

Asking too much, and so get nothing.

'Listen,' he said *sotto voce* to the squiggle. 'Sales warranty promised much.'

If I shake it violently, like old recalcitrant watch. He did so, up and down. Or like dice in critical game. Awaken the deity inside. Peradventure he sleepeth. Or he is on a journey. Titillating heavy irony by Prophet Elijah. Or he is pursuing. Mr Tagomi violently shook the silver squiggle up and down in his clenched fist once. Call him louder. Again he scrutinized.

You little thing, you are empty, he thought.

Curse at it, he told himself. Frighten it.

'My patience is running out,' he said *sotto voce.*

And what then? Fling you in the gutter? Breathe on it, shake it, breathe on it. Win me the game.

He laughed. Addlepated involvement, here in warm sunlight. Spectacle to whoever comes along. Peeking about guiltily, now. But no one saw. Old men snoozing. Measure of relief, there.

Tried everything, he realized. Pleaded, contemplated,

threatened, philosophized at length. What else can be done?

Could I but stay here. It is denied me. Opportunity will perhaps occur again. And yet, as W. S. Gilbert says, such an opportunity will *not* occur again. Is that so? I feel it to be so.

When I was a child I thought as a child. But now I have put away childish things. Now I must seek in other realms, I must keep after this object in new ways.

I must be scientific. Exhaust by logical analysis every entrée. Systematically, in classic Aristotelian laboratory manner.

He put his finger in his right ear, to shut off traffic and all other distracting noises. Then he tightly held the silver triangle, shellwise, to his left ear.

No sound. No roar of simulated ocean, in actuality interior blood-motion noises – not even that.

Then what other sense might apprehend mystery? Hearing of no use, evidently. Mr Tagomi shut his eyes and began fingering every bit of surface on the item. Not touch; his fingers told him nothing. Smell. He put the silver close to his nose and inhaled. Metallic faint odour, but it conveyed no meaning. Taste. Opening his mouth he sneaked the silver triangle within, popped it in like a cracker, but of course refrained from chewing. No meaning, only bitter hard cold thing.

He again held it in his palm.

Back at last to seeing. Highest ranking of the senses: Greek scale of priority. He turned the silver triangle each and every way; he viewed it from every *extra rem* standpoint.

What do I see? he asked himself. Due to long patient painstaking study. What is clue of truth that confronts me in this object?

Yield, he told the silver triangle. Cough up arcane secret.

Like frog pulled from depths, he thought. Clutched in fist, given command to declare what lies below in the watery abyss. But here the frog does not even mock; it strangles silently, becomes stone or clay or mineral. Inert. Passes back to the rigid substance familiar in its tomb world.

Metal is from the earth, he thought as he scrutinized. From below : from that realm which is the lowest, the most dense. Land of trolls and caves, dank, always dark. Yin world, in its most melancholy aspect. World of corpses, decay and collapse. Of faeces. All that has died, slipping and disintegrating back down layer by layer. The daemonic world of the immutable; the time-that-was.

And yet, in the sunlight, the silver triangle glittered. It reflected light. Fire, Mr Tagomi thought. Not dank or dark object at all. Not heavy, weary, but pulsing with life. The high realm, aspect of yang : empyrean, ethereal. As befits work of art. Yes, that is artist's job : takes mineral rock from dark silent earth, transforms it into shining light-reflecting form from sky.

Has brought the dead to life. Corpse turned to fiery display; the past has yielded to the future.

Which are you? he asked the silver squiggle. Dark dead yin or brilliant living yang? In his palm, the silver squiggle danced and blinded him; he squinted, seeing now only the play of fire.

Body of yin, soul of yang. Metal and fire unified. The outer and inner; microcosmos in my palm.

What is the space which this speaks of? Vertical ascent. To heaven. Of time? Into the light-world of the mutable. Yes, this thing has disgorged its spirit : light. And my attention is fixed; I can't look away. Spellbound by mesmerizing shimmering surface which I can no longer control. No longer free to dismiss.

Now talk to me, he told it. Now that you have snared me. I want to hear your voice issuing from the blinding clear white light, such as we expect to see only in the *Bardo Thödol* afterlife existence. But I do not have to wait for death, for the decomposition of my animus as it wanders in search of a new womb. All the terrifying and beneficent deities; we will by-pass them, and the smoky lights as well. And the couples in coitus. Everything except this light. I am ready to face without terror. Notice I do not blench.

I feel the hot winds of karma driving me. Nevertheless I

remain here. My training was correct: I must not shrink from the clear white light, for if I do, I will once more re-enter the cycle of birth and death, never knowing freedom, never obtaining release. The veil of maya will fall once more if I –

The light disappeared.

He held the dull silver triangle only. Shadow had cut off the sun; Mr Tagomi glanced up.

Tall, blue-suited policeman standing by his bench, smiling.

'Eh?' Mr Tagomi said, startled.

'I was just watching you work that puzzle.' The policeman started on along the path.

'Puzzle,' Mr Tagomi echoed. 'Not a puzzle.'

'Isn't that one of those little puzzles you have to take apart? My kid has a whole lot of them. Some are hard.' The policeman passed on.

Mr Tagomi thought, Spoiled. My chance at nirvana. Gone. Interrupted by that white barbarian Neanderthal *yank*. That sub-human supposing I worked a child's puerile toy.

Rising from the bench he took a few steps unsteadily. Must calm down. Dreadful low-class jingoistic racist invectives, unworthy of me.

Incredible unredemptive passions clashing in my breast. He made his way through the park. Keep moving, he told himself. Catharsis in motion.

He reached periphery of park. Sidewalk, Kearny Street. Heavy noisy traffic. Mr Tagomi halted at the kerb.

No pedecabs. He walked along the sidewalk instead; he joined the crowd. Never can get one when you need it.

God, what is that? He stopped, gaped at hideous misshapen thing on skyline. Like nightmare of roller coaster suspended, blotting out view. Enormous construction of metal and cement in air.

Mr Tagomi turned to a passer-by, a thin man in rumpled suit. 'What is that?' he demanded, pointing.

The man grinned. 'Awful, ain't it? That's the Embar-

222

cadero Freeway. A lot of people think it stinks up the view.'

'I never saw it before,' Mr Tagomi said.

'You're lucky,' the man said, and went on.

Mad dream, Mr Tagomi thought. Must wake up. Where are the pedecabs today? He began to walk faster. Whole vista has dull, smoky, tomb-world cast. Smell of burning. Dim grey buildings, sidewalk, peculiar harsh tempo in people. And *still* no pedecabs.

'Cab!' he shouted as he hurried along.

Hopeless. Only cars and buses. Cars like brutal big crushers, all unfamiliar in shape. He avoided seeing them; kept his eyes straight ahead. Distortion of my optic perception of particularly sinister nature. A disturbance affecting my sense of space. Horizon twisted out of line. Like lethal astigmatism striking without warning.

Must obtain respite. Ahead, a dingy lunch counter. Only whites within, all supping. Mr Tagomi pushed open the wooden swinging doors. Smell of coffee. Grotesque jukebox in corner blaring out; he winced and made his way to the counter. All stools taken by whites. Mr Tagomi exclaimed. Several whites looked up. *But none departed their places. None yielded their stools to him. They merely resumed supping.*

'I insist!' Mr Tagomi said loudly to the first white; he shouted in the man's ear.

The man put down his coffee mug and said, 'Watch it, Tojo.'

Mr Tagomi looked to the other whites; all watched with hostile expressions. And none stirred.

Bardo Thödol existence, Mr Tagomi thought. Hot winds blowing me who knows where. This is vision – of what? Can the animus endure this? Yes, the *Book of the Dead* prepares us : after death we seem to glimpse others, but all appear hostile to us. One stands isolated. Unsuccoured wherever one turns. The terrible journey – and always the realms of suffering, rebirth, ready to receive the fleeing, demoralized spirit. The delusions.

He hurried from the lunch counter. The doors swung together behind him; he stood once more on the sidewalk. Where am I? Out of my world, my space and time.

The silver triangle disoriented me. I broke from my moorings and hence stand on nothing. So much for my endeavour. Lesson to me for ever. One seeks to contravene one's perceptions – why? So that one can wander utterly lost, without signposts or guide?

This hypnagogic condition. Attention-faculty diminished so that twilight state obtains; world seen merely in symbolic archetypal aspect, totally confused with unconscious material. Typical of hypnosis-induced somnambulism. Must stop this dreadful gliding among shadows, refocus concentration and thereby restore ego centre.

He felt in his pockets for the silver triangle. Gone. Left the thing on bench in park, with briefcase. Catastrophe.

Crouching, he ran back up the sidewalk, to the park.

Dozing bums eyed him in surprise as he hurried up the path. There, the bench. And leaning against it still, his briefcase. No sign of the silver triangle. He hunted. Yes. Fallen through to grass; it lay partly hidden. Where he had hurled it in rage.

He reseated himself, panting for breath.

Focus on silver triangle once more, he told himself when he could breathe. Scrutinize it forcefully and count. At ten, utter startling noise. *Erwache*, for instance.

Idiotic daydreaming of fugal type, he thought. Emulation of more noxious aspects of adolescence, rather than the clearheaded pristine innocence of authentic childhood. Just what I deserve anyhow.

All my own fault. No intention by Mr R. Childan or artisans; my own greed to blame. One cannot compel understanding to come.

He counted slowly, aloud, and then jumped to his feet. 'Goddam stupidity,' he said sharply.

Mists cleared?

He peeped about. Diffusion subsided, in all probability.

Now one appreciates Saint Paul's incisive word choice . . . seen through glass darkly not a metaphor, but astute reference to optical distortion. We really do see astigmatically, in fundamental sense : our space and our time creations of our own psyche, and when these momentarily falter – like acute disturbance of middle ear.

Occasionally we list eccentrically, all sense of balance gone.

He reseated himself, put the silver squiggle away in his coat pocket, sat holding his briefcase on his lap. What I must do now, he told himself, is go and see if that malignant construction – what did the man call it? Embarcadero Freeway. If it is still palpable.

But he felt afraid to.

And yet, he thought, I can't merely sit here. I have loads to lift, as old U.S. folk expression has it. Jobs to be done.

Dilemma.

Two small Chinese boys came scampering noisily along the path. A flock of pigeons fluttered up; the boys paused.

Mr Tagomi called, 'You, young fellows.' He dug into his pocket. 'Come here.'

The two boys guardedly approached.

'Here's a dime.' Mr Tagomi tossed them a dime; the boys scrambled for it. 'Go down to Kearny Street and see if there are any pedecabs. Come back and tell me.'

'Will you give us another dime?' one of the boys said, 'When we get back?'

'Yes,' Mr Tagomi said. 'But tell me the truth.'

The boys raced off along the path.

I there are not, Mr Tagomi thought, I would be well advised to retire to secluded place and kill myself. He clutched his briefcase. Still have the weapon; no difficulty there.

The boys came tearing back. 'Six!' one of them yelled. 'I counted six.'

'I counted five,' the other boy gasped.

Mr Tagomi said, 'You're sure they were pedecabs? You distinctly saw the drivers peddling?'

'Yes sir,' the boys said together.

He gave each boy a dime. They thanked him and ran off.

Back to office and job, Mr Tagomi thought. He rose to his feet, gripping the handle of his briefcase. Duty calls. Customary day once again.

Once more he walked down the path, to the sidewalk.

'Cab!' he called.

From the traffic a pedecab appeared; the driver came to a halt at the kerb, his lean dark face glistening, chest heaving. 'Yes sir.'

'Take me to the Nippon Times Building,' Mr Tagomi ordered. He ascended to the seat and made himself comfortable.

Peddling furiously, the pedecab driver moved out among the other cabs and cars.

It was slightly before noon when Mr Tagomi reached the Nippon Times Building. From the main lobby he instructed a switchboard operator to connect him with Mr Ramsey upstairs.

'Tagomi, here,' he said, when the connection was complete.

'Good morning, sir. I am relieved. Not seeing you, I apprehensively telephoned your home at ten o'clock, but your wife said you had left for unknown parts.'

Mr Tagomi said, 'Has the mess been cleared?'

'No sign remains.'

'Beyond dispute?'

'My word, sir.'

Satisfied, Mr Tagomi hung up and went to take the elevator.

Upstairs, as he entered his office, he permitted himself a momentary search. Rim of his vision. No sign, as was promised. He felt relief. No one would know who hadn't seen. Historicity bonded into nylon tile of floor...

Mr Ramsey met him inside. 'Your courage is topic for panegyric down below at the *Times*,' he began. 'An article depicting –' Making out Mr Tagomi's expression he broke off.

'Answer regarding pressing matters,' Mr Tagomi said. 'General Tedeki? That is, quondam Mr Yatabe?'

'On carefully obscure flight back to Tokyo. Red herrings strewn hither and yon.' Mr Ramsey crossed his fingers, symbolizing their hope.

'Please recount regarding Mr Baynes.'

'I don't know. During your absence he appeared briefly, even furtively, but did not talk.' Mr Ramsey hesitated. 'Possibly he returned to Germany.'

'Far better for him to go to the Home Islands,' Mr Tagomi said, mostly to himself. In any case, it was with the old general that their concern, of important nature, lay. And it is beyond my scope, Mr Tagomi thought. My self, my office; they made use of me here, which naturally was proper and good. I was their – what is it deemed? Their cover.

I am a mask, concealing the real. Behind me, hidden, actuality goes on, safe from prying eyes.

Odd, he thought. Vital sometimes to be merely cardboard front, like carton. Bit of satori there, if I could lay hold of it. Purpose in overall scheme of illusion, could we but fathom. Law of economy : nothing is waste. Even the unreal. What a sublimity in the process.

Miss Ephreikian appeared, her manner agitated. 'Mr Tagomi. The switchboard sent me.'

'Be cool, miss,' Mr Tagomi said. The current of time urges us along, he thought.

'Sir, the German consul is here. He wants to speak to you.' She glanced from him to Mr Ramsey and back, her face unnaturally pale. 'They say he was here in the building earlier, too, but they knew you –'

Mr Tagomi waved her silent. 'Mr Ramsey. Please recollect for me the consul's name.'

'Freiherr Hugo Reiss, sir.'

'Now I recall.' Well, he thought, evidently Mr Childan did me a favour after all. By declining to reaccept the gun.

Carrying his briefcase, he left his office and walked out into the corridor.

There stood a slightly built, well-dressed white. Close-cut orange hair, shiny black European leather Oxfords, erect posture. And effeminate ivory cigarette holder. No doubt he.

'Herr H. Reiss?' Mr Tagomi said.

The German bowed.

'Has been fact,' Mr Tagomi said, 'that you and I have in times past conducted business by mail, phone, et cetera. But never until now saw face to face.'

'An honour,' Herr Reiss said, advancing towards him. 'Even considering the irritatingly distressing circumstances.'

'I wonder,' Mr Tagomi said.

The German raised an eyebrow.

'Excuse me,' Mr Tagomi said. 'My cognition hazed over due to those indicated circumstances. Frailty of clay-made substance, one might conclude.'

'Awful,' Herr Reiss said. He shook his head. 'When I first —'

Mr Tagomi said, 'Before you begin litany, let me speak.'

'Certainly.'

'I personally shot your two S.D. men,' Mr Tagomi said.

'The San Francisco Police Department summoned me,' Herr Reiss said, blowing offensive-smelling cigarette smoke around them both. 'For hours I've been down at the Kearny Street Station and at the morgue, and then I've been reading over the account your people gave to the investigating police inspectors. Absolutely dreadful, this, from start to finish.'

Mr Tagomi said nothing.

'However,' Herr Reiss continued, 'the contention that the hoodlums are connected with the Reich hasn't been established. As far as I'm concerned the whole matter is insane. I'm sure you acted absolutely properly, Mr Tagori.'

'Tagomi.'

'My hand,' the consul said, extending his hand. 'Let's shake a gentlemen's agreement to drop this. It's unworthy, especially in these critical times when any stupid publicity might inflame the mob mind, to the detriment of both our nations' interests.'

'Guilt nonetheless is on my soul,' Mr Tagomi said. 'Blood, Herr Reiss, can never be eradicated like ink.'

The consul seemed nonplussed.

'I crave forgiveness,' Mr Tagomi said. 'You cannot give it to me, though, Possibly no one can. I intend to read famous diary by Massachusetts' ancient divine. Goodman C. Mather. Deals, I am told, with guilt and hell-fire, et al.'

The consul smoked his cigarette rapidly, intently studying Mr Tagomi.

'Allow me to notify you,' Mr Tagomi said, 'that your nation is about to descend into greater vileness than ever. You know the hexagram The Abyss? Speaking as a private person, not as representative of Japan officialdom, I declare : heart sick with horror. Bloodbath coming beyond all compare. Yet even now you strive for some slight egotistic gain or goal. Put one over on rival faction, the S.D., eh? While you get Herr B. Kreuz vom Meere in hot water –' He could not go on. His chest had become constricted. Like childhood, he thought. Asthma when angry at the old lady. 'I am suffering,' he told Herr Reiss, who had put out his cigarette now. 'Of malady growing these long years but which entered virulent form the day I heard, helplessly, your leaders' escapades recited. Anyhow, therapeutic possibility nil. For you, too, sir. In language of Goodman C. Mather, if properly recalled : Repent!'

The German consul said huskily, 'Properly recalled.' He nodded, lit a new cigarette with trembling fingers.

From the office, Mr Ramsey appeared. He carried a sheaf of forms and papers. To Mr Tagomi, who stood silently trying to get an unconstricted breath, he said, 'While he's here. Routine matter having to do with his functionality.'

Reflexively, Mr Tagomi took the forms held out. He glanced at them. Form 20–50. Request by Reich through representative in P.S.A., Consul Freiherr Hugo Reiss, for remand of felon now in custody of San Francisco Police Department. Jew named Frank Fink, citizen – according to

Reichs law – of Germany, retroactive June, 1960. For protective custody under Reichs law, etc. He scanned it over once.

'Pen, sir,' Mr Ramsey said. 'That concludes business with German Government this date.' He eyed the consul with distaste as he held the pen to Mr Tagomi.

'No,' Mr Tagomi said. He returned the 20–50 form to Mr Ramsey. Then he grabbed it back, scribbled on the bottom, *Release. Ranking Trade Mission, S.F. authority. Vide Military Protocol 1947. Tagomi.* He handed one carbon to the German consul, the others to Mr Ramsey along with the original. 'Good day, Herr Reiss.' He bowed.

The German consul bowed, also. He scarcely bothered to look at the paper.

'Please conduct future business through intermediate machinery such as mail, telephone, cable,' Mr Tagomi said. said. 'Not personally.'

The consul said, 'You're holding me responsible for general conditions beyond my jurisdiction.'

'Chicken shit,' Mr Tagomi said. 'I say that to that.'

'This is not the way civilized individuals conduct business,' the consul said. 'You're making this all bitter and vindictive. Where it ought to be mere formality with no personality embroiled.' He threw his cigarette onto the corridor floor, then turned and strode off.

'Take foul stinking cigarette along,' Mr Tagomi said weakly, but the consul had turned the corner. 'Childish conduct by self,' Mr Tagomi said to Mr Ramsey. 'You witnessed repellent childish conduct.' He made his way unsteadily back into his office. No breath at all, now. A pain flowed down his left arm, and at the same time a great open palm of hand flattened and squashed his ribs. Oof, he said. Before him, no carpet, but merely shower of sparks, rising, red.

Help, Mr Ramsey, he said. But no sound. Please. He reached out, stumbled. Nothing to catch, even.

As he fell he clutched within his coat the silver triangle thing Mr Childan had urged on him. Did not save me, he thought. Did not help. All that endeavour.

His body struck the floor. Hands and knees, gasping, the carpet at his nose. Mr Ramsey now rushing about bleating. Keep equipoise, Mr Tagomi thought.

'I'm having small heart attack,' Mr Tagomi managed to say.

Several persons were involved, now, transporting him to couch. 'Be calm, sir,' one was telling him.

'Notify wife, please,' Mr Tagomi said.

Presently he heard ambulance noises. Wailing from street. Plus much bustle. People coming and going. A blanket was put over him, up to his armpits. Tie removed. Collar loosened.

'Better now,' Mr Tagomi said. He lay comfortably, not trying to stir. Career over anyhow, he decided. German consul no doubt raise row higher up. Complain about incivility. Right to so complain, perhaps. Anyhow, work done. As far as I can, my part. Rest up to Tokyo and factions in Germany. Struggle beyond me in any case.

I thought it was merely plastics, he thought. Important mould salesman. Oracle guessed and gave clue, but –

'Remove his shirt,' a voice stated. No doubt building's physician. Highly authoritative tone; Mr Tagomi smiled. Tone is everything.

Could this, Mr Tagomi wondered, be the answer? Mystery of body organism, its own knowledge. Time to quit. Or time partially to quit. A purpose, which I must acquiesce to.

What had the oracle last said? To his query in the office as those two lay dying or dead. Sixty-one. Inner Truth. Pigs and fishes are least intelligent of all; hard to convince. It is I. The book means me. I will never fully understand; that is the nature of such creatures. Or is this Inner Truth now, this that is happening to me?

I will wait. I will see. Which it is.

Perhaps it is both.

That evening, just after the dinner meal, a police officer came to Frank Frink's cell, unlocked the door, and told him to go pick up his possessions at the desk.

Shortly, he found himself out on the sidewalk before the Kearny Street Station, among the many passers-by hurrying along, the buses and honking cars and yelling pedecab drivers. The air was cold. Long shadows lay before each building. Frank Frink stood a moment and then he fell automatically in with a group of people crossing the street at the crosswalk zone.

Arrested for no real reason, he thought. No purpose. And then they let me go the same way.

They had not told him anything, had simply given him back his sack of clothes, wallet, watch, glasses, personal articles, and turned to their next business, an elderly drunk brought in off the street.

Miracle, he thought. That they let me go. Fluke of some kind. By rights I should be on a plane heading for Germany, for extermination.

He could still not believe it. Either part, the arrest and now this. Unreal. He wandered along past the closed-up shops, stepping over debris blown by the wind.

New life, he thought. Like being reborn. Like, hell. *Is.*

Who do I thank? Pray, maybe?

Pray to what?

I wish I understood, he said to himself as he moved along the busy evening sidewalk, by the neon signs, the blaring bar doorways of Grant Avenue. I want to comprehend. I have to.

But he knew he never would.

Just be glad, he thought. And keep moving.

A bit of his mind declared, And then back to Ed. I have to find my way back to the workshop, down there in that basement. Pick up where I left off, making the jewellery, using my hands. Working and not thinking, not looking up or trying to understand. I must keep busy, I must turn the pieces out.

Block by block he hurried through the darkening city. Struggling to get back as soon as possible to the fixed, comprehensible place he had been.

When he got there he found Ed McCarthy seated at the bench, eating his dinner. Two sandwiches, a thermos of tea,

a banana, several cookies. Frank Frink stood in the doorway, gasping.

At last Ed heard him and turned around. 'I had the
impression you were dead,' he said. He chewed, swallowed
rhythmically, took another bite.

By the bench, Ed had their little electric heater going;
Frank went over to it and crouched down, warming his
hands.

'Good to see you back,' Ed said. He banged Frank twice
on the back, then returned to his sandwich. He said nothing
more; the only sounds were the whirr of the heater fan and
Ed's chewing.

Laying his coat over a chair, Frank collected a handful of
half-completed silver segments and carried them to the
arbor. He screwed a wool buffing wheel onto the spindle,
started up the motor; he dressed the wheel with bobbing
compound, put on the mask to protect his eyes, and then
seated on a stool began removing the fire scale from the
segments, one by one.

15

Captain Rudolf Wegener, at the moment travelling under
the cover name Conrad Goltz, a dealer in medical supplies
on a wholesale basis, peered through the window of the
Lufthansa Me9-E rocket ship. Europe ahead. How quickly,
he thought. We will be landing at Tempelhofer Feld in
approximately seven minutes.

I wonder what I accomplished, he thought as he watched
the land mass grow. It is up to General Tedeki, now. Whatever he can do in the Home Islands. But at least we got the
information to them. We did what we could.

He thought, But there is no reason to be optimistic.
Probably the Japanese can do nothing to change the course
of German internal politics. The Goebbels Government is in
power, and probably will stand. After it is consolidated, it

will turn once more to the notion of Dandelion. And another major section of the planet will be destroyed, with its population, for a deranged, fanatic ideal.

Suppose eventually they, the Nazis, destroy it all? Leave it a sterile ash? They could; they have the hydrogen bomb. And no doubt they would; their thinking tends towards that Götterdämmerung. They may well crave it, be actively seeking it, a final holocaust for everyone.

And what will that leave, that Third World Insanity? Will that put an end to all life, of every kind, everywhere? When our planet becomes a dead planet, by our own hands?

He could not believe that. Even if all life on our planet is destroyed, there must be other life somewhere which we know nothing of. It is impossible that ours is the only world; there must be world after world unseen by us, in some region or dimension that we simply do not perceive.

Even though I can't prove that, even though it isn't logical – I believe it, he said to himself.

A loudspeaker said, 'Meine Damen und Herren, Achtung, bitte.'

We are approaching the moment of landing, Captain Wegener said to himself. I will almost surely be met by the Sicherheitsdienst. The question is : Which faction of policy will be represented? The Goebbels? Or the Heydrich? Assuming that S.S. General Heydrich is still alive. While I have been aboard this ship, he could have been rounded up and shot. Things happen fast, during the time of transition in a totalitarian society. There have been, in Nazi Germany, tattered lists of names over which men have pored before . . .

Several minutes later, when the rocket ship had landed, he found himself on his feet, moving towards the exit with his overcoat over his arm. Behind him and ahead of him, anxious passengers. No young Nazi artist this time, he reflected. No Lotze to badger me at the last with this moronic viewpoint.

An airlines uniformed official – dressed, Wegener observed, like the Reichs Marshal himself – assisted them all down the ramp, one by one, to the field. There, by the concourse, stood a small knot of blackshirts. For me? Wegener began to walk slowly from the parked rocket ship. Over at another spot men and women waiting, waving, calling ... even some children.

One of the blackshirts, a flat-faced unwinking blond fellow wearing the Waffen-S.S. insignia, stepped smartly up to Wegener, clicked the heels of his jackboots together and saluted. 'Ich bitte mich zu entschuldigen. Sind Sie nicht Kapitän Rudolf Wegener, von der Abwehr?'

'Sorry,' Wegener answered. 'I am Conrad Goltz. Representing A.G. Chemikalien medical supplies.' He started on past.

Two other blackshirts, also Waffen-S.S., came towards him. The three of them fell beside him, so that although he continued on at his own pace, in his own direction, he was quite abruptly and effectively under custody. Two of the Waffen-S.S. men had sub-machine guns under their great-coats.

'You are Wegener,' one of them said as they entered the building.

He said nothing.

'We have a car,' the Waffen-S.S. man continued. 'We are instructed to meet your rocket ship, contact you, and take you immediately to S.S. General Heydrich, who is with Sepp Dietrich at the O.K.W. of the Leibstandarte Division. In particular we are not to permit you to be approached by Wehrmacht or Partei persons.'

Then I will not be shot, Wegener said to himself. Heydrich is alive; and in a safe location, and trying to strengthen his position against the Goebbels Government.

Maybe the Goebbels Government will fall after all, he thought as he was ushered into the waiting S.S. Daimler staff sedan. A detachment of Waffen-S.S. suddenly shifted at night; guards at the Reichskanzlei relieved, replaced. The Berlin police stations suddenly spewing forth armed S.D. men in every direction – radio stations and power cut off, Tempelhof closed. Rumble of heavy guns in the darkness, along main streets.

But what does it matter? Even if Doctor Goebbels is deposed and Operation Dandelion is cancelled? They will still exist, the blackshirts, the Partei, the schemes if not in the Orient then somewhere else. On Mars and Venus.

No wonder Mr Tagomi could not go on, he thought. The terrible dilemma of our lives. Whatever happens, it is evil beyond compare. Why struggle, then? Why choose? If all alternatives are the same . . .

Evidently we go on, as we always have. From day to day. At this moment we work against Operation Dandelion. Later on, at another moment, we work to defeat the police. But we cannot do it all at once; it is a sequence. An unfolding process. We can only control the end by making a choice at each step.

He thought. We can only hope. And try.

On some other world, possibly it is different. Better. There are clear good and evil alternatives. Not these obscure ad-mixtures, these blends, with no proper tool by which to un-tangle the components.

We do not have the ideal world, such as we would like, where morality is easy because cognition is easy. Where one can do right with no effort because he can detect the obvious.

The Daimler started up, with Captain Wegener in the back, a blackshirt on each side, machine gun on lap. Black-shirt behind the wheel.

Suppose it is a deception even now, Wegener thought as the sedan moved at high speed through Berlin traffic. They are not taking me to S.S. General Heydrich at the Leibstan-darte Division O.K.W.; they are taking me to a Partei jail, there to maim me and finally kill me. But I have chosen; I chose to return to Germany; I chose to risk capture before I could reach Abwehr people and protection.

Death at each moment, one avenue which is open to us at any point. And eventually we choose it, in spite of ourselves. Or we give up and take it deliberately. He watched the Berlin houses pass. My own *Volk*, he thought; you and I, again together.

To the three S.S. men he said, 'How are things? Any

recent developments in the political situation? I've been away for several weeks, before Bormann's death, in fact.'

The man to his right answered, 'There's naturally plenty of hysterical mob support for the Little Doctor. It was the mob that swept him into office. However, it's unlikely that when more sober elements prevail they'll want to support a cripple and demagogue who depends on inflaming the mass with his lies and spellbinding.'

'I see,' Wegener said.

It goes on, he thought. The internecine hate. Perhaps the seeds are there, in that. They will eat one another at last, and leave the rest of us here and there in the world, still alive. Still enough of us once more to build and hope and make a few simple plans.

At one o'clock in the afternoon, Juliana Frink reached Cheyenne, Wyoming. In the downtown business section, across from the enormous old train depot, she stopped at a cigar store and bought two afternoon newspapers. Parked at the kerb she searched until she at last found the item.

Vacation Ends in Fatal Slashing
Sought for questioning concerning the fatal slashing of her husband in their swank rooms at the President Garner Hotel in Denver, Mrs Joe Cinnadella of Canon City, according to hotel employees, left immediately after what must have been the tragic climax of a marital quarrel. Razor blades found in the room, ironically supplied as a convenience by the hotel to its guests, apparently were used by Mrs Cinnadella, described as dark, attractive, well-dressed, and slender, about thirty, to slash the throat of her husband, whose body was found by Theodore Ferris, hotel employee who had picked up shirts from Cinnadella just half an hour earlier and was returning them as instructed, only to come onto the grisly scene. The hotel suite, police said, showed signs of struggle, suggesting that a violent argument had . . .

So he's dead, Juliana thought as she folded up the newspaper. And not only that, they don't have my name right; they don't know who I am or anything about me.

Much less anxious now, she drove on until she found a

237

suitable motel; there she made arrangements for a room and carried her possessions in from the car. From now on I don't have to hurry, she said to herself. I can even wait until evening to go to the Abendsens'; that way I'll be able to wear my new dress. It wouldn't do to show up during the day with it on – you just don't wear a formal dress like that before dinner.

And I can finish reading the book.

She made herself comfortable in the motel room, turning on the radio, getting coffee from the motel lunch counter; she propped herself up on the neatly made bed with the new unread clean copy of *The Grasshopper* which she had bought at the hotel bookshop in Denver.

At six-fifteen in the evening she finished the book. I wonder if Joe got to the end of it? she wondered. There's so much more in it than he understood. What is it Abendsen wanted to say? Nothing about his make-believe world. Am I the only one who knows? I'll bet I am; nobody else really understands *Grasshopper* but me – they just imagine they do.

Still a little shaky, she put it away in her suitcase and then put on her coat and left the motel room to search for a place to eat dinner. The air smelled good and the signs and lights of Cheyenne seemed particularly exciting. In front of a bar two pretty, black-eyed Indian prostitutes quarrelling – she slowed to watch. Many cars, shiny ones, coasted up and down the streets, the entire spectacle had an aura of brightness and expectancy, of looking ahead to some happy and important event, rather than back . . . back, she thought, to the stale and the dreary, the used-up and thrown-away.

At an expensive French restaurant – where a man in a white coat parked customers' cars, and each table had a candle burning in a huge wine goblet, and the butter was served not in squares but whipped into round pale marbles – she ate a dinner which she enjoyed, and then, with plenty of time to spare, strolled back towards her motel. The Reichsbank notes were almost gone, but she did not care; it had no importance. He told us about our own world, she thought as she unlocked the door to her motel room. This, what's around us now. In the room, she again switched on the radio. He wants us to see it for what it is. And I do, and more so each moment.

Taking the blue Italian dress from its carton, she laid it out scrupulously on the bed. It had undergone no damage; all it needed, at most, was a thorough brushing to remove the lint. But when she opened the other parcels she discovered that she had not brought any of the new half-bras from Denver.

'God damn it,' she said, sinking down in a chair. She lit a cigarette and sat smoking for a time.

Maybe she could wear it with a regular bra. She slipped off her blouse and skirt and tried the dress on. But the straps of the bra showed and so did the upper part of each cup, so that would not do. Or maybe, she thought, I can go with no bra at all . . . it had been years since she had tried that . . . it recalled to her the old days in high school when she had had a very small bust; she had even worried about it, then. But now further maturity and her judo had made her a size thirty-eight. However, she tried it without the bra, standing on a chair in the bathroom to view herself in the medicine cabinet mirror.

The dress displayed itself stunningly, but good lord, it was too risky. All she had to do was bend over to put out a cigarette or pick up a drink – and disaster.

A pin! She could wear the dress with no bra and collect the front. Dumping the contents of her jewellery box onto the bed, she spread out the pins, relics which she had owned for years, given her by Frank or by other men before their marriage, and the new one which Joe had gotten her in Denver. Yes, a small horse-shaped silver pin from Mexico would do; she found the exact spot. So she could wear the dress after all.

I'm glad to get anything now, she thought to herself. So much had gone wrong; so little remained anyhow of the wonderful plans.

She did an extensive brushing job on her hair so that it crackled and shone, and that left only the need of a choice of shoes and ear-rings. And then she put on her coat, got her new handmade leather purse, and set out.

Instead of driving the old Studebaker, she had the motel owner phone for a taxi. While she waited in the motel office she suddenly had the notion to call Frank. Why it had come to her she could not fathom, but there the idea was. Why not? she asked herself. She could reverse the charges; he would be overwhelmed to hear from her and glad to pay.

Standing behind the desk in the office, she held the phone receiver to her ear, listening delightedly to the long-distance operators talk back and forth trying to make the connection for her. She could hear the San Francisco operator, far off, getting San Francisco information for the number, then many pops and crackles in her ear, and at last the ringing noise itself. As she waited she watched for the taxi; it should be along any time, she thought. But it won't mind waiting; they expect it.

'Your party does not answer,' the Cheyenne operator told her at last. 'We will put the call through again later and —'

'No,' Juliana said, shaking her head. It had been just a whim anyhow. 'I won't be here. Thank you.' She hung up — the motel owner had been standing near by to see that nothing would be mistakenly charged to him — and walked quickly out of the office, onto the cool, dark sidewalk, to stand and wait there.

From the traffic a gleaming new cab coasted up to the kerb and halted; the door opened and the driver hopped out to hurry around.

A moment later, Juliana was on her way, riding in luxury in the rear of the cab, across Cheyenne to the Abendsens'.

The Abendsen house was lit up and she could hear music and voices. It was a single-storey stucco house with many shrubs and a good deal of garden made up mostly of climbing roses. As she started up the flagstone path she thought, Can I actually be there? Is this the High Castle? What about the rumours and stories? The house was ordinary, well maintained and the grounds tended. There was even a child's tricycle parked in the long cement driveway.

Could it be the wrong Abendsen? She had gotten the address from the Cheyenne phone book, but it matched the number she had called the night before from Greeley.

She stepped up onto the porch with its wrought-iron railings and pressed the buzzer. Through the half-open door she could make out the living room, a number of persons standing about, Venetian blinds on the windows, a piano, fireplace, bookcases . . . nicely furnished, she thought. A party going on? But they were not formally dressed.

A boy, tousled, about thirteen, wearing a T-shirt and jeans, flung the door wide. 'Yes?'

She said, 'Is – Mr Abendsen home? Is he busy?'

Speaking to someone behind him in the house, the boy called, 'Mom, she wants to see Dad.'

Beside the boy appeared a woman with reddish-brown hair, possibly thirty-five, with strong, unwinking grey eyes and a smile so thoroughly competent and remorseless that Juliana knew she was facing Caroline Abendsen.

'I called last night,' Juliana said.

'Oh yes, of course.' Her smile increased. She had perfect white regular teeth; Irish, Juliana decided. Only Irish blood could give that jawline such femininity. 'Let me take your purse and coat. This is a very good time for you; these are a few friends. What a lovely dress . . . it's House of Cherubini, isn't it?' She led Juliana across the living room, to a bedroom where she laid Juliana's things with the others on the bed. 'My husband is around somewhere. Look for a tall man with glasses, drinking an old-fashioned.' The intelligent light in her eyes poured out to Juliana; her lips quivered – there is so much understood between us, Juliana realized. Isn't that amazing?

'I drove a long way,' Juliana said.

'Yes, you did. Now I see him.' Caroline Abendsen guided her back into the living room, towards a group of men. 'Dear,' she called, 'come over here. This is one of your readers who is very anxious to say a few words to you.'

One man of the group moved, detached and approached

carrying his drink. Juliana saw an immensely tall man with black curly hair; his skin, too, was dark, and his eyes seemed purple or brown, very softly coloured behind his glasses. He wore a hand-tailored, expensive natural fibre suit, perhaps English wool; the suit augmented his wide robust shoulders with no lines of its own. In all her life she had never seen a suit quite like it; she found herself staring in fascination.

Caroline said, 'Mrs Frink drove all the way up from Canon City, Colorado, just to talk to you about *Grasshopper*.'

'I thought you lived in a fortress,' Juliana said.

Bending to regard her, Hawthorne Abendsen smiled a meditative smile. 'Yes, we did. But we had to get up to it in an elevator and I developed a phobia. I was pretty drunk when I got the phobia but as I recall it, and they tell it, I refused to stand up in it because I said the elevator cable was being hauled up by Jesus Christ, and we were going all the way. And I was determined not to stand.'

She did not understand.

Caroline explained, 'Hawth has said as long as I've known him that when he finally sees Christ he is going to sit down; he's not going to stand.'

The hymn, Juliana remembered. 'So you gave up the High Castle and moved back into town,' she said.

'I'd like to pour you a drink,' Hawthorne said.

'All right,' she said. 'But not an old-fashioned.' She had already got a glimpse of the sideboard with several bottles of whiskey on it, hors d'oeuvres, glasses, ice, mixer, cherries, and orange slices. She walked towards it, Abendsen accompanying her. 'Just I. W. Harper over ice,' she said. 'I always enjoy that. Do you know the oracle?'

'No,' Hawthorne said, as he fixed her drink for her.

Astounded, she said, '*The Book of Changes?*'

'I don't, no,' he repeated. He handed her her drink.

Caroline Abendsen said, 'Don't tease her.'

'I read your book,' Juliana said. 'In fact I finished it this evening. How did you know all that, about the other world you wrote about?'

Hawthorne said nothing; he rubbed his knuckle against his upper lip, staring past her and frowning.

'Did you use the oracle?' Juliana said.

Hawthorne glanced at her.

'I don't want you to kid or joke,' Juliana said. 'Tell me without making something witty out of it.'

Chewing his lip, Hawthorne gazed down at the floor; he wrapped his arms about himself, rocked back and forth on his heels. The others in the room near by had become silent, and Juliana noticed that their manner had changed. They were not happy, now, because of what she had said. But she did not try to take it back or disguise it; she did not pretend. It was too important. And she had come too far and done too much to accept anything less than the truth from him.

'That's – a hard question to answer,' Abendsen said finally,

'No it isn't,' Juliana said.

Now everyone in the room had become silent; they all watched Juliana standing with Caroline and Hawthorne Abendsen.

'I'm sorry,' Abendsen said, 'I can't answer right away. You'll have to accept that.'

'Then why did you write the book?' Juliana said.

Indicating with his drink glass, Abendsen said, 'What's that pin on your dress do? Ward off dangerous anima-spirits of the immutable world? Or does it just hold everything together?'

'Why do you change the subject?' Juliana said. 'Evading what I asked you, and making a pointless remark like that? It's childish.'

Hawthorne Abendsen said, 'Everyone has – technical secrets. You have yours; I have mine. You should read my book and accept it on face value, just as I accept what I see –' Again he pointed at her with his glass. 'Without inquiring if it's genuine underneath, there, or done with wires and staves and foam-rubber padding. Isn't that part of trusting in the nature of people and what you see in general?' He seemed, she thought, irritable and flustered now, no longer polite, no longer a host. And Caroline, she noticed out of the corner of her eye, had an expression of tense exasperation; her lips were pressed together and she had stopped smiling entirely.

'In your book,' Juliana said, 'you showed that there's a way out. Isn't that what you meant?'

' "Out," ' he echoed ironically.

Juliana said, 'You've done a lot for me; now I can see there's nothing to be afraid of, nothing to want or hate or avoid, here, or run from. Or pursue.'

He faced her, jiggling his glass, studying her. 'There's a great deal in this world worth the candle, in my opinion.'

'I understand what's going on in your mind,' Juliana said. To her it was the old familiar expression on a man's face, but it did not upset her to see it here. She no longer felt as she once had. 'The Gestapo file said you're attracted to women like me.'

Abendsen, with only the slightest change of expression, said, 'There hasn't been a Gestapo since 1947.'

'The S.D., then, or whatever it is.'

'Would you explain?' Caroline said in a brisk voice.

'I want to,' Juliana said. 'I drove up to Denver with one of them. They're going to show up here eventually. You should go some place they can't find you, instead of holding open house here, like this, letting anyone walk in, the way I did. The next one who rides up here – there won't be anyone like me to put a stop to him.'

'You say "the next one",' Abendsen said, after a pause. 'What became of the one you rode up to Denver with? Why won't he show up here?'

She said, 'I cut his throat.'

'That's quite something,' Hawthorne said. 'To have a girl tell you that, a girl you never saw before in your life.'

'Don't you believe me?'

He nodded. 'Sure.' He smiled at her in a shy, gentle, forlorn way. Apparently it did not even occur to him to not believe her. 'Thanks,' he said.

'Please hide from them,' she said.

'Well,' he said, 'we did try that, as you know. As you read

on the cover of the book . . . about all the weapons and charged wire. And we had it written so it would seem we're still taking precautions.' His voice had a weary, dry tone.

'You could at least carry a weapon,' his wife said. 'I know some day someone you invite in and converse with will shoot you down, some Nazi expert paying you back; and you'll be philosophizing just this way. I foresee it.'

'They can get you,' Hawthorne said, 'if they want to. Charged wire and High Castle or not.'

You're so fatalistic, Juliana thought. Resigned to your own destruction. Do you know that, too, the way you knew the world in your book?

Juliana said, 'The oracle wrote your book. Didn't it?'

Hawthorne said, 'Do you want the truth?'

'I want it and I'm entitled to it,' she answered, 'for what I've done. Isn't that so? You know it's so.'

'The oracle,' Abendsen said, 'was sound asleep all through the writing of the book. Sound asleep in the corner of the office.' His eyes showed no merriment; instead, his face seemed longer, more sombre than ever.

'Tell her,' Caroline said. 'She's right; she's entitled to know, for what she did on your behalf.' To Juliana she said, 'I'll tell you, then, Mrs Frink. One by one Hawth made the choices. Thousands of them. By means of the lines. Historic period. Subject. Characters. Plot. It took years. Hawth even asked the oracle what sort of success it would be. It told him that it would be a very great success, the first real one of his career. So you were right. You must use the oracle quite a lot yourself, to have known.'

Juliana said, 'I wonder why the oracle would write a novel. Did you ever think of asking it that? And why one about the Germans and the Japanese losing the war? Why that particular story and no other one? What is there it can't tell us directly, like it always has before? This must be different, don't you think?'

Neither Hawthorne nor Caroline said anything.

'It and I,' Hawthorne said at last, 'long ago arrived at an agreement regarding royalties. If I ask it why it wrote *Grass-*

245

hopper, I'll wind up turning my share over to it. The question implies I did nothing but the typing, and that's neither true nor decent.'

'I'll ask it,' Caroline said. 'If you won't.'

'It's not your question to ask,' Hawthorne said. 'Let her ask.' To Juliana he said, 'You have an – unnatural mind. Are you aware of that?'

Juliana said, 'Where's your copy? Mine's in my car, back at the motel. I'll get it if you won't let me use yours.'

Turning, Hawthorne started off. She and Caroline followed, through the room of people, towards a closed door. At the door he left them. When he re-emerged, they all saw the black-backed twin volumes.

'I don't use the yarrow stalks,' he said to Juliana. 'I can't get the hang of them; I keep dropping them.'

Juliana seated herself at a coffee table in the corner. 'I have to have paper to write on and a pencil.'

One of the guests brought her paper and pencil. The people in the room moved in to form a ring around her and the Abendsens, listening and watching.

'You may say the question aloud,' Hawthorne said. 'We have no secrets here.'

Juliana said, 'Oracle, why did you write *The Grasshopper Lies Heavy*? What are we supposed to learn?'

'You have a disconcertingly superstitious way of phrasing your question,' Hawthorne said. But he squatted down to witness the coin throwing. 'Go ahead,' he said; he handed her three Chinese brass coins with holes in the centre. 'I generally use these.'

She began throwing the coins; she felt calm and very much herself. Hawthorne wrote down her lines for her. When she had thrown the coins six times, he gazed down and said :

'Sun at the top. Tui at the bottom. Empty in the centre.'

'Do you know what hexagram that is?' she said. 'Without using the chart?'

'Yes,' Hawthorne said.

'It's Chung Fu,' Juliana said. 'Inner Truth. I know without using the chart, too. And I know what it means.'

Raising his head, Hawthorne scrutinized her. He had now an almost savage expression. 'It means, does it, that my book is true?'

'Yes,' she said.

With anger he said, 'Germany and Japan lost the war?'

'Yes.'

Hawthorne, then, closed the two volumes and rose to his feet; he said nothing.

'Even you don't face it,' Juliana said.

For a time he considered. His gaze had become empty, Juliana saw. Turned inward, she realized. Preoccupied, by himself . . . and then his eyes became clear again; he grunted, started.

'I'm not sure of anything,' he said.

'Believe,' Juliana said.

He shook his head no.

'Can't you?' she said. 'Are you sure?'

Hawthorne Abendsen said, 'Do you want me to autograph a copy of *The Grasshopper* for you?'

She, too, rose to her feet. 'I think I'll go,' she said. 'Thank you very much. I'm sorry if I disrupted your evening. It was kind of you to let me in.' Going past him and Caroline, she made her way through the ring of people, from the living room and into the bedroom where her coat and purse were.

As she was putting her coat on, Hawthorne appeared behind her. 'Do you know what you are?' He turned to Caroline, who stood beside him. 'This girl is a daemon. A little chthonic spirit that –' He lifted his hand and rubbed his eyebrow, partially dislodging his glasses in doing so. 'That roams tirelessly over the face of the earth.' He restored his glasses in place. 'She's doing what's instinctive to her, simply expressing her being. She didn't mean to show up here and do harm; it simply happened to her, just as weather happens to us. I'm glad she came. I'm not sorry to find this out, this revelation she's had through the book. She didn't know what she was going to do here or find out. I think we're all of us lucky. So let's not be angry about it; okay?'

Caroline said, 'She's terribly, terribly disruptive.'

'So is reality,' Hawthorne said. He held out his hand to Juliana. 'Thank you for what you did in Denver,' he said.

She shook hands with him. 'Good night,' she said. 'Do as your wife says. Carry a hand weapon, at least.'

'No,' he said. 'I decided that a long time ago. I'm not going to let it bother me. I can lean on the oracle now and then, if I get edgy, late at night in particular. It's not bad in such a situation.' He smiled a little. 'Actually, the only thing that bothers me any more is knowing that all these bums standing around here listening and taking in everything are drinking up all the liquor in the house, while we're talking.' Turning, he strode away, back to the sideboard to find fresh ice for his drink.

'Where are you going now that you've finished here?' Caroline said.

'I don't know.' The problem did not bother her. I must be a little like him, she thought; I won't let certain things worry me no matter how important they are. 'Maybe I'll go back to my husband, Frank. I tried to phone him tonight; I might try again. I'll see how I feel later on.'

'Despite what you did for us, or what you say you did –'

'You wish I had never come into this house,' Juliana said.

'If you saved Hawthorne's life it's dreadful of me, but I'm so upset; I can't take it all in, what you've said and Hawthorne has said.'

'How strange,' Juliana said. 'I never would have thought the truth would make you angry.' Truth, she thought. As terrible as death. But harder to find. I'm lucky. 'I thought you'd be as pleased and excited as I am. It's a misunderstanding, isn't it?' She smiled, and after a pause Mrs Abendsen managed to smile back. 'Well, good night anyhow.'

A moment later, Juliana was retracing her steps back down the flagstone path, into the patches of light from the living room and then into the shadows beyond the lawn of the house, onto the black sidewalk.

She walked on without looking again at the Abendsen house and, as she walked, searching up and down the streets for a cab or a car, moving and bright and living, to take her back to her motel.

PENGUIN MODERN CLASSICS

IN COLD BLOOD
TRUMAN CAPOTE

'The American dream turning into the American nightmare... a remarkable book'
Tony Tanner, *Spectator*

Controversial and compelling, *In Cold Blood* reconstructs the murder in 1959 of a
Kansas farmer, his wife and both their children. Truman Capote's comprehensive
study of the killings and subsequent investigation explores the circumstances
surrounding this terrible crime and the effect it had on those involved. At the
centre of his study are the amoral young killers Perry Smith and Dick Hickock,
who, vividly drawn by Capote, are shown to be reprehensible, yet entirely and
frighteningly human.

The book that made Capote's name, *In Cold Blood* is a seminal work of modern
prose, a remarkable synthesis of journalistic skill and powerfully evocative
narrative.

PENGUIN MODERN CLASSICS

THE HEART IS A LONELY HUNTER
CARSON MCCULLERS

'She has examined the heart of man with an understanding that no other writer …
can hope to surpass' Tennessee Williams

Carson McCullers's prodigious first novel was published to instant acclaim when
she was just twenty-three. Set in a small town in the middle of the deep South, it is
the story of John Singer, a lonely deaf-mute, and a disparate group of people who
are drawn towards his kind, sympathetic nature. The owner of the café where Singer
eats every day, a young girl desperate to grow up, an angry drunkard, a frustrated
black doctor: each pours their heart out to Singer, their silent confidant and he in turn
changes their disenchanted lives in ways they could never imagine …

Moving, sensitive and deeply humane, *The Heart is a Lonely Hunter* explores
loneliness, the human need for understanding and our search for love.

PENGUIN MODERN CLASSICS

RABBIT, RUN
JOHN UPDIKE

'Brilliant and poignant ... By his compassion, clarity of insight, and crystal-bright prose, [Updike] makes Rabbit's sorrow his and our own' *Washington Post*

It's 1959 and Harry 'Rabbit' Angstrom, one time high school sports superstar, is going nowhere. At twenty-six he is trapped in a second-rate existence – stuck with a fragile, alcoholic wife, a house full of overflowing ashtrays and discarded glasses, a young son and a futile job. With no way to fix things, he resolves to flee from his family and his home in Pennsylvania, beginning a thousand-mile journey that he hopes will free him from his mediocre life. Because, as he knows only too well, 'after you've been first-rate at something, no matter what, it kind of takes the kick out of being second-rate.'

'Updike's punch is powerful' *Newsweek*

PENGUIN MODERN CLASSICS

ATLAS SHRUGGED
AYN RAND

'A writer of great power ... she writes brilliantly, beautifully, bitterly' *The New York Times*

Opening with the enigmatic question 'Who is John Galt?', *Atlas Shrugged* envisions a world where 'men of talent' – the great innovators, producers and creators – have mysteriously disappeared. With the US economy now faltering, businesswoman Dagny Taggart is struggling to get the transcontinental railroad up and running. For her John Galt is the enemy, but as she will learn, nothing in this situation is quite as it seems.

Hugely influential and grand in scope, this story of a man who stopped the motor of the world expounds Rand's controversial philosophy of Objectivism, which champions competition, creativity and human greatness.

'*Atlas Shrugged* is a celebration of life and happiness' Alan Greenspan

PENGUIN MODERN CLASSICS

HERZOG
SAUL BELLOW

With an Introduction by Malcolm Bradbury

'Spectacular ... surely Bellow's greatest novel' Malcolm Bradbury

This is the story of Moses Herzog, a great sufferer, joker, mourner and charmer. Although his life steadily disintegrates around him – he has failed as a writer and teacher, as a father, and has lost the affection of his wife to his best friend – Herzog sees himself as a survivor, both of his private disasters and those of the age. He writes unsent letters to friends and enemies, colleagues and famous people, revealing his wry perception of the world and the innermost secrets of his heart.

'A masterpiece ... Herzog's voice, for all its wildness and strangeness and foolishness, is the voice of a civilization, our civilization'
The New York Times Book Review

WINNER OF THE NOBEL PRIZE FOR LITERATURE